PETER DI
SING A SONG OF MURDER

ERIC ELRINGTON ADDIS, aka 'Peter Drax', was born in Edinburgh in 1899, the youngest child of a retired Indian civil servant and the daughter of an officer in the British Indian Army.

Drax attended Edinburgh University, and served in the Royal Navy, retiring in 1929. In the 1930s he began practising as a barrister, but, recalled to the Navy upon the outbreak of the Second World War, he served on HMS *Warspite* and was mentioned in dispatches. When Drax was killed in 1941 he left a wife and two children.

Between 1936 and 1939, Drax published six crime novels: *Murder by Chance* (1936), *He Shot to Kill* (1936), *Murder by Proxy* (1937), *Death by Two Hands* (1937), *Tune to a Corpse* (1938) and *High Seas Murder* (1939). A further novel, *Sing a Song of Murder*, unfinished by Drax on his death, was completed by his wife, Hazel Iris (Wilson) Addis, and published in 1944.

By Peter Drax

PETER DRAX

SING A SONG OF MURDER

With an introduction
by Curtis Evans

DEAN STREET PRESS

Published by Dean Street Press 2017

Introduction copyright © 2017 Curtis Evans

All Rights Reserved

First published in 1944 by Hutchinson & Co. Ltd.

Cover by DSP

ISBN 978 1 911579 65 6

www.deanstreetpress.co.uk

INTRODUCTION

ERIC ELRINGTON ADDIS, aka "Peter Drax," one of the major between-the-wars exponents and practitioners of realism in the British crime novel, was born near the end of the Victorian era in Edinburgh, Scotland on 19 May 1899, the youngest child of David Foulis Addis, a retired Indian civil servant, and Emily Malcolm, daughter of an officer in the British Indian Army. Drax died during the Second World War on 31 August 1941, having been mortally wounded in a German air raid on the British Royal Navy base at Alexandria, Egypt, officially known as HMS *Nile*. During his brief life of 42 years, Drax between the short span from 1936 to 1939 published six crime novels: *Murder by Chance* (1936), *He Shot to Kill* (1936), *Murder by Proxy* (1937), *Death by Two Hands* (1937), *Tune to a Corpse* (1938) and *High Seas Murder* (1939). An additional crime novel, *Sing a Song of Murder*, having been left unfinished by Drax at his death in 1941 and completed by his novelist wife, was published in 1944. Together the Peter Drax novels constitute one of the most important bodies of realistic crime fiction published in the 1930s, part of the period commonly dubbed the "Golden Age of detective fiction." Rather than the artificial and outsize master sleuths and super crooks found in so many classic mysteries from this era, Drax's novels concern, as publicity material for the books put it, "police who are not endowed with supernatural powers and crooks who are also human." In doing so they offered crime fiction fans from those years some of the period's most compelling reading. The reissuing of these gripping tales of criminal mayhem and murder, unaccountably out-of-print for more than seven decades, by Dean Street Press marks a signal event in recent mystery publishing history.

Peter Drax's career background gave the future crime writer constant exposure to the often grim rigors of life, experience which he most effectively incorporated into his fiction. A graduate of Edinburgh Academy, the teenaged Drax served during the First World War as a Midshipman on HMS *Dreadnought* and

Marlborough. (Two of his three brothers died in the war, the elder, David Malcolm Addis, at Ypres, where his body was never found.) After the signing of the armistice and his graduation from the Royal Naval College, Drax remained in the Navy for nearly a decade, retiring in 1929 with the rank of Lieutenant-Commander, in which capacity he supervised training with the New Zealand Navy, residing with his English wife, Hazel Iris (Wilson) Addis, daughter of an electrical engineer, in Auckland. In the 1930s he returned with Hazel to England and began practicing as a barrister, specializing, predictably enough, in the division of Admiralty, as well as that of Divorce. Recalled to the Navy upon the outbreak of the Second World War, Drax served as Commander (second-in-command) on HMS *Warspite* and was mentioned in dispatches at the Second Battle of Narvik, a naval affray which took place during the 1940 Norwegian campaign. At his death in Egypt in 1941 Drax left behind Hazel --herself an accomplished writer, under the pen name Hazel Adair, of so-called middlebrow "women's fiction"--and two children, including Jeremy Cecil Addis, the late editor and founder of *Books Ireland.*

Commuting to his London office daily in the 1930s on the 9.16, Drax's hobby became, according to his own account, the "reading and dissecting of thrillers," ubiquitous in station book stalls. Concluding that the vast majority of them were lamentably unlikely affairs, Drax set out over six months to spin his own tale, "inspired by the desire to tell a story that was credible." (More prosaically the neophyte author also wanted to show his wife, who had recently published her first novel, *Wanted a Son,* that he too could publish a novel.) The result was *Murder by Chance,* the first of the author's seven crime novels. In the United States during the late 1920s and early 1930s, recalled Raymond Chandler in his essay "The Simple Art of Murder" (originally published in 1944), the celebrated American crime writer Dashiell Hammett had given "murder back to the kind of people who commit it for reasons, not just to provide a corpse; and with the means at hand, not with hand-wrought dueling pistols, curare and tropical fish." Drax's debut crime novel, which followed on the heels of Hammett's books, made something of a similar impression in the United Kingdom, with mystery writer and founding Detection Club member Milward Kennedy in the *Sunday Times* pronouncing the novel a "thriller of great merit" that was "extremely convincing" and the influential *Observer* crime fiction critic Torquemada avowing, "I have not for a good many months enjoyed a thriller as much as I have enjoyed *Murder by Chance*."

What so impressed these and other critics about *Murder by Chance* and Drax's successive novels was their simultaneous plausibility and readability, a combination seen as a tough feat to pull off in an era of colorful though not always entirely credible crime writers like S. S. Van Dine, Edgar Wallace and John Dickson Carr. Certainly in the 1930s the crime novelists Dorothy L. Sayers, Margery Allingham and Anthony Berkeley, among others (including Milward Kennedy himself), had elevated the presence of psychological realism in the crime novel; yet the criminal milieus that these authors presented to readers were mostly resolutely occupied by the respectable middle and upper classes. Drax offered British readers what was then an especially bracing change of atmosphere (one wherein mean streets replaced country mansions and quips were exchanged for coshes, if you will)—as indicated in this resoundingly positive Milward Kennedy review of Drax's fifth crime novel, *Tune to a Corpse* (1938):

> I have the highest opinion of Peter Drax's murder stories.... Mainly his picture is of low life in London, where crime and poverty meet and merge. He draws characters who shift uneasily from shabby to disreputable associations.... and he can win our sudden liking, almost our respect, for creatures in whom little virtue is to be found. To show how a drab crime was committed and then to show the slow detection of the truth, and to keep the reader absorbed all the time—this is a real achievement. The secret of Peter Drax's success is his ability to make the circumstances as plausible as the characters are real....

Two of Peter Drax's crime novels, the superb *Death by Two Hands* and *Tune to a Corpse*, were published in the United States, under the titles, respectively, *Crime within Crime* and *Crime to Music*, to very strong notices. The *Saturday Review of Literature*, for example, pronounced of *Crime within Crime* that "as a straightforward eventful yarn of little people in [the] grip of tragic destiny it's brilliantly done" and of *Crime to Music* that "London underworld life is described with color and realism. The steps in the weakling killer's descent to Avernus [see Virgil] are thrillingly traced." That the country which gave the world Dashiell Hammett could be so impressed with the crime fiction of Peter Drax surely is strong recommendation indeed. Today seedily realistic urban British crime fiction of the 1930s is perhaps most strongly associated with two authors who dabbled in crime fiction: Graham Greene (*Brighton Rock*, 1938, and others) and Gerald Kersh (*Night and the City*, 1938). If not belonging on quite that exalted level, the novels of Peter Drax nevertheless grace this gritty roster, one that forever changed the face of British crime fiction.

Curtis Evans

CHAPTER I

LOUIE PATRA came out of the shadows of Starling Court into Lucas Street. He was a broad-shouldered man with long arms like an ape's; his mouth was wide and thick-lipped. When he spoke, which was seldom, he used a husky, treacly voice.

The sun was shining, the month was June, and it was eleven o'clock in the forenoon; but in spite of these facts, Louie was wearing an overcoat—he always wore an overcoat. This morning it was unbuttoned and showed a gold chain looped across his blue serge waistcoat. Now and then he dabbed at spots over his ears with a handkerchief rolled into a pad.

At the corner by the barber's shop he stopped and raked the street with his boot-button eyes. A man passed whom he employed from time to time, but Louie gave no sign that he had seen him. Then he went into the shop.

Silvretti, a melancholy Italian with high cheek-bones and long black moustaches, was unpacking a carton of cigarettes. When he heard the door-bell ring he straightened up.

Louie worked his cigar to a corner of his mouth. "Well, what's the news?" His voice rumbled up from his stomach. He made an opening in the bead curtain which hung in the entrance to the saloon and looked in. The place was empty.

"There is no news, Mr. Patra. No news at all. Everything is very quiet—very quiet indeed." Silvretti spoke quickly, nervously, in a sing-song voice which had no life and held no hope. He was a melancholy optimist. A pessimist fighting against fate.

"Has there been any talk about that beat-up last night?"

"No, no. Everything was quite all right."

Louie stared out into the street. "I've got the wire that there's a chiseller hanging around. See what you can find out."

Silvretti bowed and bobbed his head. "Yes, certainly, Mr. Patra. I will make the inquiries. I will ask Tony."

"Tony doesn't know. Ask the others." Louie opened the door, went out into the street and walked along Lucas Street in the direction from which he had come. A hundred yards away he saw Detective-sergeant Leith coming towards him. His face creased in an unaccustomed smile when Leith was five yards away. "Well, how's crime this fine morning?" He paid Leith the compliment of taking his cigar from his mouth before he spoke.

"Not so bad. Might be better." Leith had the long face of a horse and a brooding eye. "Did you hear anything last night?"

"What do you mean?"

"There was a crowd beat up a black outside your place; crowned him with the lid of a dustbin."

Louie took his cigar out of his mouth and blew out a thin stream of creamy smoke. "Is he dead?"

"It takes more than a dustbin lid to kill a man." Leith pointed to the entrance to Starling Court. "Is there a way through there?" he asked.

Louie answered quickly: "No. There's only my store and my office, that's all, and the gate's locked every night." After a short pause he added: "I have to be very careful. There are very many bad men round these parts." He chuckled. "And I do not want any dead fellows in my yard." He might have added with truth that neither did he want the police nosing round his place.

The livelihood of Louie Patra depended entirely on the supply of bad men; men who climb up the face of a house; men who could pick a pocket, steal from cars, forge a signature or a five-pound note. He had a use for them all.

He took hold of his gold watch-chain and pulled a gold watch from his pocket. "It's time I was getting on with my work," he said, and turned into Starling Court.

The road beneath the stone arch was narrow and paved with kidney-shaped stones, humpy, uneven and strewn with scraps of dirty paper. Twenty yards within the entrance a flight of wooden steps led up to the door of his office.

Louie passed the steps and went on down the yard to his store. Twenty years ago it had been a chapel of an obscure faith, now it housed bales of paper. He pushed open the door of the store and went in. It was a blessed relief to get out of the heat of the streets and into the dusty, cool half-light of the store. Slits of windows set high up in the thick stone walls admitted light grudgingly through a layer of dust and spiders' webs. The remains of a dismantled pulpit lay across the rafters. There was a musty, faintly bitter smell of newspaper. Bales of it were stacked high and almost reached to the rafters. In an open space there was a bin, into which a bent old man was emptying loose paper from a sack.

For a minute or two Louie stood quite still while his eyes became accustomed to the half-light. He wasn't scared of any damn' split, but all the same he felt better here within the four walls of his store. He kicked the door shut and shot the bolt. Then he turned and walked towards the bin.

Benny Watt was old in crime and in years. He had the eager, questing, have-you-got-a-herring look of a sea-lion—an albino sea-lion, for Benny's hair was white. Sometimes his head weaved to and fro like a sea-lion contemplating a dive into its pool. He was rather deaf and had not heard Louie enter.

When Louie touched him on the shoulder he dropped the sack he was lifting on to the edge of the bin and turned his head quickly. For a split second his china-blue eyes held fear, and then he smiled.

"'Morning, guv'nor. I won't be long finishing this little lot."

"You can leave it. We ought to be getting some more stuff in one of these days."

"And high time too." Benny's voice rose to a complaining whine like that of a spoilt child. "When do you expect it in?"

"Soon, I hope; but times are slack."

"It wasn't like that when I was working, and if it wasn't for these blamed ears of mine, dammit, I think I'd have a crack at something myself." Benny laughed a crackling laugh and, fumbling in his trouser pocket, pulled out a pipe and a stick of tobacco, black as tar. "There's not the blokes going round these days half as good—no, not a quarter as good as some of the old 'uns. Take Tommy Finn now. There wasn't a job he wouldn't tackle and get away with. I worked with him once and I know."

Louie rolled his cigar across his mouth. "There's still a few left. The trouble is, the splits are getting too damn' hot."

"The trouble is, the lads don't know their job these days. Now there's Spider; he's getting on, I know, but he knows what's what. You ought to give him a try."

"What can he do?"

"Most anything he gives his mind to; he can case a job better than any other bloke I know."

"I thought he was working for the Rigger."

"He was, but the Rigger's not doing much these days. It was you froze him out of these parts."

Louie gave one of his rare smiles. "Yes, he was getting in the way, so I suggested to him that he should go some other place."

Benny laughed. "And when you finished making the suggestion he spent a week in hospital. That's what Spider told me." Benny knocked out his pipe and trod on the ashes as they fell on the floor. Then he lifted the sack of paper and emptied it into the bin and began to turn a handle. An iron plate came down and pressed on to the paper. "Now don't forget Spider, guv'nor. He's a friend of mine and he wants a job; he told me so himself last time I seen him."

Somewhere far away a bell began to ring insistently. "That damn' 'phone," Louie muttered to himself. He unbolted the door and went out into the heat of the yard. He climbed the wooden steps which led to his office; on the door was a brass plate bearing the words: 'L. Patra. Wastepaper Contractor. Office.'

He opened the door with a yale key and slammed it shut behind him. Then he picked up the receiver of the telephone, which stood on the top of a roll-top desk. He said, "Mr. Patra speaking," and stared with unfocused eyes at a calendar on the wall.

"Good morning, Mr. Patra. This is Zimmermann speaking. You remember me? Yes, of course you do." Louie heard a guttural laugh.

"Where are you?"

"At the usual place. I have a little proposition for you. It is a very good proposition too. You will like it, I am sure."

"Let's have it." Louie tapped the ash off his cigar into a saucer. Then he drew up a chair and sat down.

"I think it would be better that we meet and have a little talk together. You understand? It is safer that way, and I do not like this telephone."

"All right. Come along. I'll be waiting for you."

Louie put down the receiver and sat thinking. Zimmermann. He had had only one deal with him before, but he had paid well, and money was scarce. He leaned back in his chair and looked at the calendar. It was for the year 1933 and had a highly coloured picture of a small, curly-haired boy playing with an outsize in St. Bernard's. Louie was very fond of the picture.

He pushed back the cover of the desk and revealed a row of pigeonholes stuffed full of papers. He pulled out a handful and spread them out on the desk; then he took a steel pen from a rack and began to make entries in a ledger which was lying open on the desk.

* * *

Herman Zimmermann had a satisfied smile on his square face when he walked out of the 'phone box in his hotel in Aldgate. His hair was the colour of flax and of the texture of silk; the shoulders of his suit were padded, which added to the effect of squareness; the cloth of the suit had the appearance of being lined with cardboard. He put on his hat, a trilby with a stiff up-turned brim bound with white braid, went out into the street, and hailed a taxi.

"Take me, please, to Canton Street. It is in the district of Soho," he ordered the driver, and during the journey sat stiffly on the edge of the seat. There was no expression on his wooden face; he might have been going to have his hair cut for all the emotion he displayed. He seldom smiled unless he was drunk, and then he was apt to laugh unexpectedly and sing songs in a surprising falsetto voice.

He stopped the car when it had turned into Canton Street, and said to the driver: "All right. This will do very well." He looked at the clock and fumbled uncertainly with unaccustomed coins. When he had overpaid the driver he walked up Canton Street to Number twenty-six. On a board on the door-post was written in faded red paint, 'S. Zwolsky. Ladies' Tailor', and on the door itself there was an envelope held by a rusty drawing-pin: 'Brown one ring. Benson two rings.'

Zimmermann pressed a button twice, and a buzzer sounded in the office of 'L. Patra. Wastepaper Contractor'.

Louie put down his pen and brushed a drift of cigar ash off his waistcoat. Then he got up and pulled a handle on the wall. A catch on the door of Number twenty-six Canton Street was thereby released, and Zimmermann was free to mount a flight of uncarpeted stairs.

Louie waited until he heard a door slam and then pulled the handle in the opposite direction; a section of the wall swung outwards and he walked out on to a landing from whence he looked down and saw the flaxen hair of Zimmermann. He called out: "You didn't take long getting here."

Zimmermann saved his breath for the ascent. Beer had spoiled his wind. When he came face to face with Louie he held out his hand and said: "So! We meet again. I am glad." It would not have been surprising if he had saluted.

"Go right in." Louie pointed in the direction of the office. He followed his visitor and then operated the handle. When the section of the wall was in place he pressed on it to make sure that it was fast. He walked to the desk and picked up the box of cigars. "Have one. They're not bad; part of the last lot you brought."

As he pierced the end of his cigar, Zimmermann said: "And I hope that you did not have any trouble."

"No. I fixed it all right; sold the lot inside a week." Louie sat down and crossed one fat thigh over the other, and grasped the toe of his pointed patent-leather shoe. "When am I going to get the next lot?"

"Very soon; in two or three days, I hope, if the weather keeps fine. The *Van Wyk* does not like it when it is rough." Zimmermann got up and walked to the window. He saw the stairway leading down to Starling Court and the gate into the street. "So you have another way out; that is very convenient."

"I've got a dozen."

Zimmermann came back to his chair and sat down with his back to the window, his hands, outspread like starfish, on his knees. "And now about that little proposition that I spoke to you about. It is extra good, I assure you."

Louie showed no interest. "Go ahead."

Zimmermann took his wallet from his pocket and extracted from it a printed booklet of about twenty pages. "This, what I have here, is the catalogue of the collection belonging to a gentleman called Mr. Kimber."

"Collection? What of?"

"All sorts of things. Look, you can read for yourself." He handed the catalogue to Louie.

"Old Silver and Sheffield plate. Early English glass. Ivories," Louie read, and then he looked at Zimmermann. "Have you gone crackers?"

"Crackers? Crackers? I do not know what you mean by that."

"Barmy, looney, loco. Just plain mad. What sort of a price do you think you can get for this junk?" He tossed the catalogue contemptuously on to the desk. "Junk. That's what it is. Junk."

"One minute, if you please. I will explain." Zimmermann was tapping impatiently with a finger on his knee. He was angry at such a reception of his 'proposition'.

Louie picked up the catalogue and read aloud the description of one of the items. "'An Irish potato-ring pierced and chased with flowers, vines and coursing scenes. By Patrick O'Callagahan, Dublin.' Now what the hell is a potato-ring, anyway?"

"I do not know what a potato ring is and I do not care." Zimmermann's voice was trembling. "But this I do know. I have got a buyer for this collection. Someone who will pay well."

"Who?"

"That is my business. You will deliver to me the goods on board the *Van Wyk* and I will pay you three hundred pounds."

"Do you mean the whole of this lot?" Louie asked.

"All the collection? No, no. Just a certain number of the items. I have marked the ones I want. You will pack them in the bales of your wastepaper in the same way as you did with the diamonds in February. It will be quite easy, you will see."

"Yes, if I'm not copped. But if the splits get me with an Irish potato-ring on me, what the hell am I going to say? Tell 'em it's a birthday present for my Aunt Mabel? They'd have me cold. It was different with the rocks. I got them rough-cut right away so they couldn't be identified."

"But with your organization, Mr. Patra, what risk is there? Last time we met you told me that you had never been caught and that the police had no suspicions of you. That is why I have come here today. I know that you are safe."

"If I take it on, the price'll be a thousand quid."

"That is absurd. Quite absurd. I shall have a lot of expenses on the other side. The customs men and the police—I shall have to pay them both, and also the men who will carry the bales. It will be a big risk for them and they will want much money."

"What are you going to do with the stuff when you get it across?"

"It will go to America. Everything is arranged."

Louie stubbed out his cigar and lit another. "Where is the stuff?"

"In Mr. Kimber's house, Number forty-six Durham Square."

"In Town, eh?"

"What is that, please?"

"In London."

"Yes, of course; in London. You will not have to go far."

"It's not a question of how far I have to go, it's the risk. Pulling a smash in Town is not so damn' easy as you seem to think. And there'll be at least six of the boys to pay. A job like that'll be cheap at a thousand."

"Perhaps I can make it five hundred. What do you say?"

"Nothing doing."

Zimmermann wet his lips and tried to smile. "Five hundred English pounds. It is a lot of money. For the diamonds I only paid you two hundred and fifty."

"That was a different job altogether. If you had skipped, I could have sold the rocks myself; but with this stuff I'd be stuck."

"I will pay."

Louie stared at Zimmermann for a full five seconds. "The last man who let me down is in hospital. They think he'll live. He was a black. If he hadn't had a hard head he'd have been in a mortuary by now."

"Mr. Patra, I do not know why you speak like this to me."

"I'm just telling you." Louie's voice was low and husky. "If you want to keep your health, remember what I've said."

"Then you will take the job?" Zimmermann had difficulty in forming the words, for this talk of hospitals, mortuaries and hard heads had frightened him.

"I'll let you know about that tomorrow. I've got to have a look at the place first. If I do it, the price'll be a thousand."

Zimmermann got up. He said stiffly: "As to that price, I will consult my friends."

"All right, but don't leave it too long. I've got a lot of work on hand."

Louie released the panel in the wall and walked with Zimmermann to the top of the stairs. "Of course, you won't tell anyone you have been here."

"Of course not, Mr. Patra. I understand."

"And if anyone in the street tries to talk to you, don't have anything to do with them."

"Thank you for the warning, but I am not a child."

*　　*　　*

As Louie walked back to the office there was a trace of a smile at the corners of his thick-lipped mouth. A thousand pounds. He could just about do with that sum. He'd have to pay the boys, of course. He sat down and took a stub of a pencil from his waistcoat pocket and did a simple sum on the blotting-pad. Tony would want twenty; two Jim Crows at a fiver apiece; a man to case the joint, ten; and Benny a couple of quid. He'd want a good man to pull the job. He wrote 'X' on the pad and the figures 50 beside it. The problem now was to find X, a man with nerve who could be trusted. Benny was right enough, there weren't many of that sort about these days.

He got up and opened the door at the top of the wooden stairs, walked down to the yard, and along to the store.

"Hey! Benny! Where can I find Spider?"

Benny rose from his stool and took his clay pipe out of his mouth. "What's that?"

"Spider. Where does he hang out?"

"You could try the 'Ring o' Bells'. He might be there; or else the 'Flag'. We had a pint there last night, him and me."

Louie looked at his watch. It was twelve o'clock. There'd be time to take a look at Durham Square before he went to find Spider.

Durham Square in Bloomsbury had once been fashionable. In the days of Queen Anne it had been a shilling fare in a chair from the Royal Opera House in Covent Garden, but then you had to pay the link-boys if the night was foggy. On the iron railings which flanked the area of Number forty-six there were loops to hold the link-boys' torches.

Louie wasn't the least bit interested in the signs of the times when the house was young. He was looking at the heavy sash windows and the distance between them and the pavement. The front door was solid enough to withstand the assaults of a battering-ram and it was protected by a wrought-iron gate. That gate had cost young Kimber's father five hundred pounds and was secured with an intricate lock. There were bars on the windows in the basement, and the door had no fanlight.

It was a pleasant Square with gardens in the middle of it. It was occupied at that moment by three nurses with children, two dogs and a man wheeling a barrow. Louie noted with satisfaction that it was not apparently used by taxi-drivers as a short cut, for though he made a complete circuit he saw only one or two tradesmen's vans. The railings round the gardens were low and could easily be climbed, while there were sooty laurels in the garden which would give cover if necessary.

He walked to the back of Number forty-six and found a mews. The house possessed a small plot of ground enclosed by a ten-foot wall. There was a door in the wall which opened into the mews; it looked as though it had not been opened for years.

'Looks as though it'll have to be an inside job,' Louie thought as he left the mews in search of a taxi; he had had enough of walking. He drove to Piccadilly Circus and walked from there to the 'Flag and Lamb', a small public house up an alley off Shaftesbury Avenue. There he found Spider in the four-ale bar, sitting on a stool making a pint last until he could find someone to buy him another. Spider's finances had reached basement level.

Spider was a small man with an indiarubber mouth who had stopped growing old at the age of forty. He was proud of the fact that he could still touch his right ear with his left toe, and would give a demonstration on the slightest provocation. He always wore a blue serge suit, a bowler hat and a florid tie pierced with a fake-diamond pin. He was as cocky as a sparrow and as cunning as a monkey.

He saw Louie come into the bar, but he gave no sign of recognition; Louie did not like being addressed in public by those who were known to the police, and the police knew few better than Spider.

Louie ordered a small whiskey and when he had finished it he caught Spider's eye and gave him the fraction of a jerk of his chin. Then he left the bar and, followed by Spider, boarded a bus which was going to Ealing Broadway. He sat on one of the back seats, and when he was satisfied that there was no one on the top of that bus who knew him he signed to Spider to join him.

"How are you fixed?" Louie shot the question out of the side of his mouth.

"Nothing much doing, guv'nor."

"I want you to case a joint in Durham Square."

"That's me, guv'nor. When do I start?"

"As soon as you get yourself dolled up a bit. Get another tie and chuck that pin down a drain."

"This pin, guv'nor? It cost me a dollar and chance it."

Louie ignored the protest. "And buy yourself a black suit. Don't go to the house yourself, but hang around a pub in Little Fenton Street—it's the place the servants use. Make out that you're after a job as a kitchen hand or footman or something like that, and get all the dope you can on Number forty-six."

"What's the swag?"

"Museum stuff. It'll be in cases, I expect. I want the whole lay-out."

"How are you going to work it? Inside job?"

"Maybe, I haven't fixed anything yet."

"Then I'd better go all out for a job."

Louie thought for a moment. "See what chance there is of that, but don't fix anything until I see you again."

"What was the number you said?"

"Forty-six Durham Square, and the name of the bloke that owns the shop is Kimber."

"Kit Kimber?" Spider's rubber mouth formed an 'O' and he slapped a hand on his knee.

"Maybe. I don't know."

"Kit Kimber's got all the oof in the world. There's not a con man up West that hasn't had a try at trimming him, but there's none of 'em got more than the price of a drink out of him."

"Then he's right out of your class. Leave him alone."

"O.K., guv'nor."

They rode on in silence for several minutes, and then Spider put a hand in his pocket and brought it out empty and held it palm upwards.

Louie took out his wallet and skinned two notes off a roll. "That's how it is, is it? All right, this'll do to go on with. When you've got any dope, come round to Silvretti's and tell him you want me." Louie banged on the bell and went down the stairs of the bus.

CHAPTER II

TOOLEY WAS AS hard-hearted as a welshing bookmaker and as superstitious as a love-sick typist. He believed in lucky charms and water from wishing-wells; he wouldn't have walked under a ladder to escape from a pursuing policeman, he'd have crowned the policeman first. He got a thrill out of a black cat, and when he saw a grey horse he wished a wish and didn't look at its tail.

Few of his wishes had come true, and on the occasion of his arrest, three years before, a black cat had let him down badly.

Now, as he walked with short prison steps along a gritty country road, he fingered a small ivory pig. Anna had given it to him, and he had been thinking of Anna quite a lot during those three years.

Low dry-stone walls bordered the road, and beyond, moorland rose to hump-backed hills crowned with stone cairns. Fifty yards ahead a car was drawn up on the grass verge, and when he came close to it his heart began to beat faster and every pulse throbbed.

He had lived this moment a hundred times during the last month—the time when he would be free; every night he had lain awake thinking of it until the thought became a torturing agony and they had had to call the doctor. He had given him sleeping-draughts, but they hadn't done much good. The warder on his hall, a decent old fellow, had told him that it took 'em all that way, but that hadn't done much good either.

And now he was free! It was as though he were living that dream all over again and soon he would have to force himself to awake to escape from it.

Then he called out: "Louie?"

Louie twisted round in his seat in the car and saw a man slight of build, with the face of a young man grown suddenly old; his eyes were a curious shade of hazel green. They were eyes which held no expression, and even when he laughed with his mouth they remained strangely impersonal.

Tooley stumbled forward the last few steps, and Louie gripped him by the shoulders. "That's all right. Take it easy. Take it easy." He took a bag from Tooley's hand and tossed it into the back of the car.

Tooley settled himself down in his seat and stretched out his legs. "God! Is it true?" Then his lips trembled and he began to sob.

Louie took a flat bottle from a pocket in the dash and poured liquor into a tin cup. "Here! Get some of this down. It'll make you feel better."

Tooley's shaking fingers closed round the cup; he raised it to his lips and drank greedily; some of the liquor dribbled on to his chin, and he dabbed at it with his handkerchief.

Louie took the cup from him. "You want to go easy with that the first time." He put the cup away and took a cigarette-case from his pocket.

As the match flared up and he took a deep draught of smoke, Tooley said: "If these were a quid apiece they'd be cheap." He lay back in his seat, and suddenly felt as though the road and the sky were whirling round. He jerked himself forward and gripped the edge of the cushion. Then slowly his head began to clear and he saw the road stretching away ahead, he could hear the ticking of the clock on the dash.

Louie pressed the button of the starter. The car bumped over the uneven grass on to the road. Tooley didn't speak, he didn't want to speak. He watched Louie work the gear-lever as though he had never seen it done before. First, second, third, and then into the peace of top. One of these days he'd drive again, but not now; he'd be scared. There was a sheep on the road ahead; his feet pressed hard against the floorboards. He glanced at Louie, who had seen the movement and said: "Back-seat driver. That's a new one for you."

From a quarry came the sounds of steel on stone. Against the skyline he saw the stocky figure of a warder with a rifle slung on his shoulders and for the first time really began to savour his freedom.

Steel on stone! The clang of the muster-bell and the shrill note of the warders' whistles and that infernal, eternal rattle of keys. Keys. Keys. Keys.

He saw himself in a ragged, shambling line, silent, sullen and hopeless. It seemed far away now and yet only yesterday. . . . He'd got to forget, make himself forget. He'd got to get his nerve back. Scared to drive a car! He hadn't thought it would be like this. He had pictured himself meeting Louie and telling him all about the boys inside, and then saying, "Do you mind if I take her?" and slipping in under the wheel. Now he didn't want to say anything about the others. He wanted to forget. "I want another drink."

"Help yourself. It's something extra special. Zimmermann brought a stack of cases last trip."

"Who's Zimmermann?"

"I forgot. You haven't seen the squarehead. I've been doing quite a bit of business with him one way and another. The *Van Wyk*'s paying her way at last."

"Shipping stuff over here?"

"And across as well. It's working fine."

"How's Benny?"

"Just the same. Maybe a bit deafer, but you won't see much difference in him. Tony's coming along not so bad." Neither spoke for a time, and then Louie said: "There's some papers in the back."

Tooley half turned in his seat and picked an *Echo* off the pile on the floor. He turned to the racing page, and though the names of the horses meant nothing to him he read it all. It was funny how things had been going on just the same all the time he had been away. Three years out of his life. Three years he could never get back. And what he'd missed! Pictures, races, drinks, loafing around doing what you damn' well wanted to do. Lying in bed in the morning, meeting the boys, dances, Sundays at Brighton. He'd had some damn' good times and he'd have 'em again. He'd get back some of what he'd lost. Some of it.

He thought of Anna and wondered if she'd forgotten him. She'd only been a kid when he'd left. He took the little ivory pig from his pocket and held it up for Louie to see. "Anna gave me that. How is she?"

"She's O.K. Working for Guido."

"What's that?" Tooley snapped out the question.

"Now don't get fussed. She's doing well for herself. Dancing partner. Gets the run of her teeth, a quid or two a week and commission on the drinks. She doesn't do so bad."

"What sort of place is it?"

"A club."

"I see." Tooley slid farther down in his seat and did not speak again for half an hour. "This is a new bus, isn't it?"

"Yes, I had to change. Did a lot of country work for a while, but it's cooled off now."

"How are things going in the Smoke?"

"Slack, but I've got a job on the board. I don't know how it's going to pan out. Maybe I'll want you."

"I've got to have a lay-off before I start again." Tooley sucked hard at his cigarette. "You don't know what it's been like these last weeks. The first month and the last are the worst."

"Well, you've got nothing to worry about now. I've fixed up a doss for you at Silvretti's place."

"That mouldy old wop! Why can't I stop in your place? You got plenty space, haven't you?"

"It's not that, it's the splits. Leith's working up our way and he's hot."

"You've let him live all this time, have you?"

"I'm not worrying about him," Louie replied. "I'm being careful, that's all. You'll be on a ticket for a spell, and if he saw me going about with you it might start him thinking."

Tooley said: "I see what you mean, but you might have chosen someone a bit more cheerful than Silvretti." Then he went to sleep and did not wake until the car reached Hammersmith Broadway. The sun had gone down and he felt stiff and cold and a little sick. He looked at the crowded pavements, the cars and the buses, and drank in the smell of London, and began to live again. There was the inevitable little man carrying an umbrella running for a bus; a policeman standing with his thumbs in his belt like they do on the stage; paper-boys calling, "*Star*, *News* and *Standard*"; a seedy-looking man in a seedy-looking hat standing outside the closed door of a public house smoking a tired-looking cigarette.

"What was that job you were speaking about?"

"Spider's casing it; he's coming in tonight to tell me how he's got on."

"Spider! He used to work with the Rigger, didn't he?"

"Yes, but the Rigger's finished. I ran him out of business. There wasn't room for both of us." Louie threw the butt of his cigar out of the window. "We're getting into the thick of it now; you'd better get into the back and keep down out of sight."

It was not until the car was bumping over the cobblestones of Starling Court that Louie said: "It's all right. You can come out." He stopped the car outside the store and called out to Benny to open up the double doors. Then he drove the car inside and waited until Benny had opened a sliding door, which revealed a space just large enough to hold the car.

"I've had this built since you went away, and there's another door on to Canton Street"

As he got out of the car, Tooley said: "You don't take many chances."

"I don't take any."

Benny had followed them back into the store and had shut the sliding door before he recognized Tooley. "Well, so you've got back at last."

Tooley gave him a brief, tight-lipped smile. "That's what it looks like. How have you been?"

"Not so bad, but I get the rheumatics terrible bad when it rains."

Tooley looked at the piles of baled paper. "You've been busy."

"Paper, paper, everlasting paper. It's weeks since I packed a proper bale, but maybe now you're back we'll see something."

Tooley took the flat bottle of brandy out of his pocket. "Here! This'll make you forget."

"I hardly ever touch the stuff these days," Benny said, as he slipped the bottle into his jacket pocket, "but it'll come in handy next time I have a touch of the rheumatics."

Louie said: "And I'll bet a fiver you have an attack tonight. Come on, Tooley."

"Wait a minute, guv'nor, I got a message for you from Spider. He's done all he can and he says he'll be along as soon as it's dark, to tell you all about it." He slipped a spill of paper into Louie's hand. "And that's from Silvretti."

"O.K. Spider can come in through the shop. Now cut along and shut the yard gate." Louie led the way to the wooden stairs and up to the office. As he locked the door behind them, he said: "I'll get Guido along and we can fix up the chow." He pressed a bell-push and then he took a pound note from his wallet. "This'll do for you to go on with. I'll settle with Silvretti."

"Thanks." Tooley sat down on a hard chair and pushed his hat back on his head. "I'd like to have a run around tonight and meet some of the boys."

"No, you won't. You'll turn in early."

Tooley's hazel-green eyes closed to slits. "I'll do what I damn' well like. This is my first night and I'm going to get drunk. Do you hear that? Drunk. And then I'm going to bed and sleep till Monday."

"Like hell you are! If you work for me you'll take your orders from me." There was a hard edge to Louie's husky voice.

"And supposing I don't work for you?"

"Then you'll be in the gutter or else back in the stone jug inside of a month. Where are you going to get the dough to live on? Work for it?" Louie laughed, a low rumbling laugh. "I thought you had sense. I thought you were one of the smart boys who knew what was good for you. If I chuck you out, where are you going to? Who's going to stake you?"

"I can work single-handed. I've done it before."

"That was before you'd been inside. You'd find it a bit different now. The splits'll be on your tail all the time. They'll never let up. They'll never give you a break."

"Then what difference will it be if I come in with you? If you're right, they'll be on to me just the same."

"Listen, Tooley, and I'll tell you something, and I'm only going to tell you once." Louie leant forward and put an elbow on his knee. "If you keep in with me you can lie up at Silvretti's. You can take a walk around if you like, but you needn't do a thing a split can pull you for. I'll do all the fixing. I'll get the job and work it all out. When I have it taped I'll give you the office. There won't be any risk the way I'll work it."

"And all the time I've got to do what you tell me. Is that the way it goes?"

"It's just plain sense, and you'd see it that way if you weren't all jittered up. Take it easy for a day or two, and then think again. Wait a minute." Louie got up and pressed a bell-push. Five minutes later there was a knock on a door at the other end of the room to that used by Zimmermann. Louie eased back a spring lock.

Guido came in. He was fat and short; his jet-black moustaches were waxed to pin-points. He smiled quickly and easily, mechanically; his smile was a tool of his trade; he sold food.

"Good evening, Mr. Patra. You will be dining in tonight, no?"

"Yes, Tooley and me are going to feed."

"Tooley! Tooley!" The light was failing, and Guido peered shortsightedly round the office.

Tooley's tight lips spread in a quick smile. "What cheer, you old robber! You're fatter than ever."

Guido's smile became genuine. "That is because of my good food. Still I go to the market myself in the morning very early, and sometimes I cook him too. Now this morning I buy some very nice soles. Not many, you understand, just three; beautiful soles because Mr. Patra say that he bring with him tonight a friend who would be verry hungry."

"I've been hungry for years." The smile had gone from Tooley's face.

"That is too bad. I am sorry, but please wait and I will arrange such a dinner for you." Guido looked at the ceiling for inspiration and found it there. "I have prawns and these I will cook with *champignons* in a white wine sauce. The sauce will be worthy of the sole and the sole will be worthy of the sauce. But first you will have the small *hors d'œuvres*, and afterwards you will like a savoury? Oh yes, I remember. You like the angels on horseback." Guido looked at Louie. "At what hour will you wish to dine?"

"Half past eight. I want to see Spider first."

"He is here now in the bar. I will send him to you." Guido padded, flat-footed, out of the room.

Tooley got up and began to walk up and down the room with clipped steps. At the third turn he stopped and swore. "I can't get it out of my system, walking like this. I walked five miles every night, I worked it out. When I couldn't sleep I used to work out sums. It got so that I couldn't read, and I had to do something; I was scared to think." He caught sight of the calendar on the wall, the coloured picture of the boy and the St. Bernard. "You had that before I went; getting a bit out of date, aren't you?"

"I like the picture," Louie said.

"So do I." Tooley stared at it. "I like pictures; they make me forget things." He suddenly swung round. "But I'll never forget; never."

"Can it," Louie growled. "For Heaven's sake take a pull at yourself. Spider's coming in." Louie rose and opened the door Guido had used. Spider was waiting outside. "Why didn't you knock?"

"I was just going to, guv'nor, when you opened up."

Louie pointed to a chair. "Sit down."

But Spider had seen Tooley and he went up to him with his hand outstretched. "Why, Tooley! It's good to see you again. How are things?"

"Bloody. And you ought to know." Tooley dropped Spider's hand quickly.

"I know how you feel, lad. It took me like that the first time, but you'll feel better when you've got some decent chow under your belt." He grinned. "Is it still bacon pie on Thursdays?"

"Yes, and hash on Mondays and greasy damn' stew on Fridays and cocoa and bread and scrapings every morning for breakfast and—"

"Cut that." Louie's eyes were angry. Tooley put a hand under his chin to stop it trembling. "Sit down," Louie ordered Spider.

"I don't know what's the matter with him. I was only asking," Spider grumbled.

Louie opened a drawer and took out a box of cigarettes, which he handed to Tooley. "That's the kind you like, isn't it?"

Tooley nodded and took the box.

"Go ahead."

Spider passed his tongue between his lips. "I done all I could, guv'nor, but I couldn't get a decko at them keys. You see, the bloke that keeps them just wouldn't play. I tried everything, but he wouldn't open up."

"What have you got?"

"I've been inside. That took a bit of doing, but I managed to pal up with the bloke that does the boots and he gave me a run around." Spider leaned forward and became throatily confidential. "The crib's no blooming good. There's locks on the doors that would take a week to work, and steel shutters on every one of the blamed windows; and besides that there's rattlers all over the place. Even if you did manage to break it, what have you got but a pile of stuff even you couldn't fence?"

"Tell us what you saw, that's all I want."

"Well, the stuff's all in little glass cases in a room at the back—used to be a billiards-room, so the bloke told me. Like a blinking museum it was; there was little silver pots and china jugs and candle-sticks and plates and I don't know what all. Not but what some of 'em was pretty; there was some little cups you could damn' nigh see through and there was a figure of a girl, pretty she was, all coloured up and carrying a bunch of flowers. The bloke said it was Bristol china and worth a hundred and fifty quid, and there was a beer-tankard which he said cost his boss two-fifty. I didn't know whether he was kidding or not, but that's what he said."

"What's the lay-out?" Louie asked.

Spider fished a folded sheet of paper from his pocket and brought it over to Louie. "These are the stairs from the kitchen; this here's the hall door, that's where they feed, and this is a room where there's a lot of books. What I've drawn double is a kind of a steel shutter arrangement at the start of a passage. At the other end of the passage is this room where all the stuff is."

Louie said: "Yes, I get you. It's built out into the garden."

"That's right, guv'nor. It's got a couple of skylights I haven't marked, but they've got shutters too. There's bars on the windows thick as your wrist."

"What about the rattlers?"

"I don't know where they all are, guv'nor, but I know where they're worked from." He put a dirty forefinger on the plan. "If you was standing here just inside the front door and looking into the hall the stairs go up there. Well, opposite where the stairs start there's a table with some brushes on it and a tray of cards. Just under the table in the corner there is a wooden box with a keyhole in it. That's where they turn on the rattlers. The butler does it every night when he goes round locking up."

"What's the butler like?"

"You won't do no good with him, guv'nor, not in a hundred years. A bloke like him led me up the garden path once; I thought I had him fixed, but when I went to pull the job there was half the rozzers in the world waiting for me. I never did trust a butler after that."

"Is he the only one that has the keys?"

"No, him and young Kimber, that owns the dump. He's a young bloke, about twenty-five, and smart as paint, as I told you. Red Marcus tried to work on him once and spent a packet, but all he got was the price of a drink. When Kimber's old dad died, him that bought all this junk, there wasn't a con man up West that didn't have a go at him, but none of 'em made a touch; anyway, that's what Red told me."

"Is that all you got on him?"

"He told me a lot more, but—"

"Let's have it," Louie interrupted.

"Well, this Kimber bloke spends a lot of his time around Soho way. He's in one of them Prisoners' Help Societies and Red says he goes visiting at Brixton. He saw Red there not long after Red had had that go at him, and they didn't half have a chin. He had some scheme of a farm down in the country and wanted Red to promise to go down there after he came out and help to raise chickens."

Louie gave one of his rare laughs, which lasted some time. "He tried to reform Red, did he? He must be a sucker."

"Red told him that if he came in with him they'd clean up a packet, but he wouldn't bite; said he'd got all the dough he wanted. I told Red he was a fool, but he said he wouldn't feed chickens for a pound a minute, and there was some talk of pigs, and Red said the only way he could stand a pig was on the end of a fork, streaky."

"Anything more?"

"No, I think that's about the lot."

Louie took two five-pound notes from his wallet. "You haven't done so bad."

Spider stuffed the notes in his trouser pocket and stood up. "Well, I'll be getting along. It'll be nice working with you, Mr. Patra."

"Working with me?" Louie's voice was almost silky.

"Yes, you'll want me in the job, won't you?"

"You're finished. You've got your money. Now clear out and keep your trap shut."

"But I thought I was going to be in it. There's mighty little doing these days, and I said to Benny the other night, I said: 'If there's one bloke I'd like to work with it's Mr. Patra'; and you can ask Benny if that's not the gospel truth. He'll tell you."

Louie got up slowly and unlocked the door. "That's the way out, and if you want to keep your health you'll forget everything you've said here tonight. One squeak from you and I'll send the boys around to sing you to sleep."

Spider looked at Tooley, who was staring at him as coldly as a snake; then he slid through the door and was gone.

Tooley said: "He got the dope all right."

"Yes, but I wish to hell I'd never used him."

"Why?" Tooley took the cigarette from his mouth and blew out a cloud of smoke. "He hasn't got the guts to talk."

"It's not the splits I'm worrying about, it's the Rigger."

"You told me he was finished."

Louie unfolded a slip of paper and gave it to Tooley. "Take a decko at that."

Tooley read aloud: "The chiseller. It is the Rigger."

"Where did you get this?"

"Silvretti sent it. I got the wire that there was someone doing a bit of muscling, and I put him on to find out who it was."

"It might have been better if you'd kept Spider on a string. You'd have known where you had him."

"Yes, I thought of that; but I think he's better-right out of it. If he starts playing any funny games I'll know what to do."

"What about the job? It looks cuckoo to me."

"Zimmermann's all right. He'll pay."

"But the joint. Who are you going to get to do the smash?"

"There's not going to be any smash. I'm going to work it from the inside."

Tooley got up and pushed back his chair. "The butler's no good; Spider said so, and he's the only man with the keys."

"No, he's not. Kimber's got a set. He's the one we're going to work on."

"And who are you going to get for that?"

"You."

"What's that?" Tooley swung round and his hands closed on the back of a chair.

"You. Don't you see? It's simple. Dead simple."

"I don't get you."

"Kimber's on this reforming racket. That's what we've got to work on. You've just come out. It's easy meat."

"But you said just now that I couldn't go round on my own working up a job, and that's sense."

"It'll be all right the way I'll work it." Louie opened his coat and put his thumbs in the arm-holes of his waistcoat. "You'll pal up with Kimber and spin him a yarn that you want a chance. Tell him you'll go down on his farm or anything else he wants you to do. It'll be easy as pie, and you're just the man for the job; you might have been measured for it."

"What comes next?"

"Bring him to Guido's place and leave the rest to me. You won't have to do a thing that'll tie you up with what happens after that. You'll have nothing to worry about and there won't be any risk. I'll fix it."

"What about the last job? When I was pinched. You said that was going to be dead safe."

"And it would have been if it hadn't been for the Rigger."

As Louie spoke the words, Tooley's grip on the chair-back tightened. He didn't speak for ten seconds, and then his voice was a whisper. "The Rigger! You mean he shopped me?"

"He did."

"But why? I didn't know him hardly."

"But he knew you were working for me. And you weren't the only one." Louie tapped the ash of his cigar into a saucer. "I didn't get wise for a time, but when I did I put the boys on him, the Hoxton crowd, and after that he cleared out and went down to Balham or some place."

"And Spider knows about this job? Why not rub him out?"

"No, I'm going to leave it the way it is. Spider won't sing. Come on and eat." Louie slammed down the cover of the desk.

He opened the door which Guido and Spider had used and led the way into a narrow passage lit by one dim shaded light. There was another door at the end of the passage which Louie unlocked. "You'll see a big difference in the place. I got it fixed good."

They were in the entrance hall of Guido's Club. The carpet was thick and mossy green, the walls apricot, with concealed lighting. Tooley could hear the muffled beat of a dance band. "This is more like it," he muttered, and gave his hat to a waiter. The music came louder and then died again as a door opened and shut. The shaded light, the warmth and the drugging music; it was like getting into a warm bath after having been out in a blizzard. Tooley soaked it in, utterly content.

And then a man and a girl came in. Tooley turned away, but Louie caught him by the sleeve. "You got to get used to this, to meeting people."

"I ought to have a dinner-suit."

Louie lifted his broad shoulders an eighth of an inch. "You can come as you like here. The place doesn't warm up till ten or later. Then you'll see a crowd." He led Tooley into the cloak-room and opened a door with a yale key. Again the sound of music burst forth, and Tooley found himself in the dining-room at a table shielded by a lattice-work screen. There were twenty tables, but only three were occupied. The man and the girl who had just come in were dancing alone on a ten-foot square of floor space. The band was playing a slow waltz.

A waiter arrived with a circular dish of *hors d'œuvres*, which he placed in the centre of the table. There was crisp toast in a silver rack and butter in a silver dish. He went away and returned a moment later with two dry martinis.

Tooley speared a herring *gendarme* and ate it slowly. When he had finished he said: "You'll never know how good that tasted."

Louie said, "I hope to hell I won't," and lifted his glass. His brain was alive with a plan already half formed. It was a good idea to get Tooley to work on Kimber; it just fitted in and there were no snags as far as he could see. As long as Tooley didn't try to make a killing, Kimber wouldn't suspect anything; he'd tell Tooley to go slow, and when he'd got him going, then . . . then . . . well, he'd think of some way of getting the keys; he wouldn't want 'em for long.

"Who's that girl?" Tooley was leaning forward looking through a hole in the screen.

Louie put down his fork and laughed.

A girl, slim as a boy, with hair the colour of bleached flax and bound with a broad scarlet ribbon, was dancing. She was wearing a sheath of a dress which followed her figure, and there were sequins on it which shone like tiny diamonds as she moved.

"Who is she?" Tooley's voice trembled.

"Tommy Finn's kid. Anna. You asked about her in the car. I wondered when you were going to recognize her."

"How is Tommy? I used to have good times down at his place."

"Dead. Fell off a roof in Audley Street a couple of months back. That's why I took Anna on here, and she's doing not so bad."

"She was still at school when I saw her last. I never thought she'd turn into this." Tooley took the pig from his pocket and put it on the table before him. "She had a whole crowd of them, all sorts and sizes. She never had any dolls. I went down to see Tommy—it was a Sunday, I remember—and we had a yarn about the job I was going to pull, and he gave me a lot of tips. And then she came in and he shut up like a clam. That was when she gave me this one. I told her I was going to get a job, and she said: 'Well, here's something to bring you luck.' It was the one she liked best, and I didn't want to take it, but she made me."

Guido came padding across the floor. "Is everything all right, Mr. Patra?" He saw Tooley's empty plate. "Come. I can see that you have eaten nothing, nothing at all. A little salad? Caviare? No?"

"He's through. Bring on the fish and a bottle of Marco," Louie growled.

"Marco on a night like this! No, no. I have a bottle of champagne already iced." Guido picked up the plates.

"And tell Anna we want to talk with her."

"Anna? Yes, I will tell her. She is looking very lovely tonight. One day soon I tell her she will get married. It will not be difficult for her to find a man. And what a lovely bride she will make!"

"And I suppose you've got the wedding breakfast all worked out?"

"But of course, Mr. Patra. There will be—"

"You can tell us some other time. Get on with the dinner." Louie waited until Guido was gone, and then he said: "I don't want you to go running round with her. We got a lot of work to do."

Tooley said nothing. His eyes were fixed on Anna. The music had stopped and she was walking to a table. He saw Guido approach her and saw her look towards the table behind the screen. He saw her shake her head and sit down. Guido went on talking. Then suddenly she got up and came towards the screen.

He searched in her face for the girl he had known. She was prettier than any girl he had ever seen; her skin had the dusky bloom of a peach, and her eyes were so blue that they were almost violet.

He was in a panic and tried to think of what he would say to her, but she was by his side before he could form one word in his brain. Her hand fell on his and she pressed it quickly. Then she ran her fingers through his hair. "Gosh, it's good to see you again. I'd almost forgotten you."

He pointed to the pig by his plate. A quick smile crossed his face. "And Roderick?"

"Roderick, my poor pet! Do you mean to say you've kept him all this time? Do you remember the rest of the family? They've all gone. I don't know what happened to them."

A waiter arrived with the champagne in an ice-bucket.

"Why not sit down?" Tooley suggested.

Anna took a swift look at Louie. She said: "I've got my partner to look after."

"You can give him a miss this time."

Anna slipped into a chair. "That's lovely." Louie told the waiter to lay another place. Tooley had his eyes fixed on her, hungrily gazing. Anna plunged into a spate of protective talk. "It does seem an age since I saw you last, Tooley. I was a kid, an absolute kid. And I was very innocent then, too."

Tooley said: "Yes. I remember that. When did you find out?"

"When Father died. The dicks came." Tooley's eyebrows went up half an inch. "Leith was there. Do you know him?"

"Yes, I know Leith."

"Well, he brought a sort of matron person and she took me to a home, and later I went to a school in the country."

"That must have been a change."

"It was. I hated it."

"Who paid?" Tooley asked.

"I don't know. It doesn't matter. Anyway, I stayed there till I was eighteen. Then I fell in love with the most wonderful young man who came to teach us English and—er . . . and . . . well, then they chucked me out. That was three months ago, and here I am."

"Are you still in love with the wonderful young man?" Tooley was serious.

Anna laughed. "Good heavens, no. I had a pash for him, that was all. It was wonderful. I didn't do any work and he always gave me good marks. He blushed like anything, poor pet, when he asked me questions, and so did I, at first. Of course, when it came to exams and I knew nothing, people started asking questions. Everything came out and he went, and so did I."

The band had started again and Tooley was beating time with his fingers on the cloth. "What about a dance?"

"I'd love to." Anna spoke without feeling.

"You don't have to unless you want to." Tooley's voice was hard.

She put a hand on his. "Don't be silly, come on."

Tooley walked out on to the floor, and as Anna passed him, Louie said: "Take him easy. He's all like that." He raised both his hands and made them tremble.

As she slid into Tooley's arms, Anna said: "Louie told me about you last night. I'm frightfully sorry."

"That's all finished with. I'm forgetting about it." He held her tightly, but she resisted the pressure.

"Sorry, but I've got to breathe, or have I?"

Tooley said, "Sorry," and pursed his thin lips more tightly together. He was holding on to his memory of the kid he had known and was finding it difficult. "Do you remember that afternoon when I went away, when you gave me the pig and wished me luck?"

"Yes. Dimly." Anna was looking round the tables as they danced. People were beginning to come in. She smiled at one man and lifted the hand on Tooley's shoulder for a second to wave to another.

"I've been thinking of that afternoon for the last three years, wondering what it would be like to meet you again."

"That's a dangerous game, making pretty pictures. Sometimes they don't last, or did this one?"

"It lasted all right—until tonight. We were good pals once."

"That's right. Pals. And we'll go on that way."

When they came close to the table, Tooley said: "Let's sit down."

Louie had gone, leaving behind him a folded note. Tooley read it and then tore it up into tiny pieces. He didn't like being told when to go to bed.

A waiter came and served the sole, and when he had gone Tooley said: "I've never known anyone change as much as you have. I knew you once, or I thought I did, but now it's like talking to a stranger."

Anna sipped her wine. "I've grown up and I've been in love. It makes a lot of difference."

"I've never been in love. I've never cared for a girl in my life."

Anna pretended not to hear, and said: "This is a wonderful sole. That old robber Guido never gives me anything like this. I usually have some foul chicken mess in a casserole—yesterday's chicken."

Tooley took the bottle out of the bucket and filled her glass. "But this is a celebration." He laughed. "Some celebration. I've been thinking about this night for years. It was my idea of heaven: to eat and talk while I was eating. You don't know how good that is. We fed like animals; we each had our trough of swill. I ate because I didn't want to have a pain in my guts."

Anna put down her glass and opened her bag and took out a compact. "It must have been terrible."

"Terrible," Tooley repeated, and there was a sneer in his green eyes. "Yes. That's the word. Terrible." He finished his wine at one gulp, and then leaned back, looking at Anna. He was a little drunk. "I can't believe it. Here I am sitting in front of a beautiful girl eating sole *à la* something and drinking fizz. Come on! Let's dance. Dance. Damn you!"

She thought for one split second, and then said, "O.K.," and squashed her cigarette into an ash-tray.

"Music. I like music. It makes me feel good." A minute later: "What's that scent you're using?"

"I don't know. Mr. Patra gave it me."

"It's good. I like it." They danced for a spell, and then: "How do you get on with Louie?"

"All right. Why?"

"What do you have to do for your pay?"

"Dance."

"That all?"

"Yes."

"He's never asked you to do a job for him?"

"What do you mean?"

"Oh, nothing; forget it."

Tooley was dancing better, for he was a little drunk and Anna had found the measure of his steps. She said: "I'll have to give you some lessons. You wouldn't be bad if you'd only let yourself go. Keep your heels on the floor and your knees loose."

"Quite the little professional. You've got all the patter."

"It's what I'm paid for."

"Where's it going to take you?"

"I don't know; I don't care. It's not a bad life really."

"I suppose you think you'll get someone to marry you one of these days."

"Maybe."

"What about going out tomorrow night and doing a show?"

"I'd love to, but you'd have to ask Guido."

Tooley stopped dancing and led her to the table behind the screen. "Look here, what's the matter with you? You're as cold as a clam."

"Sorry, but three years are a long time and I'm not good at taking things up where we left off. We've got to get used to each other, that's all. And you're different to what you were."

"You've changed. I haven't." He refilled his glass. As he put it down half empty he went on: "It's like grabbing at a shadow, talking to you."

"I'll go out with you tomorrow. Guido'll let me go, I know, but I'm tired now; I want to go to bed."

Tooley leaned across the table. "O.K., kid. Thanks." He smiled, and the tight lines round his mouth were smoothed out.

Anna unlocked the door and took him into the hall, where Guido was standing. He opened a door. "Good night, Tooley. This is your best way out."

Tooley looked at the door for a second and then at Guido. "Another bolt-hole." He walked out on to the landing which Zimmermann had used, down a flight of uncarpeted stairs, past the notice on the doorpost—'S. Zwolsky. Ladies' Tailor'—and out into Canton Street. He hesitated for a moment to get his bearings and then walked south towards Shaftesbury Avenue.

At the first cross street he turned right, and at the corner by Silvretti's barber's shop a man came out of a doorway. "'Evening, Tooley. You're late for your first night out." It was Leith.

Tooley stood quite still and stared at him for a full half minute. Then he said: "Any objections?" There was a fighting glint in his green eyes and his mouth set hard.

Leith looked up at the roof of a house opposite. "No. But I'd take it easy if I were you."

Tooley's hands were gripping the edges of his coat and a pulse in his head was beating like a goldsmith's hammer. "I'll please myself about that."

"Who's staking you?" Leith's tone was deliberately casual.

"Nobody. I'm working on my own from now on."

"You're not going back into the game, are you?"

"Why shouldn't I?"

"Because you'll lose."

"No, I won't."

"You did last time."

"I was framed."

Leith snapped open his cigarette-case and held it out. "That's very interesting. Who was it?"

Tooley took a cigarette and lit it. "Don't you worry. I'll look after him."

"Sounds bad." He took a pace forward and passed his hands over Tooley. "Thought you might be carrying something." He put his hands back in his trouser pockets.

"Looking for a chance to pull me in again? Why can't you let a bloke alone?"

"You asked for it, talking like that. You know, Tooley, I'd a damn' sight rather stop you doing something stupid than I'd pull you for it."

"Is that why you're still a sergeant?"

"Maybe it is. I never thought of it that way before."

"Oh, go to hell!" Tooley turned and unlocked the door next to Silvretti's shop.

Leith walked a hundred yards and then he stopped under a street lamp and took out his note-book. He wrote with a stub of a pencil: '12.30 a.m. Met James Hope, *alias* Tooley, convict on licence. Seen to enter Number two Lucas Street.' Then he went to his lodgings and slept soundly for eight hours.

Tooley hardly slept at all.

CHAPTER III

KIT KIMBER was so rich that at the age of twenty-five he had reached a state of boredom which even the spending of money in large quantities failed to alleviate. He owned a yacht, an aeroplane and several motor-cars. He had failed to kill himself in a number of different ways, and had reached the peak, or rather the depths, of utter boredom when a charity hound ran him into a corner of his club.

Kit knew the signs of a legal touch better than most men, and clutched at the best weapons of defence against importunity, his chequebook and fountain-pen. The professional charity hound waved them aside.

"How much? And what is it this time? Fallen women or our black brothers? Bibles or maternity homes?" He filled in the date at the top right-hand corner of the cheque. "Or do you want me to become a life member of a *crèche*?"

"My name is Brooking and I'm the secretary of the Prisoners' and Convicts' Aid Society. We would like money, of course."

"How much? I've got an appointment in ten minutes."

"Mr. Kimber, you are a young man of—er—character and energy. You have no—er—ties."

"No job, you mean, and you're quite correct." Kit put down his pen and pressed a bell-push in the wall. "I think a drink's indicated."

"Not for me, thank you. A glass of beer with my supper. That is all I allow myself."

"A glass of beer with your supper?"

"Yes, and in winter-time a glass of stout."

"And you find that that mild potion sustains life?"

Mr. Brooking laughed dutifully. "It is my one dissipation."

"Do you mean to say that you call one glass of beer with your supper or one glass of stout in the winter-time a dissipation?" Kit sighed and waved away a waiter who wore knee-breeches and a striped waistcoat. He sighed again as he saw the retreating back of the waiter. One word, or perhaps two, would have brought a welcome measure of alcohol. Kit was aching for a pink gin.

Mr. Brooking had produced a sheaf of pamphlets. "If you will take these and read them you will learn of our objects."

Kit took the papers and stuffed them into his pocket. "Yes, rather. Splendid show. I am sure you do a tremendous lot of good." He fingered his fountain-pen.

"We do some good, yes," Mr. Brooking admitted diffidently. "But the results have been a little disappointing. Too many of those we have tried to help have failed us. We have given them money and clothes and have found them work, but that has not been enough, apparently."

"But what else can you do?" Kit was vaguely interested.

"Their environment, I believe, is the trouble, or at least that is what we decided at our last meeting. Colonel Truscott, our president, has suggested that we should start some sort of establishment in the country far away removed from their old associations. He is very keen on the open-air life. One might almost say that it is part of his religion."

"One might," Kit agreed. "I know Colonel Truscott and I suppose he gave you my name?"

"Yes, and he said that you were just the man for the job."

"What is the job exactly?"

Mr. Brooking beamed, for he thought he saw victory ahead. "It is very interesting work; really absorbing. You visit the various convict establishments and make contact with those prisoners who are shortly to be discharged; make friends with them and get them to promise to work on one of your farms when they are discharged."

And Kit Kimber agreed; he didn't quite know why. Later, when Mr. Brooking was but a curious memory, Kit cursed Colonel Truscott and almost decided to break his promise to Mr. Brooking. But there was something in the idea which attracted him; he had often wanted to meet criminals and find out what they were really like. Up to date his only experience of the class had been confined to encounters with gentlemen who sought to interest him in gold mines, orange groves and cast-iron schemes for getting money out of bookmakers.

It was unfortunate that he was abroad at the time of Tooley's release—unfortunate for Tooley—but as soon as he returned to London, Mr. Brooking got busy. "The name is James Hope, but he is known as Tooley," he told Kit. "I've asked one of the police, a man called Leith, to get in touch with you. He can tell you more about him than I can."

Leith called at Durham Square and drank much beer and told all he knew about Tooley. "He's a curious fellow and I doubt very much if you'll be able to do anything with him. If you'd caught him a week ago it might have been different, but I have an idea that he has joined up with one of his old crowd."

"I'll give him a try."

Leith lifted a silver tankard to his lips and drank deeply. "When you first meet him you think he's as hard as nails; got a surly manner like a stray dog that's had to look after itself; doesn't trust anyone, but like a lot of his kind he's got a sentimental streak. I met him once taking toys to a kid." Leith grinned. "And he was furious that I'd seen him. Not long after that he was pinched. About three months later I found out that the kid was the daughter of Sharkey Finn. He fell off a roof and killed himself, and I had to go to his house. There were a lot of kid's books with Tooley's name in them."

"Film stuff."

"Yes, I know; but there's quite a lot of it in real life. You'd be surprised at the number of crooks, real hard nuts, who beg me to keep their names out of the papers so that their mothers won't know what they're doing. They say that everyone has a skeleton in their cupboard, but there's a lot who've got a pretty picture there too, which they don't want anyone else to see."

"What sort of line do you think I should take with this man Tooley?"

"I don't know, but whatever you do, go slow. He's a shy bird. I met him the other night and I could see that his nerves were all to hell. This stretch he's just done must have shaken him a lot. It would be fine if you could get him away into the country for a spell. It would give him a chance to find himself."

"That's the trouble with all the men I've dealt with so far. They'll take money and sometimes work at a job for a while, but they don't like leaving Town; personally, I don't blame them. I had three down together some time ago and they spent all their time in the pub taking money from the yokels at crown and anchor."

"Yes, it's a heart-breaking business, Mr. Kimber." Leith finished his beer and put down his tankard. "I'm sorry I can't help you much. You'll have to work it out your own way."

"Where can I meet him?"

Leith thought for a moment. "Well, now, the best thing you can do is to call in at the 'Bear'—it's a small pub in Lisle Street, about two doors away from a gramophone shop on the north side—any time between eleven and one. Don't tell him you know me."

As he accompanied Leith to the front door, Kit said: "I wonder really if it's worth my meeting the chap. If he has joined up with his old pals he'll be damned hard to shift."

"Yes, it's a slim chance, but if you've got nothing else to do it's worth trying."

And so at eleven o'clock Kit Kimber went to the 'Bear' in Lisle Street, but he saw no one there remotely resembling Tooley, for the very good reason that Tooley was in a 'phone box calling Kit's house. The butler thought that Mr. Kimber would be back shortly, so Tooley went for a walk, and half an hour later tried again. Louie had been insistent that he should get to work on Kimber that day, for the *Van Wyk* was on her way across and Zimmermann was anxious to return as soon as possible. At noon Tooley said, "To hell with Kimber!" and went to the 'Bear'. Kit saw him come in and thought, 'That's my man,' and caught him before he reached the bar.

"I say, is your name Hope—James Hope?"

Tooley froze. The last man who had used that name had been the prison governor. One glance told him Kit was not a policeman, but that was all. "What d'you want?" Tooley's lips hardly moved.

"Have a drink?"

Tooley didn't answer for a minute, then he climbed on to a stool and put his feet on the brass rail. There was nothing to lose by accepting a drink. "O.K. Mine's a black label."

"My name's Kimber."

"What's that?"

"Kimber. Heard it before?"

"No. No, of course not. Why should I have?"

"I thought Brooking may have told you. He asked me to look you up."

"I've heard of him. He's in one of them help societies."

"I am, too."

"All right, then. Fire away. Do your stuff."

"It doesn't look as though it's going to be worth my while."

Tooley stared at his glass. "You're wrong there. I want a chance the same as any other bloke. What do you want me to do? Get down on my knees to you? Spin a hard-luck yarn?"

"No, I think I've heard most of them."

"Well, that's something. Same again, miss."

"I can get you a job that'll pay a fair wage, but you'd have to—"

"Yes, I knew there was a string to it," Tooley sneered.

"Just go into the country. That's all."

"It's enough, isn't it?"

"Better than where you've come from."

"Maybe." Tooley picked up his glass. "Here's how."

"I don't want you to promise me anything except that you'll stay for a fortnight; give it a fair go. You needn't do any work during that time, but if you want to stay on it'll mean doing a job."

"It's easy for you to talk. I've got all my pals here."

"And what good are they going to do you?"

"And the Smoke. I've been in these parts all my life. How'd you like it if you had to clear out to some place you didn't like, where you didn't know anybody?"

Kit hitched himself up on a stool and reached for the cheese. "Well, have you got any ideas? What do you want to do?"

Tooley tapped on the counter as thoughts raced through his brain. It was true enough. His only chance was to get right out of it. He'd told Louie he wanted a time off to get his nerve back. Why shouldn't he go? It needn't be for long. Get out of it. Maybe Anna would come with him; it wouldn't be so bad if he had her. He gave a little laugh at the picture of himself as a respectable married man, settled in the country. And then he recalled his meeting with her, and muttered: "She'd never come. At least, not just yet. I'll have to take her easy."

He turned to Kit and spoke aloud. "You see, mister, part of the trouble is that I've been away the hell of a long time, and I've been reckoning on hitting it up a bit. You don't know what it means to me just to stand here in a pub and talk, and know that you can't be ordered about. You've never eaten and worked and lived to the stroke of a bell or the blast of a whistle. Every place you go you have to shuffle along, treading on the heels of the bloke in front. That's all you see, another bloke's back. Or sit in your crib knowing you won't see a soul for another eighteen hours. That's what it is in the wintertime. And nothing to do but think, until you go nearly crazy. You get so that you can't read, and you want to scream, it's so quiet. Sometimes a bloke breaks and starts shouting and beating on the door with his pail. And then all the rest of 'em start up too. It's not much to begin with, and then it gets louder and louder and you can't stop and they come and take you away, four of 'em, and lock you up in solitary. Bread and water's all you get. And then they haul you up before the boss and he drools on about rules and discipline. He's got it all pat like a kid saying a lesson. You don't listen to him. You get like that. Like as if part of you's dead. Well, that part of me's waking up. I want people round me all the time. People I can talk to. I want a band playing all the time. And you ask me to go down to the country. You call that giving a bloke a chance."

"Then what can I do?"

"I don't know. Nothing for blokes like me. Start with the kids. You've some chance with them."

Without thinking of what he was saying, Kit said: "Come out with me tonight. Forget what I've said."

"Where?"

"I don't mind. You choose. We can have dinner somewhere and do a show."

Tooley forgot to sneer when he replied: "O.K., I'll meet you here at eight."

On his way to his club Kit ran into Leith near Piccadilly Circus. Leith said: "Well, how did you get on?"

"I don't know if I'll be able to do any good. He's all on edge."

"I was afraid it would be like that."

"But there's something about the man I like. I don't know what it is. If I keep on I think I might be able to do something."

"He's out of the general run. That's the difficulty—to know how to handle him. Roughly speaking, there's two kinds of crooks: the ones that are just naturally that way—you can't do anything with them except shut 'em up and keep 'em shut up. And then there's the crowd that are weak and conceited. They like spending money, but they hate making it. As long as they've got plenty of dough it's all right, they keep straight, but when they go broke you can start looking for trouble. They look for the easy way out and find themselves inside and wondering how they got there. There's plenty of that sort in your class. They go to good schools, but all they learn is how to spend money, not how to make it."

"What about Tooley? How does he come in?"

"He's different, as I said. He's one of what I call the bitter sort. He went into crime for pure devilment and now the devil's got him and won't let go. And he's bitter because he's been inside. He can never forget, and he's not too good at forgiving. That spell he's had has turned him real bad—leastways, I'm afraid it has." Leith stopped outside the Criterion. "Well, I'll have to be getting along. Let me know how things go."

*   *   *

As he walked northward, Tooley was thinking: 'He wasn't such a bad guy. Maybe I could give it a go. Soon as we pull this job; soon as it's all cleared up and if there isn't any stink. I won't say anything to Louie, I'll just clear out, and maybe by that time Anna'll come too; it'd be just fine if I could get her.'

He called in at Silvretti's and said: "Tell the guv'nor I want to see him."

Silvretti was sitting on a stool behind the counter smoking a cigarette. "All right. I tell him. Come back in one hour." He picked up a paper and began to read.

Tooley went into the street and stood for a moment looking up and down. Then he put his head in at the shop door. "Where'll I find the boys these days?"

"You can try the 'Marquis'; that's where some of 'em go."

Tooley went to the 'Marquis', a public house in Wardour Street, but he fed alone at a table in the corner. There was no one there whom he knew and he was shy of asking questions.

At two o'clock he returned to Silvretti's and found the Italian shaving a customer and making gloomy conversation. As he parted the bead curtain Silvretti looked up and took a slip of paper from a pocket in his dirty white coat. "And he say, 'Don' be late.' You understand. Don' be late."

"O.K." Tooley took a packet of cigarettes off a pile and said, "Put these on the slate," and went out. On the pavement he unfolded the paper and read: 'Goodge Street Tube. 2.30.' Then he struck a match and shielded the flame until the paper was a film of black ash. He knew the rules.

He had been waiting for three minutes in the entrance to the station when Louie passed him but gave no sign. He followed, and at the first bus stop saw him board a bus and climb the stairs. There were no police in sight and as the bus moved off he ran and jumped on to it.

As Tooley sat beside Louie on the back seat, Louie said: "How'd it go?"

"Not so bad. We've fixed to go out tonight."

"Where?"

"Nothing settled. I'm meeting him at the 'Bear' at eight o'clock."

"All right. Steer him into Guido's round about midnight. I'll have Slipper there and Mabel to pair up with him. Guido'll show you where to sit so that they can keep tabs on you. When Anna walks past your table, ask her to join you."

"Can't you keep her out of it?"

"Why? She works for me. I pay her, and she's smart as paint."

"Still—"

"She's only going to dance with him. That's all." Louie leaned back; his coat was open and he put a thumb in the armhole of his waistcoat. "Anna is Tommy Finn's kid; she's bred in the game, and if she doesn't kick, then it's nothing to do with you. Leave her alone or else there'll be trouble. Savvy?" Louie's eyes were as cold as a cat's and his voice hardened as he uttered the threat.

Tooley's lips set in an obstinate line. Then he said: "O.K. I'll play your game this time, because I said I would."

"This time? What's biting you? Scared of the Rigger?"

"I'm not scared of anyone."

"Sounds like it to me. But you've got no worry. Anyone that works for me gets looked after, and this is a peach of a job the way I'm going to work it. And there'll be plenty dough. Yes, a peach of a job." Louie's voice was husky again and held no bite. He took his thumb out of his waistcoat and buttoned his coat. Then he banged on the bell. As he got up he said: "Don't forget. Have him at the club at midnight and introduce him to Anna. That's all you've got to do."

As the bus jolted on after the stop, Tooley muttered to himself: "I'll never get away from him, so what the hell's the good of sweating about?" He had the pig in his right hand. "Maybe it'll bring me luck this time."

CHAPTER IV

LOUIE PATRA had plenty to do in the few hours left at his disposal. It was the quick, secret work that suited him best and fed his vanity. He was as efficient as a watchmaker, oiling microscopic wheels, ensuring that the cogs would engage smoothly.

He sat back in his chair, thinking for a while, his white hands outspread on the desk, his small eyes half shut. He was rehearsing the scene that was to be enacted that evening at Guido's Club. He was choosing his tools.

His choice for the star role fell on a craftsman called Slipper. Slipper was, at the moment, at liberty. He was deft and reliable. Slipper was the man.

A brief interview with the gentleman in question, summarily whisked from one of his haunts to Louie's office, proved that Slipper was willing. He listened moodily to his instructions, pulling at the lobe of one ear and nodding mechanically.

"Got a dinner-jacket and all the duds?" snapped Louie.

Slipper was facetious. "My tailor got it just now, for alterations. I can get it out if I . . ."

"Here you are." The money was put into Slipper's ever-ready hand. The fingers—unusually long and delicate fingers—spun each coin in the air dexterously.

"Do I get my chow?"

"You'll get your chow, and as much drink as you'll need," Louie replied, adding softly: "when you've earned it. That's all."

Louie himself, oily and debonair in his dinner-suit, was at the club before eleven. He was a little bit anxious lest Tooley should not handle Kimber properly. Tooley was still jumpy and not altogether to be relied upon yet. A little light work should give him back his confidence, Louie considered. But it would be a fiasco indeed if the victim should fail to appear, when the trap was so delicately set.

He showed no sign of anything but confidence to Guido, however, to whom he issued the usual curt, concise instructions, without vouchsafing any unnecessary information. Louie believed that each tool should work independently and more or less blindly, content with their own orders and their wages. Ignorance spelt not so much bliss, as a measure of safety from possible squealers.

Punctual to the moment, Slipper appeared in the foyer of the club at 11.30, shuffling and looking self-conscious in a dinner-jacket which had long since forgotten its tailor.

Louie's thick lips parted in a fraction of a smile, and he said: "Go right in. Mabel'll be along in a minute. And don't start hoofing it till Anna gives you the office." As Slipper advanced towards the door with the wariness of a fox in a hen-roost, Louie whispered to Guido: "Give him that cheap wine, nothing else, and table number seven. You won't have any trouble."

When Guido had anchored Slipper in the obscurity of table number seven, he returned to the lobby to keep a lookout for Mabel.

Mabel was apt to be conspicuous. She possessed a head of hair as wonderful as it was false, a fiery vocabulary of some two hundred words, and a reputation coveted by none. She also had a florid taste in lipsticks.

But tonight she was a faded reproduction of the usual chromeo. Also she was nervous, and even overawed by Guido as he escorted her heavily to where Slipper was sitting, looking moodily at a bottle of wine.

"Well, do you always look like this at a party?" She opened a bead bag and took out a compact which had seen years of service.

"I never worked in a dump like this before." Slipper rubbed his chin nervously and puffed quickly at his cigarette.

"Soft pickings if you know your way about. Your tie's crooked." She leaned across the table and straightened it with one pull. "And your collar's a size too big, but you can't do anything about that now." She picked up the bottle of wine and filled her glass. "Tastes of vinegar to me."

Slipper shuddered and caught a passing waiter by the sleeve. "Get me a double gin, mate."

He saw the waiter talk to Guido, and as Guido shook his head his hopes were dashed.

The waiter went away and did not return. Slipper put his hand across his face and sighed.

"Kind of funny, you working in a place like this," said Mabel. "Of course, it's different for me."

Slipper lit a cigarette, and as he blew out the smoke he said: "You got a neck. Different for you! Different from Holloway. Different from the 'Nag's Head', where you got the push for selling swipes. Different! I'll say it's different"

"That's what I said, different; but you don't need to make a blinking anthem out of it. You're ignorant that's what you are. Dead ignorant, just the same as a kid that hasn't been to school. I don't know what the guv'nor was thinking of, getting you here, honest I don't."

"Well, I'll tell you." Slipper leaned on his elbows, sprawling across the table. "He knows who's the smartest worker north of the river."

"Then it's a damned shame he didn't get him along."

Slipper groped in an inside pocket and produced a very old and dirty and greasy pocket-book. He took from it a bunch of yellowing newspaper cuttings.

"There you are! Take your pick, where you like, any one you like, I don't care. They're all good."

Without any interest Mabel selected one of the cleanest. Slipper edged round the table and, breathing hotly, read over her shoulder. "That's what the Common Serjeant said just before he sent me down for a stretch. And up at the top is what Leith said. 'One of the most dangerous and daring criminals known to the police.'"

Slipper knew the words off by heart, for he was as proud of them as a servant is of his character.

"Most daring criminal known to the police," he repeated. "There you are; there's no getting away from that, it's in print; and here's a piece one of them reporter blokes put in one of the Sunday papers. Got a mug of me too. See?"

"Pity you didn't wash your face before it was took," was Mabel's comment, but Slipper wasn't listening. He was basking in the brilliant light of his past.

He was aroused by Mabel, who nudged him with a sharp elbow. "That's them."

Slipper looked up and said: "I didn't know Tooley was out."

"Last Thursday. You know what you got to do?"

"Yes, I know all right." Slipper was watching Kit Kimber as he walked across the dance floor. "We'll wait till there's more of a crowd."

"You got to do it tonight, the guv'nor said so."

"I know, I know." Slipper filled his glass with wine and drank it off without tasting it It His fingers clasped and unclasped round the stem of the glass.

"Got the wind up?"

"'Course I haven't. I've pulled hundreds of jobs tougher than this. It'll be easy meat. We've just got to work him into a corner, give him one bump, that's just to take his mind off what I'm after; not that it's necessary, you understand, but I'm not running any risks."

"What would happen if we was caught?"

"We won't be; don't you worry. All the same, I'd like it a lot better if I had a winger; a bloke who could kind of steer him round my way. That's the way I work mostly. I told the guv'nor that, but he said—" Slipper stopped talking suddenly.

"Well, what did he say?" prompted Mabel.

A hint of a grin came over Slipper's face. "He said that two crows in the place in one night was plenty."

Mabel sniffed. "Two crows! I'll have a word with him about that afterwards."

"No, you won't; you'll keep your trap shut and stay healthy."

"They've clicked." Mabel took out her powder-puff, gave it a little shake and put it back into its compact.

"What's that?"

"Anna." As Anna walked across the floor, Mabel said grudgingly: "She's a smart kid all right, but harder than a flint road. Look at him goofing at her. She's got him going all right. Give 'em time."

"When do we start?"

"Plenty of time. They'll talk for a bit and have a drink. Wait till he's got some of that fizz inside of him." Kit was raising his glass and looking at Anna; he was smiling at her.

A waiter arrived with a ragout in a casserole. As he set down the dish he slipped a folded piece of paper into Slipper's hand.

When he had gone, Slipper read it slowly twice, then he gave it to Mabel.

"See what he says, wait till there's a waltz and the lights go low. Can you waltz?"

"I can waltz all right, can you?"

"I've never tried, but I expect I can make a go of it."

"And I've got on my light slippers." Mabel looked down at Slipper's feet. "What you got to do is to keep those boats on the floor. If you lift 'em I'll kick your shins. Get that?"

"I can dance all right."

"Then for Heaven's sake don't try; just shuffle around and let the others do the fancy steps. I got corns. Any funny business and I'll stamp holes in your feet with my heels. If I'd known I'd have put nails in them."

Slipper spooned the ragout on to his plate and then pushed the dish across to Mabel. "What do they call this?"

"Stew."

Slipper pointed to the menu. "There's nothing about stew written here."

"That's what it is, stew. And it's what I've had for the last three days."

"I could have done with a steak."

"I could have done with a nice bit of fish."

Slipper gave the bottle of wine a nasty look. "And the guv'nor said we'd have a slap-up feed."

They watched Kimber dance three times before the top lights were switched out. The band started a waltz and the floor began to fill. Slipper rubbed the palms of his hands on his trousers. Mabel gave her face a quick dusting of powder, and then closed her compact with a snap which made Slipper look up.

He said: "We'd better get going."

"I'll tell you when." Mabel watched Anna and Kit walk on to the floor and slide into the waltz. "Let 'em get warmed up first."

The room was full of diners and most of them were dancing when Mabel touched Slipper on the arm. "Come on, and don't forget what I said about keeping your plates on the deck, or else—"

Mabel could dance, and she steered Slipper with a firm grip on his shoulder. Slipper had stopped being nervous and he was cold as ice.

Mabel whispered a word to him. He dropped his right hand to his side. There was a couple on each side of them and one behind them. They bumped, and Slipper's right hand moved faster than a lizard's tongue. He breathed, "O.K."

They made one more turn of the floor and then returned to their table. There was a waiter standing there. Slipper's hand passed over that of the waiter's, and then he and Mabel sat down.

Slipper took a handkerchief out of his pocket and wiped his face and forehead. "I'm glad that's over."

Mabel looked at the menu and beckoned to a waiter. She ordered a *pêche melba*. Slipper said, "Bring me a brandy." Then he lit a cigarette and drummed on the table with a forefinger.

Five minutes later a waiter brought Slipper his brandy and again something passed between him and Slipper. Again the lights went low and the same scene was played. Mabel manoeuvred Slipper so that he was close to Kit Kimber. Again Slipper whispered, "O.K.," but this time he and Mabel did not return to their table. They walked out of the room and met Louie in the hall. He said: "That was fine. Very nice piece of work." He purred like a cat and his voice was husky and full of syrup.

He gave Mabel a pound and handed two to Slipper. He pointed to a door. "That's your best way out."

*   *   *

Benny Watt was in the chapel sitting hunched over his desk, a watchmaker's glass in his right eye and a row of blank keys laid out before him.

Louie came in and stood behind his left shoulder. "How are you getting on?"

Benny picked up a key and held it up to the light. "That's finished very nearly. Just got to buff him up on the wheel and he'll be O.K."

"Will it fit?"

Benny grinned. "He'll fit all right. You don't want to worry about that."

"I'd like 'em all tomorrow."

"You'll have 'em tomorrow." Benny picked up a piece of yellow soap. "See that print? Lovely and clean, ain't it?" He put the glass back in his eye and chose a file.

"Finish the door-keys first."

"That's what I'm on now."

Louie stood for a moment pulling at his cigar. "I'll tell Guido to send you in some chow."

"And beer."

"You can have all you want." There was an oily smile on Louie's face as he stepped out into the yard and walked towards the wooden stairs which led to his office, but before he was half-way there he changed his mind. There was a line of light showing under the garage door. He walked to the door and pushed it open.

Tony loved engines. He also loved bright colours.

He was eighteen years old and tall and slim and lanky, and moved awkwardly like someone who has not got complete control of his limbs. He was never really happy unless he had a wrench in his hand.

When Louie opened the door of the garage Tony was standing at a work-bench. He was wearing a mauve silk shirt and trousers of a startling shade of blue. In front of him were scattered the parts of a carburettor. He was passing a thin silver wire through the hole of a jet.

He swung round quickly at the noise of Louie's entry, and there was a frightened look on his face.

"You got to take something for these nerves of yours, Tony." Louie kicked the door shut. "Who did you think I was?"

"Sorry, Mr. Patra, but I wasn't expecting you, and I was so busy on this that you gave me a fright."

"Always on the job," Louie purred. "That's fine."

"I'm going to fix it so that I can get eighty out of the big car."

"That's fine. Maybe we'll need it one of these nights. When are you going to finish?"

"Tonight if I keep at it."

"Friday morning'll do. I got a job Friday night."

"I'll need to give her a test first. I'd like to have a try-out at Brooklands."

"O.K. But you got to have her ready on the dot." Louie rolled his cigar across his mouth. "That's a fine shirt you're wearing."

"Like it?"

"It's fine. Maybe you'll be able to buy a lot more if we pull this job."

Tony screwed a nut on to a bolt. His fingers were long and slender like those of a musician.

"And we won't have far to go," Louie continued. "Durham Square. Know it?"

"It's just west of Soho Square, isn't it?"

Louie took a map from his pocket and spread it out on the bench. "From here you turn right, and left at the top, second on the right and straight ahead for a couple of hundred yards."

"Yes, I know. There's gardens in the middle of it."

"That's right. The house is Number forty-six, in the middle of this block. You've got to be at this corner at ten minutes past eleven o'clock on Friday night, facing south. I'll be at the corner of Stenning Street, so look out for me, and if I'm reading a paper you'll know that it's all O.K. and you can go right ahead. There'll be a man opposite the house and when he flashes a light go ahead. That'll mean that the job's finished, and he'll come out of the house and get into the bus. Circle the gardens and pick me up and then come straight back here as hard as you can lick. There'll be nothing to it."

"I'd have liked it better if there'd been a longer run. I'd like to show you what she can do when she's opened up."

"Maybe it'll be far enough." Louie took a couple of steps towards the door. "And then on the Saturday I'll maybe want you to take the lorry down to the creek. Is she O.K.?"

"Yes, she's O.K., Mr. Patra. Going fine."

"Maybe you'll be able to buy half a dozen silk shirts and a couple of new suits." Louie allowed himself a grin as he said, "Good night," and moved towards the door.

When he entered the lobby of the club the band was still playing and the floor was still crowded. He sent a waiter to find Guido, and when the fat man came padding flat-footed across the mossy carpet, he said: "That'll be all for tonight. Send Tooley along to the office."

He had finished one cigar and started on a second before the door of the office opened and Tooley came in. He poured whiskey into a glass and pointed to a chair. "It's worked out fine. You done well."

"I didn't do anything. He asked me to take him to a night-club."

"Lucky it was so easy; it don't always work out that way. Soda?"

Tooley nodded, and as he took his glass, he said: "I could trim him."

"Who?"

"Kimber, of course. I've got him going."

"And what the hell would be the good of that? What would you get? Ten, twenty, thirty, fifty perhaps, and that would be the finish. You'd have to run and keep on running, and before you had time to spend the dough the dicks would have you and you'd be inside for another stretch. That's how it would go. The dicks have got you taped all ways. If you want to win you got to work my way." Louie reached for the whiskey and refilled Tooley's glass. He gave Tooley the map that he had shown to Tony.

"It'll be best if you walk to the house by yourself. You'll have the keys to all the doors."

"How are you going to get them?" Tooley asked.

Louie laughed, a deep rumbling belly laugh which lasted half a minute. "That's something I'll fix. You'll have the keys and there'll be nothing for you to worry about there." Louie took a folded piece of paper from his pocket. "This is the plan of the lay-out inside. You remember? The one Spider brought the other night. Take it home with you and get it into your head. Don't forget the rattlers; you'll have to turn them off before you start work, and the outer hall is tiled, so you'll have to wear rubber-soled shoes. I tell you it's going to be a sweet job, one of the smoothest I've ever worked."

"All the same, I'd rather be out of it." Tooley's face was hard-set and the line of his lips was thin. "Kimber knows who I am; he knows I am on a ticket and the first thing I'll know is that Leith'll be putting me over jumps, and I don't want that."

"Kimber got on to you first, didn't he?"

Tooley nodded.

"Well, then, why should they think you have anything to do with it? You've never been to the house. You've only seen Kimber twice, and, besides that, remember that the dicks have one-track minds. You've never pulled a job like this before. They'll round up all the screwsmen and grill them all they know. They'll never even think of you. And besides, I'll fix you with an alibi no one'll crack."

"If it's going to be so damned easy why not get someone else?" Tooley gave a quick tight smile. "Or do it yourself?"

"Because I haven't got your education, Tooley." He produced Zimmermann's list of the articles that were to be stolen. "What I want you to do is to take a run down to the Victoria and Albert Museum tomorrow, and mug up on this lot. Find out what a potato-ring looks like. And here's another one. Have you ever heard of a mazer bowl?"

"It's a wooden bowl with a silver rim."

"There you are. That proves what I was saying. You understand this sort of language. I don't."

Tooley folded the catalogue and put it in his pocket. "And what about the get-away?"

"That'll be easy. As soon as you come out of the front door Tony'll come past with the big car."

Tooley thought for a moment and then he said: "I was just thinking about that front door. What am I going to do if it's bolted?"

"It won't be. Kimber'll be dining out and we'll pull the job about eleven. Now run along and get a good night's sleep. You got to look after yourself."

Tooley went back to the club to find Anna, but she had gone. Louie had seen to that.

He went out of the Canton Street entrance into the cool air of the night. His brain was drumming and he wanted to walk and walk until he was exhausted. Sometimes he could think better while he was walking, and he wanted to think. Now that he was out of Louie's influence the job did not seem so attractive, and he wanted to find out if there was anything wrong with it. "You got to look after yourself." That was what Louie had said, and it was true enough.

He was frightened. If the job didn't work out right he'd be in a bad jam; back on the Moor. Louie had never been there; he didn't know what it was like. It was easy for him to talk. Louie hadn't given him time to think. And then there was Anna. He wanted her worse than he had ever wanted anything before in his life.

Tooley walked as far as Oxford Street, crossed and continued north. He was free. He could go where he liked and as far as he liked. He was free. He told himself that. He could do what he damn' well liked and there would be no one to stop him.

The stones of the pavements were hard and his head was hot with wine and food. He would go on and on. He could go where he damn' well liked. He didn't give a toss for Leith or for Louie or any of the crowd. If he felt like it he would clear out and he wouldn't care what any of them thought or said.

From now on he was going to please himself—If only Anna would come away with him it would be all right. He could buy her if he had the cash. He knew that. He'd sensed that the first night at the club. She was on the make. She'd stay with him as long as he could feed her and keep her and pay for her clothes. And all the same he wanted her—not just wanted, but craved her, as in prison he had craved the right to talk. He'd make her like him. He'd—A police-man loomed up, as wide and as solid and as immovable as a pillar-box. He caught Tooley by the arm. "Just a minute, sir. Where are you going?"

"Home," Tooley snapped.

"And where's your home?"

"Buckingham Palace."

The policeman did not smile. He looked at Tooley with appraising and fish-like eyes. He drew down his jaw and scratched his cheek with a finger while he studied Tooley. He looked at his face, at his clothes and his shoes, and, having completed his examination, he stopped scratching his cheek and said: "The station's just round the corner. Do you mind stepping there? I'd like to check you up."

A sleepy sergeant sitting at a desk in the charge-room listened to the policeman's report. Before he could ask a question Tooley said: "My name's James Hope. I'm a convict on licence and here's my papers."

The sergeant took them and mumbled: "Thought I'd seen your mug before." When he had finished reading he gave them back and said: "Better for you not to be out at this time of night. Why don't you go to bed?"

"Because I want to walk. There's no law against that, is there?"

"You'd better go back to where you're staying." The sergeant signed to a man in plain clothes, who was sitting on a bench reading a paper. "This officer will go along with you, just to see you're not bothered again."

When Tooley reached his room over Silvretti's shop he sat on the bed and took off his shoes. "I'm free; like hell I'm free!" he muttered. "I can do what I like; like hell I can do what I like!"

CHAPTER V

WHEN SPIDER HAD left Louie's office he had had ten pounds in his hand and the knowledge that he wasn't going to be in on the big job. The money made him feel good, but Louie's curt dismissal rankled in his brain, and he fed the germ of discontent with several pints of old-and-mild, laced with gin.

Now old-and-mild will not do anyone much harm unless taken by the bucketful, and gin on its own is a good enough drink, but the combination is apt to have the effect of a particular brandy sold in the Cape, which is known as Fight-your-mother-Mrs.-Brandy.

The mixture certainly raised the fighting spirit in Spider, and he very soon was in the state when he would have felt like pushing a bus over. Sober, he would have kept away from Lucas Street after what Louie had said to him, but now he did not care.

Next day he went to Mrs. Hoskins' café in Canton Street, which was not ten yards from the doorway bearing the board: 'S. Zwolsky. Ladies' Tailor.'

Mrs. Hoskins was a small woman, whose face was always red because she cooked all day, and it was round because it had been made that way. Two of the most important of her front teeth, important both from the point of view of scenic effect and as an aid to efficient mastication, had been lost in battle with a customer whose stomach had found fault with her cooking.

The customer had backed up the judgment of his stomach to the extent of throwing a bottle of sauce at Mrs. Hoskins.

When Spider walked into the café Mrs. Hoskins was having what she termed a 'good clean up'. That is to say she had put all the dirty dishes into a copper of hot water and was stirring them with a wooden stick.

A wisp of grey hair was hanging over her forehead. When she saw Spider she swept back the wisp with a hot, wet, red hand and grinned. "'Ullo, mate. It's a long time since you've been round here. You hain't been sick, have you?"

"No, I'm all right. What have you got to eat?"

Mrs. Hoskins wiped her hands on her sacking apron and walked to the window, where a double line of enamel trays were ranged over gas burners. "There's sausages and beans and onions and potatoes; and there's a bit of stewed steak somewhere if I can find it." She poked about among the sausages with a two-pronged fork. "Yes, here it is, and a nice bit it is too; fourpence."

"That'll do me, and I'll have some mashed to go along with it." Mrs. Hoskins, glad of an excuse to leave her dish-washing operations, leaned on the counter. "It's a pity you wasn't in before."

"Why?" Spider asked.

Mrs. Hoskins' voice sank to a windy whisper. "I think the boss has got something on. If you'd been about, you might have picked up something. Mind you," she added hurriedly, "I don't know nothing; it's just what I've guessed, and don't tell anyone I said anything to you about it, or it might get me into trouble; you know what the boss is like."

Spider pulled up a stool to the counter and picked up a knife and fork. "You can trust me," he lied. "Where's Mr. Benny Watt?"

"Just gone down the street not a couple of minutes before you come in. Looked as if he'd been up half the night."

Spider sawed at the 'nice' bit of steak. "I'd like to have a crack with him. We used to work together once."

"Then maybe if you had a word with him and he spoke to the boss something might be fixed."

"I could do with a job."

"He gives me the creeps; the way he looks at you."

"He's all right," Spider mumbled, as he soaked up gravy with a piece of bread. "You got to know him, that's all there is about it."

The street door opened and Benny Watt shuffled in. He was on his way to the door which led to the passage when Mrs. Hoskins shouted at him: "There's a friend of yours here, Benny."

The questing seal-like gaze wavered to and fro and at last found Spider. He said: "Glad to see you; where have you been?"

"Knocking around."

"Did you do that job for the guv'nor?" asked Benny.

"Yes. It was easy as kiss your hand."

"That's fine, that's fine," Benny mumbled. "It was me put him on to you. You ought to make a good thing out of it."

Spider thought for a minute before he replied: "Yes. When does it come off?"

"Didn't he tell you?" There was a note of suspicion in Benny's high-pitched voice.

"No, he said he'd let me know later," Spider lied.

"You haven't got a lot of time. He told me to be ready for Friday night. That's tomorrow."

Spider concealed his surprise. He said: "He knows where to find me."

"Tooley's going to be in it, and Tony's driving the big car; he was working on it all last night."

"Durham Square?"

"He didn't tell me that; just to be ready at eleven o'clock, that was all he said. I've got to have the gate open at half past ten for Tony. I don't know nothing else."

"It's one of these foreign jobs," said Mrs. Hoskins.

"What do you know about it?" queried Benny angrily. "You oughtn't to know nothing about it."

"I got my eyes, haven't I? And my ears? And there ain't no laws that I know that says I ain't got to use them."

"The guv'nor don't care about laws," Benny sniggered. "You ought to know that by this time."

"I sees what I sees, and I hears what I hears."

"Well, what did you hear, and what did you see?" Benny taunted her.

"I saw a foreigner go in at the door of twenty-six, and I heard him go up the stairs and I heard him go along the top passage and go into the office. And it was the same bloke that was here just before the job you was all in at that place down in Kent. Three months ago it was, very near."

Benny was interested. "Did you hear who he was, and who he worked for?"

"It was none of my business," Mrs. Hoskins retorted. "And I didn't ask no questions."

"I'll bet you didn't ask no questions; you got some sense." Benny Watt took Spider by the sleeve. "Don't say I told you anything. The guv'nor's funny that way; he likes to give all his orders hisself and he don't tell anyone any more than he has to."

"O.K." Spider winked an eye which had the effect of making his face look more like that of a rubber doll than ever.

"I'm going to have a drop of shut-eye now, I was up most of the night." Benny got up off the bench and shuffled towards the door. "Maybe I'll be seeing you later."

Spider paid Mrs. Hoskins fivepence and went out into the street.

* * *

John Carson had almost forgotten his own name, so long had he been addressed as the Rigger.

When young and fairly honest, he had worked in a shipyard. That is how he had got the name of the Rigger.

On the day after that on which Spider had been dismissed from his position as first assistant to Louie Patra, the Rigger was standing wondering how he was going to pay for his next drink.

All around him was a collection of old iron, which the Rigger, in moments of alcoholic optimism, was pleased to call motor-cars.

He was in the market for any old bus whose wheels went round. It was unnecessary that they should go far or fast, but it was a condition of every sale that the purchase should carry the Rigger and the vendor up a neighbouring hill. At the top of this hill was a public house, and if the sale did not come off at any rate the Rigger was sure of a free ride and at least one free drink.

He had had no free rides nor drinks for a week, and his pony, a sad animal with no ambition, being sick and unable to drag its cart round the back streets of Balham in search of rags, bottles and bones, the Rigger was sitting on the running-board of a car which had started life as a Morris Twelve, and now was but a miserable hybrid.

A bus stopped at the corner, but the Rigger was not interested. He was very thirsty. A man got off the bus and walked in the direction of the yard. "Looks like Spider," the Rigger muttered to himself. "Got his walk and all." He rubbed his chin to assist his brain in deciding this problem. Then the gloom on his face lifted. It was Spider, and he was wearing a new suit and a collar and a tie. "Maybe he'd be good for a wet"

"What cheer, me old dear. How she go?" Spider looked round the yard with affected interest. "Got plenty of 'em?"

"You can have the lot for a tenner and chance it" The Rigger took a battered packet of cigarettes from his pocket and held it out to Spider. He took one himself and worked the flattened cigarette between finger and thumb until it was more or less round. "No one's buying drags like these. They've got to have something that'll beat these new lot they've got at the Yard."

"Why don't you try to knock off a couple of real good 'uns?" Spider suggested.

"So I would, quick as kiss your hand, if there was any place where I could lay 'em up. The dicks are always nosing around here. Why, only last week they came asking about a few pounds of lead that had been stripped off the roof of a house just opposite here. I told 'em they could look where they liked, and they didn't half have a party."

"Was they lucky?"

The Rigger smiled. "What do you think?" He pointed towards the gate. "Do you see that lump that's keeping it open?"

Spider nodded.

"Well, that's what they was looking for."

"So you're not finished yet, eh?" Spider chaffed.

"Finished? Like hell I'm finished. If I could only get a chance I'd be right back in the money and not peddling balloons." The Rigger leaned forward, his elbows on his bony knees. "The only bloke that's stopping me is Louie Patra."

Spider said: "I didn't know you had anything to do with Louie."

"Had anything to do with him? I brought him up. I taught him all he knows. He worked with me for five years and when I copped my first stretch I left him to carry on."

"Did he make a go of it?"

"Wait a minute and I'll tell you my own way what happened. Louie was a drain-pipe worker when I met him first, and I fenced a lot of stuff for him. I treated him fair, but he wasn't never satisfied. He always thought he could do better his own self. Well, anyway, I left him to run the show while I was away. He ran it all right. When I come out what did I find but the rat had set up for himself, up West, and had got all my trade. Of course, there was nothing I could do. And I've never been able to make a proper go of this place since."

"He's making a lot of money these days."

"I know that. I went up West a week ago to see if I couldn't drum up a spot of business. Of course, Louie got to hear I was about, and he sent me word by a barber that I was to lay off. He told me to lay off! Me, that had brought him up as you might say!"

Spider knocked the ash off his cigarette. He thought for a full minute before he said: "I can tell you something about Louie. I just done a job for him. I done it well too, and got chucked out on my ear."

"You been working for Louie Patra?"

"I got to eat and drink. There's not a terrible lot doing these days."

"I know that. Get on with it. What happened?"

"He sent for me and said he wanted a joint cased; a house in Durham Square."

"I know Durham Square," the Rigger put in. "There used to be a lot of dough in those parts, but it's mostly all offices nowadays."

"This place isn't an office. More a museum than anything else." Spider spat. "I don't know, it's a funny business altogether. You wouldn't have any use for a china dog, now, would you?"

"China? What are you talking about?"

"China and glass and a bit of silver. That's all that's in the place, as far as I could find out."

The Rigger was interested. "And he's going to bust it?"

"Yes, on Friday night. I had a word with Benny Watt. He said Tony was going to drive for them, and he thought that Tooley was in it too."

"Who else?"

"I don't know, but that's enough, ain't it?"

"It is and it ain't. I dunno. How much have you got?"

"'Arf a thick 'un."

"What say we take a ride up the hill?"

"If you've got anything that'll go up the hill."

The Rigger nodded and then walked to a shack at the end of the yard. He came out with a tin of petrol, which he emptied into the tank of an alleged motor-car. He turned the starting-handle as one would that of a sewing-machine. Suddenly there was the noise as of many small guns being discharged irregularly in a tin shed. Spider got into the seat next to that of the driver. "You've got to hold that door shut. The catch is broke." The Rigger roared up the engine until the whole body shook like a well-set jelly. "She's all right once she gets warmed up."

There were three public houses nearer to the yard than the 'Cock and Hoop', but none boasted a snug so private, so select, and with windows which fitted so securely that the smell of beer and stale smoke was preserved from one year's end to the next.

The Rigger drove the car into a yard and switched off the engine, which died with two asthmatic coughs and a shattering backfire. He explained that she had got a bit hot coming up the hill. "Got a lovely set of tyres on her too."

Spider reminded him that he was not in the market for a car and, with an instinct that never had failed him yet, led the way down a well-worn path to a side door.

There was no one in the box of a room.

"Got the doings?"

Spider handed over a ten-shilling note. "That's got to see me through the week."

The Rigger shouted the order into the passage, and a minute or two later a silent beery man came in with two tankards.

If he had walked up the hill the Rigger could not have shown his appreciation more clearly nor more noisily. As he put down his tankard he said: "Now tell us all about this job."

"There's no more to it than what I've told you," Spider protested. "All I wants to know is how Louie's going to shop the junk. That's got me beat."

"There must be money in it, and it doesn't matter where." The Rigger winked.

"I don't get you."

"You heard that saying about letting the other chap pull the chest-nuts out of the fire for you."

"Yes, that's all right when the chestnuts aren't mouldy, like these ones."

"If he wants 'em real bad, he'll want to buy them back again. That's sense, ain't it?"

"Not with Louie Patra it ain't. I'd rather dicker with a man-eating tiger. You said yourself he's scared you out of his territory."

"I didn't say he'd scared me. I couldn't fight a dozen of 'em, that was all." The Rigger took a plug of tobacco out of his pocket and began shaving it in thin flakes. "You'd like to put it across Louie, wouldn't you?"

"Sure I would if there was a chance of doing it and keeping my health."

"Louie's smart, isn't he?"

"Of course he is."

"And I taught him all he knows. I can handle Louie. Once we get our hands on that stuff we'll have him where he'll have to pay our price."

"What car are they using for the job?" the Rigger asked after a pause.

"The big one. A Buick, and it can't half shift, 'specially with that wop Tony driving."

The Rigger finished his beer and suggested eloquently but silently that he could do with another. Spider refused to take the hint.

"When did you say Louie's fixed to pull this job?"

"Friday. Benny's been told to be ready from half past ten, and to open up the yard gate then."

The Rigger filled his pipe and lit it. "Then we haven't got an awful lot of time. Come on and see a pal of mine. He's got a van I sometimes borrow."

The car, refreshed and cooled, coughed into life at the third turn of the handle, and the Rigger turned her nose northward into a maze of small streets, and finally drew up at a corner shop which apparently sold everything from firewood to bacon and mousetraps. A cat was asleep on a box of candles and the Rigger had to stoop low to clear a bunch of boots and frying-pans hanging from the ceiling.

The vibrant clang of the door-bell drew the proprietor from his earth at the back of the shop. He was a gingery, weasly little man with greedy eyes. A pair of steel-rimmed spectacles were serving no useful purpose on his forehead.

He glanced at the Rigger and then stared at Spider.

"He's all right, Mr. Williams. We done lots of jobs together." The Rigger took a dried apricot from a box and began to eat it. "What we was after was that van of yours. We wouldn't want it for long; a couple of hours maybe."

Mr. Williams fingered his scrubby little ginger moustache and continued to stare at Spider for half a minute; then he took his eyes off Spider and walked round the counter, opened the shop door and stood there for a minute or two.

The Rigger whispered to Spider: "He's all right, but he's a bit scared of the coppers. We'll take him easy."

Mr. Williams closed the door slowly so that there was only a faint tinkle from the bell. He walked back behind the counter. There was a crafty, doubtful expression in his cunning little eyes. "What's it going to pay me?"

"I haven't worked it out yet," the Rigger replied. "But I reckon that your cut will be something round about a fiver."

"How long did you say you wanted the van for? And who's going to drive it?"

"Not more than a couple of hours, and Spider here'll be the jockey."

"When?"

"Tomorrow night about ten."

"It's a big risk for me," Mr. Williams objected. "If you're caught it means that I lose a hundred pounds; that's what the van's worth to me."

The Rigger leaned on the counter. "Now look here, Mr. Williams, this job's going to be as easy as kiss your hand. All we're going to do is to take a little run up West and—"

"Now don't tell me what the job is. If I don't know anything they can't pin anything on me; that's right ain't it?"

"You've got nothing to be afraid of, Mr. Williams," the Rigger assured him. "Give me the key of the shed and go to bed, and in the morning you'll wake up with a ten-pound note in your till."

"I'll think it over and let you know in the morning," said Mr. Williams cautiously. "And there's another thing; who's going to pay for the petrol? I don't know how far you're going to drive."

"I'll fill the tank. So long, Mr. Williams, I'll be around after supper tomorrow." He took Spider by the arm. "Come on, let's get going." As he settled down in the driving-seat the Rigger said: "I wish to hell I didn't have to deal with a little runt like that, but there's nowhere else I can get the sort of bus I want, and it's a good idea, using a van."

"What have I got to do?" Spider asked.

"Just wait round the corner of Wardour Street with the engine running until Tony goes by, then take her into Penton Street, south-east corner of Durham Square, and park her so that nothing can get past you. He's certain to come back that way, and as soon as he stops I'll hold 'em up and grab the stuff."

"Got a gun?"

"Yes, I got a gun all right."

"And if they don't come back the way you say, what'll we do?"

"Try again some other time. I'm going to trim Louie. I'm going to put a snarl in his works. Told me to lay off, did he? Me, that taught him all he knows. I wish I'd thought of this before. Instead of sweating around here I might have been living easy. I wish I'd thought of it before."

"If Louie's in the car you won't have an easy job."

The Rigger laughed. "Catch Louie being in on a job. He'll be waiting at Starling Court, and when Tooley comes back with naught I'd give quids to see his face. He never risks burning his fingers. Gets other blokes to do the work."

Spider might have said that that had been the Rigger's policy too, but he didn't. He didn't want to start an argument; he was too busy trying to work out what would be the risk to himself.

Suddenly he said: "Tooley's tough."

The Rigger grinned. "He'll stop being tough when he sees the gun."

"I don't like it. Why can't you cut out the gun? What if it goes off?"

"It won't go off. I've pulled plenty of jobs like this before."

"I've never carried a gun, and I've never worked with a bloke with one, and I don't want to start now. If anything happens I'd be for it same as you."

The Rigger braked as they came to the hill and he did not reply for few moments. Then he said: "It won't be loaded. I'm not going to take any risks either. You can search me before you start if you like."

Spider thought: 'If anything goes wrong I can beat it and leave the van.' He had a map of the streets in his mind and he worked out the route he would take. He said: "And afterwards you've got to do the dickering with Louie."

"That's what I'm looking forward to. I want to see his face when I tell him who's got his stuff."

A slight shiver ran down Spider's spine. Some blokes had queer tastes. "I'm going to lay up until you get everything fixed."

"You can do as you like."

"What about a doss?" Spider asked.

"What do you mean, tonight?"

"Now. I didn't hardly get me head down last night; I was waiting round most of the time to see if I could get a hold of Benny Watt."

"Aren't you going back to the Smoke?"

"No, not for the hell of a long time, except for this job. I don't want to see anything of Louie, and I don't want him to see hide nor hair of me."

The Rigger rubbed his chin with a rasping sound. "You can bed down in any of that lot." He pointed to a row of cars. "The Daimler's the best; I had a bloke in last week and he paid me a tanner a night for her, but I won't charge you nothing. The dicks pinched him this morning."

Spider grinned. "That's fine; got any more good news just to cheer me up afore I goes to sleep?"

"You never know how things are going to turn out," replied the Rigger gloomily. He was gloomy because he had not had enough to drink. Leaving Spider to fend for himself, he threaded his way through the graveyard of cars and unlocked the padlock of a tin-roofed shack. It was dark inside until he had lit the wick of a hanging oil-lamp. He waited until the glass had warmed up before he turned up the wick; then he sat down on an orange-crate and pulled out a box from under an iron bedstead.

"I thought you might come in handy some time," he muttered to himself, as his fingers closed on the butt of a blue-black automatic. He pressed a spring and the magazine fell into the palm of his left hand. He filled it with cartridges from a cardboard box.

Then he put the pistol back into the box under the bed, covered it with an old shirt and pushed it out of sight with the toe of his boot.

As he stood up and took off his jacket there was a hint of a smile on his broad red face. "So Louie thinks he can keep me out of the game does he? Maybe he'll change his mind before I'm finished with him."

The plan grew in the Rigger's brain as he lay on his back, staring into the darkness. He became mildly drunk with the thought of success, whilst difficulties and the power of Louie dwindled. It was going to be dead easy, he told himself. No risk, and fat profits. He'd screw Louie down and tell him where he got off. He'd make Louie work for him. That would be jam. Easy money. Why hadn't he thought of it before? No more running around after a few pounds of lead off a house roof. And the dicks wouldn't have anything on him. He'd stop down here in Balham and have Spider to do the dirty work. He'd give him a fiver a week and the run of his teeth.

Spider, curled up on the back seat of the Daimler, was trying to comfort himself with the thought that the Rigger could handle Louie Patra. He did not succeed very well, and he slept uneasily.

CHAPTER VI

LOUIE WALKED into Silvretti's shop. The barber was sitting reading an Italian paper, a pair of steel-rimmed glasses on the end of his nose. When he saw Louie he became at once obsequious, bobbing his head, and said "Good afternoon" three times.

"Is Tooley in?"

"Yes, Mr. Patra; in his room. I will call him."

Louie brushed through the curtain into the saloon. He heard Silvretti climbing the stairs, heard the murmur of voices; two minutes later Tooley came in, putting on his coat. He jerked his head in greeting.

Louie said: "Turn round a minute." He stared at the back of Tooley's head. "Yes, I think it might work. . . . Silvretti!"

"Yes, saire?"

"See if you can hunt up Slipper."

Tooley lit a cigarette and sat down, sprawling on a bench. "I thought you were finished with him."

"No, not exactly." Louie smiled. "He's going to be your stand-in."

"What do you mean?"

"He's going to fix your alibi so that no lousy copper can break it."

"That's fine." Tooley's tone was contemptuous and cold and hard. "I can just see him in the box. Anybody would believe him. So you're going to fix my alibi with Slipper. Like hell you are! What do you think the beak's going to say when he sees Slipper? They won't believe a word he says. He's got a record as long as a three-year stretch; every dick in the Smoke knows him."

"I know that." Louie's voice came rumbling up from his belly. "There won't be no need for him to give evidence. I tell you I've got I it all taped out."

"And he's going to be my alibi!"

"You'll see how it's going to work before you pull the job, and if you don't like it you can back out then."

Tooley turned on his back and sucked at his cigarette as he stared at the ceiling. After a minute or two he said: "Well, if that's the way it is . . ."

"You know you can trust me. Your end of it's simple. You'll bring Kimber to the club tomorrow night. Anna'll be there and—"

"I told you I want her kept out of it."

"That's for her to decide." Louie's voice was silky smooth.

"She doesn't know what she's doing."

"I think she does. You're forgetting that she's Finn's kid."

"Maybe she is, but that doesn't mean anything."

"I know Anna; she's been working for me for the past year. You know it would be a lot better for you, and for her as well, if you were to forget Anna till we've finished this job. It's going to mean plenty dough to you and to me, and she'll get her share as well. And you can't do anything without dough."

"If she does this job, will you let her go?"

"If she wants to. Of course I will."

"I didn't like the way Kimber was carrying on with her the other night."

"I'll look after him. Don't you worry about that end of it."

There were footsteps in the shop and Louie called out: "That you, Slipper?"

It was Slipper. He sidled through the bead curtain and stood blinking in the light. "You want me, guv'nor?"

"Sit down." He pointed to a chair. "Tooley, you sit along-side him."

Louie got up and walked behind the two men. "Yes," he muttered to himself. "I think it can be done. . . . Silvretti! Get your shears and snippers out, and get these two just as near the same as you can manage."

"The same? The same what? I do not understand." Silvretti looked like a puzzled, beaten dog.

"Cut their hair the same way. I don't care how you do it, but that's what I want."

"Ah! I see what you want. You want them to look all the same."

"That's the idea. Now get busy." Louie leaned back in his chair and pushed his hat on to the back of his head.

Silvretti, like an artist enraptured by his own skill, stopped his work from time to time and stood back with a critical look in his coal-black eyes. "Just a leetle more from the left side, yes," he muttered.

Ten minutes later he said to Louie: "Now if you please, what do you think of that? It is good, no?"

Louie got on to his feet and examined Silvretti's work. "Not bad, but you'll have to fix the colour. Slipper's a lot fairer than Tooley. Got anything to fix that?"

Silvretti looked thoughtful. "I think so, yes. One minute if you please." He chose a bottle from a row on a shelf and poured some of its contents into a saucer.

Five minutes later he finished dabbing at Slipper's head with a wad of cotton wool. Louie took his cigar from his mouth and said: "That'll do." He gave Silvretti a pound note. "Go and buy yourself a pail of macaroni."

Silvretti bowed as though he had received a knighthood. "Thank you, Mr. Patra. Thank you very much. It is not nothing that I do."

Louie turned to Slipper. "Be at the club at ten o'clock tonight and bring Mabel. I'll give you further orders when you get there. Now get going."

Slipper went off, touching his hair like a girl at a party.

"Tooley, you'd better keep out of sight till tomorrow. You'll have to get a hold of Kimber and get him to the club. I'll give you a call and let you know how you're to do that later." Louie pushed through the bead curtain, leaving it jangling for seconds after he had gone.

"Thinks of lots of things, don't he?" Tooley muttered.

Silvretti, who was putting the cork back in the bottle of dye, heard him and said: "He is a very clever man, Mr. Patra."

Tooley was fingering his ivory pig. "This time he's got to be extra special clever. If things don't go just right I'm not going to be the one to take the can back."

"The can back? What do you mean?"

Tooley was half-way up the stairs to his room, and did not hear the question.

*   *   *

Tooley's task was simple, for he found that Anna had already made a date with Kimber for Guido's Club the following night.

Although this simplified his task, the news annoyed him intensely. He disliked seeing Anna and Kimber dancing together, and he was not at all satisfied that Anna's interest was only a matter of business. She seemed to be earning her wages from Louie with unnecessary gusto.

He scowled when Anna told him of the date, but reflected that it was very much better so, since, when Kimber was questioned by the police as to why he had gone to Guido's, his, Tooley's, name would not have to be mentioned. He therefore swallowed his protests with a bad grace, and contented himself with sulking.

"After all this is over, you're coming out with me. D'you understand?"

Anna eyed him with a trace of curiosity behind her complacency.

Tooley was a much more suitable partner for her than was Kit Kimber. She knew that. And yet there was something about Kimber which fascinated her. He was only the common victim, she knew—the pigeon ripe for the plucking; but the fact that he obviously admired her, and admired her genuinely, made her a little ashamed of herself. It was only her looks that he admired, of course, but he treated her with a gentle courtesy which was new to Anna. New and very pleasant. She loved to hear him talk, even though she could not hope to keep up a conversation with him.

It was fun—and it was tough on Tooley. She knew that. She wasn't in love with Tooley, but she appreciated his attentions, and she was sorry for him. He was rough-tongued and clumsy, and he treated her like the dirt she knew herself to be in his company. With Kit Kimber she saw herself as somebody very different.

She was feeling the very essence of this new self when she met Kimber at the club the next evening. She gave him that smile which girls like Anna give to men when they meet them for the second time, and think that they may become regulars. On the first occasion she had been cautiously gracious. Now she was friendly, and Kit Kimber felt that he had known her for quite a time. Which only shows that Anna, in six months, had achieved the technique of the dance hostess. She was a clever girl and liked herself very much.

Kit asked her if she knew if Tooley was coming to the club. "I want to see him."

"Why?"

"We had a talk the other day and I wanted to continue it."

"What about?"

"I offered to fix up a job for him."

Anna laughed a little, and said that she didn't think that Tooley would be very keen on a job.

It was Kit's turn to ask why.

"Oh, I don't know, but I don't think he's that sort. You see, he's been—"

"In prison?" Kit suggested. "Yes, I knew that."

"Then you ought to let him alone. You won't do him any good." The gutter was showing through.

"What does it matter to you? Why shouldn't he have his chance if I'm willing to give it him?"

If Anna had been honest she would have replied that she didn't want Tooley taken away. She wanted him, and she didn't want him. She was a woman.

She thought with all the brain she had in her head.

"Do you mean he could get away from here?"

Kit nodded. "That was the idea. I want to get him away to the country."

Anna sighed, and it was a sigh of envy. It would be very nice to get away to the country. She wished she had been nicer to Tooley. Sometimes she hated the club—She said: "Don't say anything tonight. Wait till I've had a talk to him. He's coming here later on."

Kit agreed, and suggested a dance, and while they were dancing Tooley and Mabel came in. Tooley came over to Kimber's table, nodded to Anna, and spoke to Kimber for a minute or two. "Sorry I can't stay," he said, and pointed to Mabel. "This is an old date and I couldn't put her off."

Kit said, "Perhaps I may see you tomorrow"; and Tooley answered easily: "Yes, sure. I'll give you a ring before lunch." Then he rejoined Mabel.

Louie was sitting at his own particular table. Slipper was at his side. Louie had his watch cupped in the palm of his hand. He said to Slipper: "You know what to do. Sit at that table till Tooley gets back. Don't make a move or I'll skin you."

Slipper nodded. "I know what to do, boss."

Louie pressed a bell-push in the wall and almost at once the lights were dimmed and the band started a slow foxtrot. "All right, go ahead."

Slipper went round the screen, and as Tooley slipped from his seat at the table Slipper took his place.

*   *   *

Durham Square was almost deserted when Louie took up his position on the corner by the pillar-box. Fifty yards away the big car, with its parking-lights burning, was standing by the kerb. Louie could see the red pin-point of Tony's cigarette as he sat behind the wheel, waiting; he heard the throb of the running engine.

It was a few minutes to eleven when Tooley passed and walked up the steps of Number forty-six. Louie looked at his watch and walked slowly up the street in the direction of the car. He did not therefore see the figure which crossed the street and disappeared into the shadow of the branches of a tree, overhanging the railings of the gardens in the centre of the Square.

Louie stopped by the car and spoke through the open near-side widow: "Everything O.K.?"

Tony took his cigarette from his mouth. Louie could see the glint of white teeth. "Yes, guv'nor. I'm all set."

"Good. Look out for the signal." Louie straightened and stood still for a moment. Then he walked back the way he had come, past the house, past the figure lurking in the shadows, and on to the corner. A taxi spun by. There was no other movement in Durham Square, no noise except the distant hum of traffic in Shaftesbury Avenue.

"A sweet job," Louie muttered to himself. "It can't go wrong."

Inside the house Tooley was working quickly, silently, surely, as he moved from case to case. At last his bag was full. He checked over the items and then set the bag down on the floor and fastened the catches.

In the hall all was quiet, dark and silent as a tomb. He tiptoed over the tiles and felt for the handle of the front door. At that moment his nerve began to slip. The palms of his hands became wet with perspiration. He pulled a handkerchief from his sleeve and passed it across his forehead. He trembled, and his hand slipped on the knob. He rubbed it on his coat, and gripped the knob again.

Fiercely he told himself that there was nothing to be scared of. Tony would be there with the car. He opened the door slowly and waited for a moment, listening. He could hear nothing. He stepped out and pulled the door to behind him. He heard the lock fall and walked blindly towards the steps.

Then he saw the bulk of the car, heard the sound of its engine and tyres whirring on the smooth wood blocks of the road. As he ran down the steps the bag bumped against the railings. It was as though someone was trying to grab it from him.

He saw the white of Tony's hand as it shot out to open the rear door. There was only the breadth of the pavement between him and safety.

He jumped, stumbling, into the car and lay on the floor, panting, as though he had run a mile. Then he rolled to one side as Tony swung round the Square and headed back. He half turned his head, and shot the question: "All O.K.?"

"Yes. Fine." Tooley drew himself on to the seat and lay back luxuriously. He cursed himself for the bad moment and blamed Louie. "He ought to have let me have a lay off." He dabbed at his head with his handkerchief. "I'd have been all right next week." He was filled with a great elation now that it was over, and in his mind phrases formed that he would use when he got back to the club. "Yes, it worked all right. Of course, it wasn't too easy working on stuff like that, but I got everything. I got it all in my head. Clean as a whistle.

"I'd do the same tomorrow. No, I wasn't scared. I'll bet that'll give the rozzers something to think of. I'd like to see Leith's face when he hears of it. A sweet job."

Tony took his foot off the accelerator as he came to a corner and, as the car slowed, he saw Louie come out of the shadows. The big car lurched, swaying, to a standstill, and Louie got in.

"Everything all right? Thought I'd better just make sure." He groped for the seat and sat down beside Tooley.

The car started forward and was gathering speed when Tony swore, and Louie leaned forward in his seat. "What's the matter?"

"I don't know. There's something ahead."

"Don't stop."

The car swung to the right and jolted on to the pavement. There was a crash as the off-side mudguard hit some railings.

"Go right ahead." Louie spat out the words, but they had not left his lips before Tony rammed on the brakes, and Tooley and Louie fell on to the floor.

As Tooley's fingers clutched at the rim of the door it swung open and he felt a jab in his ribs, and a voice: "Keep still if you don't want to die. Where's that bag? The stuff?"

"So it's you?" Louie's voice was as calm and unhurried as though he were in his office asking someone to have a drink.

The Rigger froze, his gun-hand wavered, and in that split second Tooley's right hand flashed under his left armpit for the weapon which he carried there. He struck, and the gun which the Rigger held fell.

The Rigger! He struck again and, like a half-filled sack, the Rigger fell sideways, his head hanging loosely like that of a broken doll.

Louie slid out of the car and put his arms round the body. "Come on, Tooley, get him inside. We got to travel."

And, a moment later: "All right, Tony. Get back to the yard. Give her all you've got."

Tony slipped the lever into reverse and trod on the accelerator. With whining gears the car ran backwards to the corner, straightened, and then shot ahead.

"The Rigger!" Tooley muttered.

Louie put a hand on his shoulder. "Yes. I had an idea he might be around. Anyway, you settled him all right. Nice work. He won't do no more shopping. Not for a very long time." Louie chuckled, and the noise seemed to come from his belly.

"Is he hurt bad?"

"What does it matter? No one saw you do it."

Tooley shivered as though he were cold and his hands pressed hard down on the seat cushions. A sweet job. That's what he'd called it, and now—"Do you think he's dead?"

"It'd take more than that to put the Rigger out."

"I've got to know." Tooley's voice was shrill and like a frightened child's.

"I've got hold of this job. You don't want to worry any more. Leave it all to me."

Tooley fumbled for his cigarette-case, and as he pulled it out of his pocket Louie snapped a lighter. His hand was rock steady as he held the tiny flame to Tooley's cigarette. He said: "From now on you've got to follow me. You can't risk a slip now."

Tooley drew in the smoke gratefully. "As long as he's not dead," he muttered. "As long as he's not dead."

"Dead! Forget that." Louie put out a hand and turned the Rigger over. A trickle of blood had dried already on his forehead. His skin was paper-white,

Tooley shuddered and turned his head away. He felt suddenly sick. "I never slugged a bloke before."

Louie laughed. "Well, you haven't made a bad job of it for a first try-out."

The car turned into Lucas Street and Louie peered ahead. There was no one in sight. "You can go right in," he ordered Tony.

As they passed in under the archway Louie saw the figure of Benny, waiting. He told Tony to drive right into the chapel and, as Tony pulled on the hand-brake and switched off the engine, he opened the door. "Come on, Tooley, you've got to get back to the club and act as if nothing has happened."

Tooley laughed.

"Get moving. It's your only chance."

Louie gripped him by the arm and pushed him towards the door. Then he stopped and took a pill-box from his pocket. "Take a couple of these."

Tooley's throat was dry, but he managed to swallow the pills. He was aching for a drink.

Louie stared at him for a moment. "Go back to your table. Have a drink, a couple of drinks if you like. Talk to Kimber, and then you can clear out and go to bed, and if you don't want to swing keep your trap shut. I'll do all I can, but if you squawk you're sunk. Got that?"

"I'll be all right." Tooley put a hand on the door-post to steady himself.

Louie pressed a key into his hand. "Here's the key of the office. Go in that way and don't forget to lock up as you go through. Give Guido the key, and tell him I'll be up soon."

Louie watched Tooley as he walked unsteadily down the yard and up the wooden stairs to the office. Then he went back into the chapel and called out for Tony. Benny Watt was closing the sliding doors.

"Where's Tony?" His voice was harsh and urgent.

"Fixing the car."

Louie pushed Benny aside. "Tony!"

The slim figure straightened at a rear door. "Get out. I'll fix everything. He isn't hurt much."

In the light of Benny's torch Louie saw Tony's frightened face and swore. "Get out, I tell you."

Tony's mouth was working and he looked as though he were going to cry. Louie gripped him by the shoulder with a grasp which hurt. "He's unconscious, that's all."

Tony said nothing, but as Louie loosened his grip he faded like a shadow and was gone.

The sidelights of the car were still on and in their light Louie saw Benny Watt standing quite still by the slit of the door. He did not look like anything human, and for an instant the fringes of the cloak of fear touched Louie Patra.

His step was not quite steady as he walked across the floor of the chapel, and as he said, "Come on, Benny, get a move on," his voice was not quite steady.

Benny turned his questing head towards the sound, and moved as a man awaking from a dream. When he spoke, his voice was high-pitched and complaining. "They've croaked him, guv'nor."

"He's not dead."

"No, but he will be if you don't get a doctor quick."

"We're not going to have any doctors here. Come on, you've got to give me a hand. Fetch me some rope."

Louie went into the garage and waited until Benny had followed him. Then he shut the sliding doors.

Benny said: "It's a good thing you sent Tony away. He's no good."

"He can drive a car, and that's all I ever want him for." He switched on a torch and stood looking at the Rigger for half a minute.

"Isn't there nothing we can do for him, guv'nor?"

"He'll be all right. Here! Take this." He gave Benny the bag which Tooley had brought from the house in Durham Square. "Get on with the packing. Have you got the boxes?"

"They're all ready, guv'nor." Benny picked up the bag and shuffled towards the door.

Louie waited a minute and then he dropped the stub of his cigar on the floor and trod it out. He flashed his light on the face of the Rigger. "So you thought you'd put over a double-cross, did you?"

A smile twisted his mouth. "And all you've got out of it is a headache, and that isn't the finish." Louie trained his light on the dash. The indicator showed four gallons of petrol in the tank. He thought for a minute and then muttered: "That ought to be plenty."

He lashed up the heavy body with the rope, pinioning arms and legs, then picked up an empty sack and threw it over the Rigger. Then he went back to the warehouse and said to Benny Watt: "I'm going to take the car out."

The old man, raising a questioning face, asked: "Where to?"

"Never mind about that," Louie snapped. "Open up."

The engine started at the first turn of the starter, and Louie backed the car through the chapel, turned in the yard and drove out into Lucas Street.

* * *

Tooley walked through the lounge of the club and pushed open the door leading to the bar. "I'll have a double White Horse." The barman gave him the eighth part of a glance before he turned to take a bottle from the shelf.

"Cleaned it up?" he asked, as he pushed the glass across the counter. Tooley nodded and then looked away. He didn't feel like talking. His hand, as it clutched the glass, was shaking. The neat whiskey burned his throat and he coughed. "Haven't got used to it raw yet," he muttered, and splashed in water from a jug.

Then he walked to a corner of the room and lifted a six-inch trap in the wall. Through it he saw Anna's head. She was dancing with Kimber. As he watched them he drank again from his glass, slowly; his hand was steadier now, and he was beginning to feel better.

He saw Slipper and Mabel sitting at their table. It seemed a very long time ago since he had gone out, but the minute hand of his watch had not advanced so very far.

He finished his drink and went out into the lounge, down the passage, and entered the supper room by the door behind the trellis screen. The band was still playing and Anna and Kimber were still dancing. He chose the moment when they were out of sight amongst a knot of other dancers and moved from the screen. Slipper's roving eye saw him and as he left his chair Tooley took his place. "All okey doke?" Slipper whispered, and Tooley nodded.

Mabel smiled with the mechanical smile of her kind, and poured wine into a glass. "Is the boss coming up?"

"I don't know. Later perhaps. Why?"

Mabel fitted a cigarette into a foot-long holder. She didn't answer the question, but looked quite steadily at Tooley for a minute. Then she said: "What you want is one of Bob's corpse revivers. It's the only thing that's kept Slipper out of the deadhouse this last month."

"I'm all right."

"Then I'll have to get my eyes tested."

"Do you think it worked all right?"

"Yes, you needn't worry about that. They've been too busy goo-gooing to bother what you did." Mabel became ruminative. "You know I was like that kid once, and I threw myself away on a bloke with a lovely moustache. He said he was a salesman, but he couldn't have sold a pint of iced beer to a bloke that was dying of thirst in the middle of the Sahara desert. He'd have drunk it hisself first. That's the kind he was. But the kid's got brains, or something that does the same thing. She's got that gooper on a string."

Tooley glowered. "She doesn't give a damn for him."

Mabel stole a quick glance at Tooley. Then she said, "Perhaps not, but she's got him on a string all the same, and any time she wants him he's hers."

When the dance stopped and Anna and Kimber returned to their table, Tooley joined them. With an effort that made him sweat he smiled at Anna and nodded to Kimber.

Kimber told the waiter to bring another glass, and when it was filled he said: "You don't look too well. What's the matter?"

"I'm all right." Tooley tossed off the drink. "Out of training, that's all."

"Have you thought over what I was saying the other day?"

Tooley's face was blank.

Kimber looked surprised, and hesitated before he continued: "You know; about taking a little run to the country."

"It's too late," Tooley muttered.

"What's that?" Kimber asked.

"Nothing." The band struck up again. Tooley got up suddenly and said to Anna: "What about just one, before I hit the hay?"

"All right."

As he put his hand on her shoulder she felt it tremble. His face was set like a mask. She tightened her grip on his right arm. "Didn't it go all right?" Her voice was but a whisper.

"Yes, everything was O.K." His voice was toneless.

She knew that he was lying, and was frightened as she sought in her brain for a question that would draw him.

When they had been round the floor once she said: "I haven't seen Louie. Is he back?"

"Yes, he'll be up later on. He's—he's just clearing up."

"Leith was in, but he's gone now."

Tooley snorted.

Anna gave it up. Tomorrow perhaps she would get it out of him what had happened.

Suddenly he stopped dancing. "I think I'll go home." He gave her hand a quick squeeze and pushed through the crowd to the door.

In the lounge Guido was standing. He touched Tooley on the arm and whispered: "Everything is all right, yes?"

All right. Everything all right? All right. The words beat mockingly in his brain. He felt a sudden urge for action. He wanted to shout, and most of all he wanted to punch Guido's smug white face.

He, Tooley, was the only man who took the risks while the others stood back and waited for their share of the spoils. He was the goat; he was the one to take the can back.

He found himself on the steep wooden stairs which led to Canton Street, and it was very quiet there. He felt for the wall for support, and went down the stairs like a sick man.

As he reached the street he stopped, for he wanted to go back and find Louie and ask him about the Rigger. But then he thought of the laughing, giggling crowd, and realized that he could not face them. Perhaps he could go in through Mrs. Hoskins' shop. He walked a few yards in that direction before he remembered that it would be shut at that time of night.

He looked at the blank face of the window, and the labels announcing the prices of ham and eggs, and pork and beans, and sausages and mashed, and toad-in-the-hole. He knew that

Mrs. Hoskins lived in a room at the back, and he had his hand upraised to knock on the door before he changed his mind. A stupid thing to do at that time of night, and, besides, she'd never hear him; only bring the police round, asking questions.

And yet to go to bed and not know what was happening was hell. He told himself that Louie was in it as much as he was himself—and Tony. If they got him they would get the others as well. Louie must know that, and Louie had never been caught yet, and wouldn't be if there was the thousandth part of a chance of getting away with it. Tony was the weak link. He was only a kid really, and he would never stand up to questioning.

If he could only see Louie; just for a minute or two. Indecision held him puttering up and down, three steps this way, three steps that.

The gate into the yard from Lucas Street would be locked; there was no other way in. He was tired; his body was aching from tiredness, but he was not sleepy. He thought of walking, but the memory of his experiences of the night before halted his steps before he had gone ten yards.

He was free. Like hell he was free!

CHAPTER VII

AT MIDNIGHT Mr. Williams was anxious, and at one o'clock he was worse. He had been trying to read for more than an hour, but his mind took in nothing.

He had taken off his coat and was sitting in his shirt-sleeves. His shirt was flannel, of a dirty grey colour. He was reading a tattered paper-backed copy of one of Phillips Oppenheim's books. He held the book high so that it would catch the light from the gas mantle by his right shoulder.

Outside the window of the back room was the yard, littered with shavings and scraps of packing paper and straw bottle-covers. There was always a great pile of empty wooden boxes. When trade was slack and his liver was troubling him he used to take down a meat-chopper which hung just inside the back door and smash up the boxes. The work always gave him satisfaction. They smashed so easily.

He was restless now and he would have liked to have taken down the meat-chopper and gone to work on the boxes, but of course that would never do. He would have the neighbours hanging out of the windows calling for the police.

The Rigger had said he would be two hours with the van, and three hours had already passed since Spider had driven out of the yard.

It was a big risk to take for ten pounds. If they broke up the van the insurance company would ask a lot of questions and they'd want to know why the van was out in the middle of the night.

It was stupid to get into a panic, he told himself. The Rigger had taken the van before and had brought it back and paid the sum he owed promptly. There was no reason to think that he would not do the same tonight, or rather this morning, for the clock on the mantelpiece had just struck two.

At last he made a move to the room across the passage which was his bedroom, undressed and got into bed, where he lay for a long time, cold and apprehensive, until he drifted into a state which was not sleep, for he was never completely unconscious of his surroundings.

With the first light of day he got up, shivering but relieved at action, struggled into his shirt and pulled on his trousers.

It had started to rain, and the light in the sky was grey and the wind made a moaning sound round the chimney-pots. The faces of the houses were blank as though they were dead. He was alone in the world and he was frightened.

The woodwork of the door of the shed was wet and it had warped, so that he had to brace the tips of his fingers on the edge to prise it open. With a faint protesting creak it swung open. The van was not there. All the time he had known it in his mind, but the realization of the truth struck him so that he just stood and stared as though his brain had failed him.

He was shocked, and as the minutes passed he became angry as a man tricked. Everything was going to have been so easy.

The van would be away for two hours and then it would be re-turned and he would be paid ten pounds. He felt like a gambler when a 'sure thing' had been beaten by a short head.

He would not believe, he could not believe, that disaster had overtaken him, for the loss of his truck was a disaster; for Mr. Williams was a mean man. He swore, nastily, and with a venom which twisted his mean mouth to a thin line.

If he could tell the police about the Rigger, without incurring their suspicion, he would; and in that cold, wet, windy yard his little brain worked as the brain of a weasel. He would go and tell them that his van had been stolen and that he suspected the Rig-ger. And then at once difficulties came crowding into his brain. They would ask him questions. How did he know the Rigger? Why did he think that he had stolen the van? They would take him down to the station and sit him in a chair in the charge-room. It had happened once before over some silly business about some wooden boxes which he had known nothing about.

And the Rigger had been to the shop; perhaps someone had seen him enter. Of course, he could deny that he knew the Rig-ger, but he knew how the police looked when they suspected you. He didn't want to be questioned.

But if he didn't go to the police they would come to him. They would find the van, and his name was painted on it in twelve-inch letters.

He went to the cupboard which served him as a kitchen and put a kettle on the gas-ring. And as he stood looking at the flick-ering circle of blue flames he rubbed the bristles on his chin and wondered if he were due for a new razor blade.

The day opened slowly with children coming in for pints of paraffin and bundles of firewood, and quarters of sugar and tea.

When the boy came with the paper and shouted loudly, "Good morning, Mr. Williams," he scowled at him and made no reply. He was thinking: 'Bob Davis'll be along in a minute and I'll have to tell him.' Bob was the lad who drove the van and who did odd jobs about the shop. He talked too much; thought he could run the place on his own and was always trying to teach

Mr. Williams his own business. One of these days he would tell him where he got off.

There was a case of corn flakes that he hadn't unpacked, and he went out of the back door with the meat-chopper in his hand; and then the shop bell clanged and he heard a man's footstep on the boards of the shop. It wasn't Bob; he never came in through the shop.

Mr. Williams retraced his steps slowly and uneasily, and was reassured by seeing a man in a yellow raincoat and a trilby hat with the brim turned down all round.

He said, "Well?" querulously.

Leith said, "Are you the owner of this place?"—and at once caution came to Mr. Williams; caution shot with fear.

He replied slowly: "Yes. What do you want?"

"Picked up your van last night. Who had it out?"

Mr. Williams summoned up all his powers of acting. "My van? It's in the shed out at the back."

"No, it's not," Leith snapped. "We've got it at the station. It's been standing in Penton Street all night."

"I can't think how that can be. The boy, Bob Davis, put it away last night round about six. He'll be in soon and you can ask him yourself."

"Was the door locked?"

"Yes. I locked it myself before I had my supper."

"What time was that?" Leith asked.

"I don't know." Mr. Williams was still cautious.

"Let's have a look."

For a second Mr. Williams' ferret's eyes stared at Leith and he did not move. Then he turned and said, "It's this way," and lifted the flap of the counter.

In the yard Leith asked: "Do you shut the gate at night?"

Mr. Williams barely hesitated before he replied that he never shut the gate.

Leith looked into the shed, and then looked for a lock and found none. Mr. Williams explained that he used a padlock and that it was missing. He remembered quite clearly leaving it on the hasp when he had opened up on the previous morning. He showed Leith the key, which he kept on a ring with others.

"Who's this boy Bob you spoke about?"

"He drives the van; quite a steady lad."

"Has he ever borrowed the van without asking you?"

"No, never, and I would never have lent it him if he had asked." Mr. Williams was quite definite.

Leith looked at the stones of the yard, and the pile of boxes, and two other sheds the doors of which were locked. Mr. Williams explained that he kept some of his stock in them. But about that the grocer displayed no anxiety. He said: "Oh, that'll be all right."

"Better have a look all the same," Leith persisted. "Perhaps some of that lot was taken the same time as the van." He was watching the grocer closely and Mr. Williams sensed the danger and hurried to unlock the other two sheds.

He quickly examined the contents of the sheds and said: "No, they have taken nothing."

Leith nodded, but said nothing. He scratched his jaw. "Took the van out of the shed? Looks odd to me. What do you think?"

"Me? I don't know."

"It was your van. You don't seem to be worrying much."

"But I am."

"When did you find out it had gone?"

"This morning."

"What time?"

Mr. Williams hesitated. Stupid of him, but he was in difficulties already. If he said 'Early', then Leith would ask why he had not rung up the police earlier to report his loss. He wondered if he had shown sufficient alarm and consternation when he had inspected the shed with Leith. It was difficult to think when a policeman was standing by your elbow, asking you questions.

Then he remembered with a shock that he had said that the van was in the shed at the back when Leith had first questioned him about it. Though he was cold, sweat beads formed on his forehead, and he said, in answer to Leith's question, that the first he had known of the loss of the van was when Leith had told him that it had been picked up in Penton Street. It was easy to make mistakes, and he sighed his relief as he spoke, and dabbed at his head with a padded handkerchief.

"Anything ever happen to you like this before?" Leith asked.

"Happen before? What do you mean?"

"Didn't someone ever borrow your van without asking you, and return it?"

"No, never."

Leith walked over to the door of the shed where the van had been and examined the hasp. 'Nice clean job,' he thought, but he said nothing to Mr. Williams. He asked him where he slept, and looked at the room, and he also looked into the living-room, and asked a number of questions as to what he had done the night before and when he had gone to bed, and what time he had had his supper and whether anyone had been in to see him. Then he returned to the yard and met Bob Davis, the boy who drove the van, and asked him questions which Mr. Williams could not hear. Then he went to the yard gate and looked at it and at the ground all around and beneath it.

He said nothing for quite a long time and then he told Mr. Williams that he was going to have some breakfast, as he had been up since midnight and was feeling peckish.

Mr. Williams was so glad to hear that Leith had finished his investigations that he almost asked him to share his own breakfast, but a long period of selfish parsimony restrained him, and he had the pleasure of seeing a back view of Leith retreating from the shop.

It was quite true that Leith was peckish; in fact, he was devilish hungry, but the hint of a clue removed all thought of breakfast. He went straight to the local police-station and told the sergeant that he must see the inspector, and he sat on a hard chair and read a morning paper until the inspector appeared.

Then Leith asked a lot of questions about Mr. Williams, and he obtained a lot of information which would have surprised Mr. Williams, who had no idea that the police interested themselves in him at all.

The Rigger had been seen to enter Mr. Williams' shop on seven separate occasions, and on none of these occasions had he been seen to have made any purchase.

Mr. Williams' van had been seen in the respectable streets of Balham at hours when no respectable grocers' vans should have been seen in the respectable streets of Balham.

The boy, Bob Davis, had been questioned, and his life probed by the police lancet, but the results, regarded from the criminal point of view, had been less than negligible. The character of the boy, Bob Davis, was whiter than a sheet washed by one of the more widely advertised soaps; there was no tell-tale grey about him.

The background of Mr. Williams, on the other hand, was regarded with watchful suspicion by the police, but as they had plenty of other work to do they had left Mr. Williams alone.

So Leith, whose hunger was beginning to overpower his interest in the riddle of the stranded grocer's van, repaired to a coffee shop to fortify his inner man with bacon and eggs before making his report at the Yard.

CHAPTER VIII

"THEY'VE DONE IT AGAIN." Leith was greeted with these words as he came into the room of Chief Inspector Harley at Scotland Yard.

"Country job?"

"No, right under your nose. I wonder you didn't smell it. It's the Kimber collection, or at least a bit of it; the best of it, of course."

"Kimber collection? Durham Square?" Leith's mind was visualizing a map, from which he could see at a glance the proximity of Durham Square and Penton Street. Was there any connection between the two, or was it mere coincidence? A policeman's training tends to produce about as much credulity in coincidence as in fairies. Harley was talking.

"That's the place. Kimber says he knows you. How's that?"

"He's been trying to reform that chap Tooley, and I helped him to find him."

"Why?"

"I was asked by the secretary of one of these Prisoners' Help Societies to introduce Kimber to Tooley, as Kimber was willing to give him a job."

"Did anything come of that?"

"I don't think so, but he hasn't had much time."

"You'd want more than time to reform Tooley, you'd need a mallet," said Harley. "Tooley—we'll have a talk with him and that'll make a start." He called a number on the 'phone, and gave a few brief orders.

When he had put down the 'phone he said: "I've told them to pick Tooley up and bring him along here. I'd like to see him myself. He's the only link we've got with Kimber at present. But the bloke I really want to get my hands on is the one who was staking Tooley before he was pinched—and maybe is doing so again now. He's got an organization that is getting rid of a hundred thousand pounds' worth of stolen goods every year. I suppose you haven't got any line on him yet?"

"No, but, as the kids say: 'I'm getting hot.'" Leith's smile was cut short.

"Hot be damned! You're still in the ice-chest. All you know is that the man we want probably hangs out within half a mile of Soho and that he may be staking Tooley, who may have had something to do with this Kimber job. We know that this job is the same as half a dozen others that are still open, as far as we are concerned." Harley paused to scratch his jowl. "In all the other cases it's been rocks and odd sort of stuff the ordinary screwsman wouldn't touch, and now look at this little list. It's on the back of that report. 'One old Pretender Goblet, with twisted stem, waisted collar and large-domed foot, value £234.' Two hundred and thirty pounds for a glass! Can you beat that? And here's another: 'An Irish potato-ring, pierced and chased with birds, swans and dolphins. By Hector Flaherty, Dublin. Value £354.' And the rest are all the same."

"What I should say is that some collector has commissioned the theft," Leith suggested. "It's happened before."

"Yes, with single items, but never on this scale. I wouldn't mind betting every one of these pieces is known to the trade and couldn't be sold. All the same I'll have circulars printed."

"Who's gone to the house?" asked Leith.

"Simmons and all his gang, with their cameras and blow-pipes and a dozen note-books." Harley crossed one fat thigh over the other. "You know, I'm beginning to wonder if we're not being a bit too scientific. My old aunt in Maidstone, she wouldn't have had any truck with it. That woman had a lot of common sense, and she was a nailer at third degree. The power of the bare human eye; that was her strong line . . . that and a slipper."

A hint of a smile brightened Leith's wintry face; the connection between the fat Harley, the aunt from Maidstone, and a slipper, amused him.

Half an hour later there was a knock at the door and a police-man, looking very strange without his helmet, announced that Tooley had arrived.

"Good God man, bring him in, bring him in."

The door shut quickly and reopened a moment later to produce Tooley. He was carrying his cap and looked very small and slight; a slip of a man.

"Well, what the hell have you been up to?" Harley shouted at him. "You've only been out a week, and here you are mixing it again."

Tooley's eyes were cold and green as a winter's sea. "I haven't been doing nothing. What are you talking about?"

"What did you want with Kimber?" Harley was not in the mood to answer questions.

"I didn't want anything with him. He wanted me." Tooley stood with his cap clutched tightly in both his hands.

Harley had to twist in his chair to see him. He pointed to a low chair by his desk. "Come on and sit here," he snapped, and as Tooley came within arm's reach he snatched the cap out of his hands and tossed it on his desk.

Leith moved his position so that he was half facing Tooley.

"Where were you last night?"

"What time?"

"From eight o'clock onwards."

"I was in the club—Guido's Club—from about ten-thirty. Before that I was in my rooms."

"You're staying with Silvretti, aren't you?"

"It's on my papers."

"Who's paying the bill?"

"I had a bit laid by."

Harley leaned back in his chair and raked the ashes from his pipe with a dead match. After a minute, he said: "No, no, Tooley. That won't do. You'll have to think up something better than that."

"It's the truth."

"Got a bit twisted, hasn't it?"

Harley tapped his pipe on the palm and then blew through the stem. "I want to meet the man who's staking you."

Tooley said nothing, and Harley went on: "He's bought you a nice new suit, I see, and a cap to go with it. I suppose he's promised you all sorts of things. Told you he's got a job that's as easy as kiss your hand; no risk to you, and all you've got to do is this and that; no risk at all. Is that what you were told the last time you were pinched?"

"That was different, I was framed."

"Were you, now?" said Harley gravely. "And who was the villain who did that?"

"You needn't worry about him." Lights flashed in Tooley's green eyes and he almost smiled.

"Why, have you killed him?"

Tooley's hands dropped to the sides of his chair and his knuckles became white points. Fear froze his brain, and he felt suddenly very sick. Harley became as unreal as a shadowy figure in a dream. He seemed to be very far away. He fought to control his senses, and slowly feeling returned, and he could see clearly and he could hear.

Harley was still talking. "Nine out of every ten of my clients imagine that their pals have given them away, but that is nothing but an insult to the skill of myself and my able assistants. I remember your case, and it was a fair cop. Nobody gave you away."

"You've got a year and a bit on your ticket," Leith said. "You don't want to forget that."

"You blokes won't let me do that."

Leith leaned forward in his chair. "Who did you say framed you?"

"I didn't say anybody did."

"Yes, you did. Who was it?" Leith gripped the lapel of Tooley's coat. "Come on, let's have it. Maybe we might be able to help you."

"Help me? That's funny." Tooley drew back, trying to free himself from Leith's grasp.

Harley spoke. "You said you were in Guido's Club last night. Who saw you there?"

Tooley hesitated, for he wasn't ready for that question. Should he mention Kimber?

"Come on, you must know who was there."

"Guido was there. He saw me."

"Anyone else?"

"And Mr. Kimber; he was dancing with Anna Finn."

"Oh yes, now I remember. That's who it was." Leith leaned back in his chair and put his thumbs in the armholes of his waistcoat. He turned to Harley. "I saw her in the club last night. She was with Kimber."

Harley asked, "Did you see him?" and pointed to Tooley.

"No, but he might have been there."

"I was there; you can ask Kimber."

"All right, don't get excited." Harley relit his pipe, which had gone out for the tenth time. Through the smoke he said: "You couldn't have had a better alibi if you had fixed it all up beforehand; now could you?"

"It wasn't fixed," Tooley spat out.

"I didn't say it was. Alibis are dangerous things. If they crack they're apt to land you in a jam."

"I'm not worrying."

"That must be a nice change for you. I hope you keep that way for a long time." Harley uncrossed his legs and took up a pencil. "Now just let me have the times you were in the club, and then you can go."

The tension on Tooley's face relaxed and his hands became still. "I got there about 10.30 and didn't leave until after midnight."

As he jotted down the words, Harley said: "That covers the period nicely; couldn't have been better."

He looked at Leith and asked, "Got any questions?"—and when Leith shook his head he said to Tooley: "All right, you can go." Seconds passed before the words registered in Tooley's brain, and then he got up as though there had been a spring in the seat of his chair. He hesitated for a moment, and then turned and walked quickly towards the door with clipped steps.

When the door shut behind him, a smile came over Harley's face. "Takes them a long time to get rid of that walk." And after a short pause he added: "Poor devils!"

"It'd be a good thing to have a word with Kimber and find out if Tooley really was at Guido's Club last night."

"Just what I was thinking myself," Harley replied, as he picked up the 'phone. "I'll ask him to call round here right away."

He rang up Kimber's house and spoke for ten minutes, first to Kimber, and then to Simmons, who was in charge of the investigation. When he had finished he said to Leith: "Simmons says that it's an inside job; either that or they had the key to the front door. The burglar alarm had been turned off."

Leith did not answer.

Harley glared at him a little truculently. He wasn't paying a proper amount of attention.

"What's wrong with you?"

"I was thinking—"

"No."

"A grocer's van was found this morning, about 2 a.m., abandoned in Penton Street. That's only just round the corner from Durham Square."

Harley grunted. "Why the hell didn't you tell me that before?"

Leith might have replied that he hadn't been able to get a word in edgeways, but he contented himself with a succinct account of his interview with the owner of the van.

"Williams?" Harley tapped his teeth with the mouthpiece of his pipe. "Williams. Williams. Do we know him?"

"No. There's nothing definite against him. Shady bit of work, I should say, but an inexperienced liar. Couldn't make up his mind about his own story. He knew the van was out last night all right."

"Did you make inquiries about him?"

"Yes. There's nothing definite. It seems that he's a friend of the Rigger."

"The Rigger? That's an idea."

Leith shook his head dubiously. "Nothing's been seen of the Rigger for a long time. I think he's shot his bolt."

"You never know. The Rigger may be the man we want." Harley raked in the bowl of his pipe with a match. "Why shouldn't it be the Rigger?" he demanded.

"I told you; he only touches small stuff these days."

"Maybe he's changed."

"He's got the guts but not the brains. He could never have fixed up all this inside work. His lay was smashing or drain-pipe work." Harley grunted.

"And there's another thing. The Rigger's never been seen up West for the last three years."

"That proves nothing. You might have missed him or he had someone working for him."

"There's a chance of that," Leith admitted.

"You'd better get a photo of the Rigger and go to Kimber's house. Show it to the servants and see if they recognize it. Put two or three good men on to working the district, questioning the tradesmen and postmen, and the man on the beat. Find out if there's been any suspicious characters hanging around."

"Is that all I've got to do?" Leith picked up his hat, but Harley said:

"I've asked Kimber to come along here. You'd better wait and see him and hear what he has to say first." Harley cocked an eye at the clock. "They're not open yet."

Leith met the insult with a wooden face. He didn't care who knew that he liked beer.

They did not have long to wait, for with commendable speed Kimber answered the summons.

All the way in the taxi he had been looking forward to this visit to Scotland Yard, but the long walk along miles of bare corridors killed his enthusiasm for crime. Bloodhounds, handcuffs and racing-cars had been his idea of the Yard, and he was disappointed to find that the interior of the building itself might have been inhabited by the staff of the Ministry of Shipping, Agriculture and Fisheries for all the signs of crime it bore. It was also very cold.

Harley gave him a fish-like stare, and pointed to a chair. He said: "You've given us a lot of trouble, Mr. Kimber. Why don't you look after your stuff better?"

"Because I've never thought anyone would want to steal it. All the same, I've got locks on all the doors, and burglar alarms and steel shutters on all the windows. The insurance company told me what they wanted, and I had it all fixed up in accordance with their specifications."

Harley rubbed his flabby cheeks with a white starfish hand. "And a fat lot of good it's done. They just walked in and took what they wanted, and as far as I can make out never left a trace."

"Well, you ought to know about that sort of thing. Where did I go wrong?"

Harley, as was his habit, ignored the question, perhaps because he couldn't answer it.

"Did you go to Guido's Club last night?"

"Yes."

"Was that your first visit?"

"No, I went there on Wednesday night with a friend."

"Name?"

"He called himself Tooley. I don't know what his real name is. At least, I did know, but I've forgotten."

"Well, I happen to know his name. It is James Hope, and he is a convicted criminal. Did you know that?"

Kimber looked at Leith and smiled. "Of course I did. Leith can tell you the story."

"I'd like it from you."

"Well, there's not much to it; I work for one of these Prisoners' Help Societies, and I was given Tooley's name. My idea was to find him a job, and so Leith told me where I would meet him and—"

"When and where did you meet Tooley first?"

"Wednesday, in a pub in Lisle Street. We had a talk and went to a show in the evening, and later on we went to this club—Guido's."

"What did you do there?"

"Oh, just the usual thing, sat and drank, and danced a little."

"Who with?"

"A girl called Anna. I don't know what her last name is."

"I see. She was one of that sort, was she?"

"I liked her. She was different." Kimber's hackles were beginning to rise.

"All right, all right; don't get excited. You're not the first nor yet the fifty-first that's danced with Anna Finn."

"You know her?"

"Her father used to be a client of ours, and now it looks as though you've tumbled right amongst them. Who suggested you should go to this club?"

"Tooley."

"When was that?"

"On Wednesday, as I told you."

"And what about last night?"

"I'm not sure if he said anything about it or not. He may have. I went to join Anna, really."

"Tell me everything that happened last night from the time you got to the club."

"Well, I just went there and met this girl Anna, and I danced with her and—"

"What was Tooley doing while you were dancing?"

"He was with someone at another table—a terrible-looking woman."

"Did he dance with her?" Harley asked.

"I suppose he did."

"Did you see him dancing with her?"

"I can't say that I did."

"How long were you in the club?"

"Until after midnight."

"Was he there all that time?"

"No, I think he left shortly before I did. About half an hour, I should think."

"Yes, I see." Harley stared at the bowl of his pipe for a moment, and then he asked: "Can you swear that Tooley did not go out of the club between the time you first got there and when he finally left, say at half past eleven?"

Kimber laughed. "Yes, I think I can, because I remember wondering what he could find to talk about to such a woman. I was talking about him to Anna while we were dancing. He had a table where I could see him most of the time." He paused, and then said: "He may have slipped out for a couple of minutes, but I shouldn't think he could have been away for much longer than that."

"Who has the keys of your house?" Harley asked.

"I have a set, of course, and the butler has another." Kimber pulled a key-case from his trousers pocket and laid it on the desk.

Harley examined it carefully. He held each key in turn up to the light, turning it so that he could see all sides of it.

Without looking at Kimber, he asked: "Do you carry soap in your pocket?" Kimber shook his head. "Or wax of any kind?"

"No, of course not."

Harley detached a key from the ring and laid it on a sheet of paper. "I should like to borrow this one for a short time, if I may."

"Yes, certainly. I can borrow Brooks's key."

"Brooks? Who's Brooks?"

"My butler."

"Is he a reliable man?"

"Absolutely. He's been with the family for twenty-five years."

"We'll check up on him," Harley muttered, and made a note on a scrap of paper. He completed his examination of the keys and gave the ring back to Kimber. "I understood you to say in your first report that you fixed the time of the robbery as between ten and midnight. How did you do that?"

"Well, when I got home I shot the bolts on the front door and on the grille, and Brooks assured me that when he went to open up in the morning they had not been interfered with."

Harley said to Leith: "Have all the locks stripped down and get a man to examine the bolts and fastenings, if Simmons hasn't done it already." He scratched his chin and thought for a moment. Then he asked: "Did you ever have this man Tooley into your house at any time?"

"No, I only met him in the pub in Lisle Street and at the club in Lucas Street."

"Have you had any tradesmen working in the house lately?"

"No."

"Have you ever lent your keys to anyone?"

"Never in my life."

"Do you carry them about with you all the time?"

"Yes, and at night I put them on a table by my bedside."

Harley got out of his chair with difficulty. "Well, I think that's about all for the moment. But, of course, when we've completed our inquiries I'll probably want to see you again."

Harley continued to stare at the door for seconds after Kimber had gone.

Leith picked up the key which Harley had taken from Kimber. "I can't see any wax on it."

"You're getting old; your eyes are failing you," said Harley offensively. "And besides, I didn't say that there was any wax on it, but all the same there's been something very like wax, or maybe soap, on that key. It's greasy."

"I wonder when that could have been done."

"What about Tooley?"

Leith shook his head. "No, no, it couldn't have been him. I've known Tooley for years and he's never worked the dip, that I'll swear to. Besides, it's an expert's job to get a bunch of keys out of a trouser pocket without being nabbed, you know that."

"He might have borrowed them just to have a look at it."

"Kimber said he never lent them to anyone."

"I know, but he might have forgotten." Harley sat down in his chair and began to twiddle his thumbs. He looked a little like a fat, brooding Buddha. "My guess is that it's the Rigger."

"He hasn't got the brains."

"Then what does that leave us with? Your mystery man?" Harley put quite a lot of contemptuous disagreement into his tone. "The master mind."

"I still don't think it's the Rigger, but we'll get him in if you feel like that about it."

"Yes, send someone down to that dump of his. I'd like to have a yarn with him again. Someone told me he'd developed a thirst these days."

"Yes, he laps it up when he gets the chance, but that isn't often. I tell you, he couldn't touch a job like this. He'd have to have a lot of help and pay 'em well. He hasn't got the cash."

"He could have promised them a cut."

"Well, whoever it was, he pulled a nice clean job. There's not a loose string anywhere as far as I can see—except for the van."

"That's the way it always looks when a good man has been on the job. It's the way it looks when you see top professionals playing tennis. It all seems as easy as pie." Harley chose a pipe from a pocketful and filled it. "All that had to be done in this case was to get hold of the keys and make copies of them. Then arrange for Kimber to be out of the way, and choose a time when you know that the servants will be somewhere else; you have to know where the stuff is and what is the best of it, and fix where you'll sell it afterwards. You've got to know where the burglar alarms are and turn 'em off; fix up for a car to meet you and someone to keep a good look out. All as easy as kiss your hand. Nothing to it. Sometimes I wonder what we're paid for." Harley sat back in his chair and pulled at his pipe complacently. "Now you run along and find out all about it."

Leith did not run; rather did he move to the door with the gait of a constipated crab. The question which exercised his mind at that moment was what Harley was paid for, and he could not think of an answer.

CHAPTER IX

THIRTY OR FORTY wrecks, standing in a sea of mud, are not an inspiring sight at 11.30 of a rainy morning. Rusting iron, sodden tyres, showing all their tread in the form of white cords; forlorn, inert and depressing. Otherwise the place was deserted.

It was lucky for Leith that he had no imagination, otherwise he might have shot himself.

He did not shoot himself. Without haste and without embarrassment he lugged around a detective from the local division, with whom he combed the yard from bonnet to tail-light.

He noted the lump of lead which had been used to keep the gate open, and wondered why such valuable metal had been used for such a lowly purpose.

He spent quite a long time in the shack which the Rigger had used as a living-place, observing the primus and bottle of methylated spirit and can of paraffin; the dirty plates and scaly frying-pan and bucket of dirty water; the rumpled grey blankets on the iron bedstead; the pile of magazines, tumbled and without a semblance of cover among the lot of them. They were mostly American, and pretended to deal with scientific and mechanical matters: 'How to make a rocker out of a molasses-barrel', and, 'Seventeen tips for the keen auto owner'.

Leith thought that more than seventeen tips would be needed to get the inmates of this junk-yard rolling on the highway.

He went on to poke through a cupboard in which were a rubble of empty cigarette-packets and papers, tobacco, and bits of cotton waste and copper gauze and wire, and two pairs of pliers and an old overall suit.

He spent quite a time in the Rigger's shack, for he was anxious to get a picture of him, as accurate a picture as he could

make, and he was used to making pictures out of empty cigarette-packets and old handkerchiefs and discarded shoes and
magazines. As a tracker in the desert of Sinai can tell stories
from the marks in the sand, so Leith could sometimes read
a character, if not a life story, from the room in which a man
lived. He stood still for some time, staring out of the dirty little
window across the chaos of the yard. What he was thinking was
this: the grocer's van had had something to do with the robbery from Kimber's house, otherwise why should it have been
abandoned? Mr. Williams was a twister and a liar. He knew or
suspected what his van had been used for, but would not speak;
and it would take a lot to make him speak because he was badly
frightened, and a frightened man is a tough man to handle from
the police point of view. But what was he frightened of? And
how and where did the Rigger fit into the picture—if at all?

The problem was so difficult that Leith decided it needed
beer to lubricate it. Lots of beer.

The dump seemed to be deserted, and for the moment he
had done all he could, and little of the Rigger's life and habits
was hid from him.

He dismissed the local detective with the injunction to put
a man on to watching the place. "There's quite a lot of things I
want to say to the owner, when—and if—he shows up."

Leith had little difficulty in finding a bar near by, and ordered his pint and thought quite a lot. He thought much better
when he was in a place where people were making noises and
clinking glasses. Being a townsman, the background of silence
froze his thinking-machine.

As he lifted his tankard to his lips and took the first long steady
pull of a war-horse in an interlude of the battle, Leith was trying
to figure out what had happened, from the time the man who had
stolen the goods from Durham Square had left the house.

Why had the van been abandoned? There had been nothing
wrong with the engine, and no one had been on its trail at the
time; in fact, he could find no one who had seen anyone near
the van at any time. There had been petrol in the tank and oil in
the sump; then why leave it like that? Why? It was a Why that

bothered Leith quite a lot, and for the moment he could get no closer to a satisfactory answer. He glanced at his watch and ordered a 'chaser' quickly. Presently he must go back to the Yard, and report to Harley.

He hated conferences unless he knew all the answers and could get away soon. He would rather work for six hours than attend a conference—much rather.

He wanted to be able to give Harley the answer and not have Harley giving it to him, for Leith was a human man who, like all other human men, liked to be right, and who did not like to be told where he got off. He was not told that very often; neither was Harley, which was why they were an extremely efficient team of police officers.

He was not worrying about the end of the case, because his reason and his experience told him that the Rigger would, in the course of time, return to his yard, and there he would be arrested and then he would talk—not a great deal, perhaps, but enough to put the police on the track of those he had employed in the robbery, and piece by piece the puzzle would be assembled for the edification of an Old Bailey jury.

There would, of course, be many interviews and a thousand questions and answers, and a great deal of talk; but it would all come out in the end and give the evening papers something to spread themselves on for a whole page, perhaps, and maintain their circulation.

But all the same, Detective-Sergeant Leith, in the publicity of that public bar, would have liked to have got a line on the story, so that he could have handed it to Harley on a figurative plate; for he was a curious man as well as human.

*   *   *

Probably Leith himself did not know whether it was ambition, curiosity, pride, or merely a sense of duty which made him gulp the last of his beer without proper appreciation, and took him back to the Rigger's shack.

As he turned in at the gates, with a jerk of his head towards the plain-clothes man on duty there, he heard the shrill voice of a small boy telling someone that the boss had gone away. Leith traced the owner of the voice to the top of an old Morris Cowley. He was flourishing a wooden stick which for the moment was a sword.

Then he heard Spider's voice and hurried his pace through the rubble of old hoop-iron and junk.

When Spider saw Leith his mouth formed in a sudden 'O' of surprise, and he stopped talking to the boy on the top of the Morris Cowley. He looked frightened and gave a quick glance round as though he were going to run away. But he changed his mind, and while Leith approached him he stood quite still. He said, "Good morning," nervously, and there was a pause before he continued, forcing a smile: "kind of funny, meeting you here, guv'nor."

Leith asked: "Where's the Rigger?"

Spider became suddenly voluble: "That's just what I'm wanting to know myself. 'Where's the Rigger?' I said to myself this morning. 'It's been a long time since I've seen him,' I said. And then I thought I'd take a dander down here and see what he was up to." Spider looked at the boy on the car. "He says he hasn't been round this morning."

"You're his mate, aren't you?"

"That was a long time ago, guv'nor. I haven't set eyes on the Rigger since—"

"Last night," Leith interrupted. "When you and he pulled a job in Durham Square."

Spider fought to put an expression of innocent and injured surprise on to his face. "Durham Square? Why, I don't even know where it is."

"Yes, you do." Leith took two paces forward, until he was a foot away from Spider. Spider remained dumb. Leith eyed him steadily.

"You and the Rigger worked it out between you and you pulled the job last night. You used a van which you stole from a shopkeeper near here, a man of the name of Williams."

"Williams? Never heard of him."

"I'll get him to have a look at you and see if he hasn't heard of you."

"We didn't pull no job, Mr. Leith. If we had, would I be here at this very minute? I asks you, is it sense?"

"You've got a new suit. Where did you get the dough for that?"

Spider licked his dry lips. "I've been lucky. Had a good day at Ally Pally last week."

"Come on, we'll take a walk."

They walked as far as Mr. Williams' shop and gave that man another fright. His ferret's eyes darted from Leith to Spider and back to Spider again. His hands crumpled his dirty white apron.

"Ever seen this man before?" Leith asked.

Mr. Williams said he hadn't.

"Are you sure of that?"

"Yes, yes, quite sure."

"You haven't seen him hanging around at all?"

"I've never seen him before in my life."

Spider's face was as a wax dummy's, clean of expression. Suddenly he felt very relieved.

When they came out of the shop, Leith said: "All right. You can hop it."

Spider beamed. "Good-bye, guv'nor."

"Au revoir," said Leith softly, which subtlety was luckily wasted on Spider.

*　　*　　*

Leith went back to the Yard. Harley was putting on his hat, about to go out to lunch. "Well, did you get anything?"

Leith told him about the absence of the Rigger, and of his interview with Spider.

"Looks as though I may be right after all," Harley said. "And it was the Rigger who pulled the job, since he's cleared out. What about the van?"

"Nothing more about that. But I don't get the hang of it. What did he want to leave the van for? It doesn't make sense."

"When you're dealing with men like the Rigger you don't look for sense. Something might have scared him. You know how it is with a ticklish job like that. One little thing goes wrong; someone isn't there on the dot, and they get jittery and run for it. We'll put out the hooks for the Rigger. He's our man all right." Harley pushed his hat on the back of his head and thrust his hands deep into his trouser pockets. "And even with all this you won't admit it."

Leith was looking very mulish. "It wasn't the Rigger."

"I was waiting for you to say that. Now just tell me why it wasn't the Rigger?"

"Because he's got guts. If it had happened the way you say, and some little thing turned up to put 'em off their stroke, the Rigger would never have run for it. He's got guts, but he hasn't got the brains to work the job out, nor the patience either. That's why he gave up the burgling lay and turned fence. He was spending too much of his time inside."

"I still think it was the Rigger. We'll have that dump of his watched all the time; that's where he'll make for. And Spider—why did you turn him loose?"

"We'll get more out of him that way than keeping him locked up. He's not the kind that can run far, even if he wanted to."

And that was exactly how Spider was feeling at the moment when Leith had left him. He wanted to keep as far away from Louie Patra as possible, but he knew no other town than London. He wanted to find out what had happened to the Rigger, because he wanted the cut which the Rigger had promised him.

It was true that he had deserted the van when the Rigger did not return to it, but that hadn't been his fault. Something had happened. The moment he had seen Patra's car turn and speed away he had feared the worst.

Spider's legs took him northward from Trafalgar Square, as he tried to make some decision. He looked at the models of ships in the windows of the shipping companies in Cockspur Street. He was nearly picked off by a taxi as he crossed to the Haymarket. He mooched through the crowds, propelled by his homing steps to the hub of the Universe, and the hub of his own little world—Piccadilly Circus.

And as he neared it he began to feel better. It was like coming home after having been abroad for a couple of years. Even the thought of Louie Patra could not keep him away. The smell of the buses, and the hot tar oozing up between the wood blocks, and the shouts of the paper-boys, and staccato hoots of the taxi horns, and, above and behind it all, the roar and the rumble of the traffic; the sound of tyres on the roadway, whining gears and the noise of revving engines, as they roared away in low gear. . . .

He stood for a time at the corner of Shaftesbury Avenue, soaking it all in, infinitely content. At the back of his brain was forming the thought that it would be nice to sit on a high stool in a cool dark bar, and hold a pint pot in his hand, with a dish of cheese by his elbow that he could nibble.

He bought a midday paper and turned up Shaftesbury Avenue, took the first to the right, past Hemm's, and then left and right again. That unconscious will of his turned his steps into the bar of the 'Flag and Lamb'.

"A pint of mild-and-bitter, if you please, miss."

He hoisted himself up on to a stool and drew over a plate of cheese. He took a long drink of beer and had turned his paper to read the racing page when the kaleidoscopic colours of Tony's habitual attire disturbed the cool dark monotone of the bar.

Tony ordered a mixed vermouth. He was wearing a light-coloured felt hat with a dark band. His shirt was dark blue and he had a purple tie.

Slowly Spider took his eyes from his paper. He knew Tony and he knew who he worked for.

Tony sucked in smoke from an Egyptian cigarette. He had the fingers of a pianist and the grace of an animal or a ballet dancer.

The mild-and-bitter didn't seem to taste so good now.

"The boss wants you." The words came silky and smooth from Tony's lips. He drank from his glass and then took a bit of cheese.

"I'm not working for him any more."

"This morning he said that he wants to see you. I do not know anything else."

"Then he can ruddy well want. I've not got anything to do with him."

"I'll tell him what you say."

Spider stared at a bottle on the shelf and read the words on the label. 'Distilled from the very finest ingredients and guaranteed absolutely pure.'

Suddenly he said: "What's it all about?"

"Last night perhaps—I do not know."

"I don't know nothing about last night."

"Then you have nothing to fear."

"I didn't say I was scared, did I?"

Tony finished his drink and ordered another. He stubbed out his cigarette. "I think it would be better if you go."

Spider looked round the bar as though he were looking for a way of escape. A smile came to Tony's lips. He took another cigarette from his case and lit it. "He is a very good friend, but it is better not to make him angry, you understand?"

Spider understood, but he did not say anything. He crumpled up his paper and finished his drink. Then he slid from his stool. "You can tell him from me that—" Then he stopped.

Tony was smiling. "Yes, what is your message?"

"Oh, go to hell." Spider pushed through the swing door into the sudden light of the street.

*   *   *

Like an animal, long caged and suddenly loosed in a strange country, Spider did not know where to go. London had been his cage for forty years.

He walked aimlessly westward, crossed Charing Cross Road and St. Martin's Lane and reached Covent Garden; went on past the Opera House and turned right, into the Strand. He had three pounds in his pocket, all that remained of the ten pounds which Louie had given him.

He was frightened to go away and frightened to stay.

Half an hour later he was back in Shaftesbury Avenue. What was there to be scared of? Louie wouldn't do anything to him. He hadn't done anything wrong. Maybe Louie wanted him for another job. Anyway, he had nothing to lose and he might get a line on the Rigger.

He had no love for the Rigger, but there was still that business of his share, and the three pounds wouldn't last him for ever.

So Spider went to Mrs. Hoskins' shop in Canton Street.

He found Benny Watt there. Benny was sitting at a table eating beans with a spoon out of a tin plate. Mrs. Hoskins was not in sight. Benny looked up slowly when the door-bell rang, and, when he saw who it was, put down his spoon and wiped his mouth with the back of his hand. All his movements were unhurried and deliberate. "You ought to keep away from here."

"The boss sent for me."

"He sent for you? Why?"

"That's what I want to know. That's what I've come to find out."

Benny reached out a hand and pulled Spider to a chair by his side. "I thought you was in that job last night. That's what you told me."

"I couldn't get there in time."

"A good thing you was out of it."

"Didn't it go right?"

Benny looked towards the shop door; then he opened the door into the back room, looked inside, and shut it again quietly. When he came back to the table he said: "You and me's pals, Spider. We've worked together and I've never squeaked on you, and you've never squeaked on me."

Spider said, "That's right," and pulled a flattened packet of cigarettes out of his pocket.

"The best thing for you is to get out of here, right away, and stop away. Everything may be all right, but I don't know, it may turn out all wrong." Benny ate a spoonful of beans and then pushed the plate away from him. It grated on the bare wood.

But one part of Spider was monkey, and monkeys are curious. Louie couldn't do anything to him. He said: "I'm going to see the boss. Is he in his rooms?"

Benny nodded. "Yes, and maybe it'll be better if you was to find out what he wants, and specially as he sent for you. He don't like being crossed."

Spider stared at the door at the back of the shop for a long time before he said, "Got the key?" and got up and walked across the floor, like a man going to have a tooth out.

Benny went into the back room and came back with the key in his outstretched hand. As his trembling fingers felt for the keyhole he said: "She's still asleep and she don't seem to care that I've been up half the night—most of the night you might well say." But Spider brushed past him and went up the flight of steep wooden stairs.

It was dark in the upstairs passage and his fingers felt on the wall for the door to the office. Then faintly he heard footsteps, the door swung open suddenly and he found himself a foot away from Louie Patra.

"I wondered if you'd come." He put out a hand, drew Spider in and slammed the door shut. He went to the window overlooking the yard, and when he spoke he did not turn. "So you thought you could put on a double-cross, did you?" The words sounded to Spider like the purring of a tiger seeing its dinner. He felt a bit sick and wished he hadn't come. Louie turned slowly. He rolled his cigar from one corner of his mouth to the other. His coat was open and he had his thumbs stuck in the armholes of his waistcoat. "Well, what's your story?"

"Look here, guv'nor, I ain't done nothing wrong, and I don't know what you mean about a double-cross, honest I don't."

"Then who gave the Rigger the office?"

"I don't know."

"You work with the Rigger, don't you?"

"Used to, months ago; but he's finished."

A ghost of a smile came to Louie's face, widened his mouth for an instant and then was gone. "Yes, he's finished all right."

"And besides, how was I to know that you was going to pull the job last night?"

"Who said anything about last night?"

Spider hesitated for a moment and then said: "I guessed it was last night. It must have been last night, the way I figured it out."

"And didn't you tell the Rigger what you'd figured out?" Louie began to walk slowly across the room. "Of course you did, and you and the Rigger fixed up as nice a little double-cross as ever I've seen."

Spider retreated until his back was against the wall. His eyes were on Louie's, and he was as frightened as he had ever been in his life.

"And you've got that nice new suit on that I told you to buy. It'll be a pity to spoil it."

Spider could not move nor make a sound. He tried to swallow but couldn't.

Louie spat out his cigar and trod on it; then slowly his hands came up. "Nice new suit; pity to spoil it"

Spider pressed against the wall. His face was the colour of the ashes in the saucer on Louie's desk.

"But perhaps there's another way." Louie's voice was a whisper. With his left hand he grasped a bunch of Spider's shirt, just below his collar. With the other he unbuttoned the jacket and pulled it off. "I'll send you out as good as new. No one'll know you've been a naughty little boy; not unless you tell them, and I wouldn't do that if I were you."

Spider fought for words. "I won't squeak, I swear it. Just let me go, just let me go. I'll do anything you want me to. I'll—"

Louie lifted his right hand and struck him across the face with the palm. Spider started to cry.

"Keep your breath. You'll have plenty to shout about in a minute." He opened a cupboard door and put in his hand. When it came out it was holding a short black strap. "You've had one warning; this is the last."

*   *   *

Spider lay in the passage outside the office for half an hour before the pain eased and he moved his arms and slowly sat up. "The swine," he muttered, and put a hand against the wall to steady himself as he got to his feet. He shuffled along the passage and went down the stairs one foot at a time.

Benny was still sitting at his table with the empty dish in front of him. Spider had to knock loudly on the door before he realized that anyone was there.

As he opened the door Benny said: "What did he have to say?" Then he saw Spider's face. "Good heavens!—what's he been doing to you?"

Spider took two steps to a chair and sat down. He was still feeling sick and faint.

Benny put the key in his pocket and then went to the door which led to Starling Court. "You wait there. I'll be back in a minute." When he returned he was carrying the flat bottle Tooley had given him. "Take a drop of this." He drew the cork and gave Spider the bottle. Then he went to the street door, opened it and looked out, shut the door again and swore when the bell clanged. He looked towards the door of the back room and stood still as though he were waiting for something. "We don't want her around," he muttered, and looked at Spider.

Spider was letting the liquor run slowly down his throat. He shuddered as though he were cold, shuddered all over; his head fell suddenly on the table on his crossed arms. The bottle fell on its side and the liquor ran slowly over the table. Benny Watt picked it up and put back the cork. Then he stooped over Spider:

After a little while he touched him on the arm. Spider raised his head very slowly and turned it so that he looked at Benny Watt. He said: "Can I stop here for a bit?"

"What's that?" Benny cupped a hand to his right ear.

"Can I stop here? In the chapel?"

"No, no, you can't do that; he comes in there nearly every day." Benny didn't speak for a minute and then he pointed to the door of the back room and said: "Maybe she could fix something for you. Wait a minute."

He shuffled across the floor and, opening the door slowly, went inside. Dimly Spider could hear people talking, very far away.

Then the door opened again and the voice of Mrs. Hoskins broke through his consciousness. He made an effort and sat upright.

Mrs. Hoskins tucked in a straying rat-tail of grey hair, and said: "Well, what have you been up to?"

"Had a night out. Want a doss," Spider mumbled.

"Just for a couple of hours," Benny explained.

Mrs. Hoskins looked back at her room and said: "Well . . ." She moved over to the window and stared at the trays of food. Then she looked at the clock and yawned. "Can if you like, but you got to be out by nine."

Benny Watt nudged Spider. "She says it's O.K." He took Spider by the arm and led him into the back room. Mrs. Hoskins followed them and began to straighten the clothes on the bed. The bed almost filled the room. A cupboard door hung open crazily. None of the drawers of a pine chest were properly shut. The top of it was a litter of buttons and brushes and trays and wisps of hair and rumpled crochet mats.

Spider lay down on the bed and stretched himself with a little contented sigh. He muttered, "Pull down the blind," and shut his eyes.

*　　*　　*

That evening Leith had to make an unsatisfactory report at the Yard. He had made but little progress, and his conference with Harley failed to elucidate matters. Harley put his papers together in a neat pile and placed them on one side. Then he took a report from a basket by his right hand. "Here's another case that's been put on my plate. The body found on the burning dump."

Leith said: "I saw something about it in the paper tonight. What do the farriers say?"

"That the man died from wounds on the head. There was no trace of carbon in his lungs, so he must have been dead before he was put on the dump."

"Murder! That's interesting." Leith took the typewritten sheet; his eyes ran swiftly over the lines. "Age fifty to fifty-five . . . well developed . . . brown hair, grey eyes . . . dressed in a blue serge suit from which the name-tab had been removed. No name or laundry marks on underclothing . . . no hat." He put the paper on the desk. "Doesn't seem much to go on there."

"I've had a man checking up on the Missing Persons register, but he doesn't tally with any of them."

"What about a circular?"

"It's being printed now."

"With a photograph?"

"No. The face was too badly burned."

"What about finger-prints?"

"All the skin was burned off both hands." Harley lit a pipe. "They had been pressed down into the burning refuse."

"Pressed down?" Leith showed a sudden interest. "Are you sure about that?"

"That's what Forsythe said. He made the first examination, and he's pretty sound."

"That looks as if this man was on our books."

"Yes, I'm waiting for a report from Records now." Harley picked up the 'phone on his desk and asked for a number. He spoke for a minute or two and then put back the receiver. "The general description fits three men, and the Rigger is one of them."

"The Rigger! And you were thinking that he had pulled the job, or at least that he'd been mixed up in it."

"We know he's disappeared." Harley scribbled two names on a piece of paper. "These are the other two possibles. Check up on them."

As he took the paper Leith said: "I wonder what the hell happened."

"Wondering never got a policeman any place." Harley tamped down on the tobacco in his pipe and lit another match. "The Rigger had guts but no brains, as someone said. The bloke who pulled the Durham Square job had brains. Find him and we'll find out who killed the Rigger—if it is the Rigger's body."

"That's all you want me to do, is it?"

"That's all," replied Harley through a cloud of grey smoke.

CHAPTER X

THAT AFTERNOON Tooley had spent sleeping in his bed in the room over Silvretti's shop. At three o'clock he woke slowly and after a while swung his feet to the floor and yawned and stretched.

A bar of light came through a slit in the drawn blind. He looked at his watch stupidly; rubbed his eyes and ran his fingers through his hair. Then he went to the mirror and put on his tie. Sleep had soothed his jangling nerves, and in the fastness of this frowzy room he felt secure. That morning he had been questioned by the police and they had let him go. That meant something; it meant a lot; they hadn't got anything on him. All he'd got to do now was to collect his share: he wouldn't have to work for months.

His hand went out to his hair-brush and then drew back. He'd give the wop a job. Louie would pay. He was smiling a tight smile as he entered the saloon below and called out to Silvretti and sat down in one of the chairs.

When Silvretti came through the jangling bead curtain he said: "Shave and a shampoo and anything else you've got."

Silvretti filled a mug from the tap and began to work up a lather. "You have had a good sleep, no?"

"I slept all right." Tooley tilted his head back on the rest and stretched out his legs. It felt fine; one of the things he had been looking forward to. He looked at the Italian. "What's on your mind? You look like a horse with croup."

Something that was meant to be a smile twisted Silvretti's mouth beneath his drooping black moustaches. He waggled his head and replied in a sing-song voice: "I am very well and I am very happy; very, very happy." He began to soap Tooley's face.

Tooley looked at the ceiling veined with wandering hair cracks like a crazy map, like a map a kid would draw; that bit in the corner was just like Africa or Australia, he didn't know or care; he still felt sleepy. Then he heard Silvretti talking.

"It is terrible, terrible. The same thing every day: yes, every day it is the same."

"What the hell are you yapping about?"

"This piece I read in the papers not five minutes before you call. I sit down for two, three minutes and what do I see but that someone has been killed."

"Well, why not? You've got to die sometime."

"But not like this; it is terrible." Silvretti put down the brush and went into the saloon. He came back with a paper, which he handed to Tooley. "There in the Stop Press; you read him for yourself, and if you do not think that . . ."

But Tooley wasn't listening; his eyes were racing over the smudged type. "A body of a man has been found on a rubbish dump near Walthamstow. No particulars are available, but it is believed that the police have a clue."

"Keep still if you please." The razor cut smooth swathes of white cream. "Quite still."

Tooley re-read the announcement and then let the paper drop on the floor by his side.

"That is the second time that such a thing has happened. The first time the murderer was caught. Perhaps it will be the same this time. The police are very clever. Keep quite still if you please." Silvretti cleaned the razor on a sheet of coarse brown paper and bent again to his task. "No doubt tomorrow we will read something else. It will be very interesting." He paused and then asked: "Don't you think so?"

"Yes, damned interesting. Now get a move on, I'm in a hurry."

"The shampoo? The haircut?"

"Cut them out. I tell you I'm in a hurry."

Five minutes later Tooley stepped out of the shop into Lucas Street and looked up and down, but saw no sign of the enemy. He was looking for Leith. He walked south to Crompton Street, turned left, left again and came back into Lucas Street through an alley.

The entrance to Starling Court was twenty yards away, and as he passed in through the arch his heart eased down its furious beating. He felt safer now. He mounted the wooden stairway and knocked on the door of the Wastepaper Company's Registered Office.

A chair scraped inside and almost immediately the door was opened.

Louie said nothing until Tooley was inside and the door was shut and locked. "I thought you knew better than to come up this way." He went to the window and looked out.

Tooley lounged against the wall. He said: "It's O.K. You needn't sweat." He took his cigarette from his mouth and blew out a cloud of smoke. He watched it drift slowly upwards.

Louie sat down at the desk. He still looked sulky. "What do you want, anyway?" He was hot and tired after his recent interview with Spider.

Tooley tossed the crumpled newspaper on to the desk. "It's all in there. You stuck him on a dump, didn't you? So you stuck him on a dump."

Louie pushed aside the saucer on the desk and spread out the newspaper. "Where is it?"

"On the back page; Stop Press. They say the police've got a clue."

When he had finished reading, Louie said: "They'd got to find him sometime. But he won't tell them anything. I pushed his hands right deep down and the stuff was hot. They won't get a finger-print off him."

"You might have been seen by someone," Tooley suggested.

"I don't think so." Louie folded the paper and put it into the waste basket.

"You ought to have put him some place where he wouldn't have been found."

"And where would that be?" Louie didn't speak for half a minute, and then he continued: "You've got to leave it all to me. Every single thing."

Tooley couldn't remain still any longer. He began to walk up and down the room with clipped steps. His head nodded forward on his breast and he drew so hard on his cigarette that the smoke tasted hot. Suddenly he wanted to get out of the room, and he fumbled with the lock of the courtyard door.

"Other way," Louie barked. "I told you not to use that door."

There was a curious light in Tooley's green eyes. "I want my cut. I want to get out of it."

"You're all worked up. All worked up. Take it easy, Tooley." Louie's voice was syrupy smooth. He gripped Tooley by both his arms above the elbows and forced him backwards away from the door.

Tooley felt the line of a chair at the back of his knees, and sat down.

Louie stood in front of him with his hands deep in the pockets of his jacket "If you run away, if you make a single solitary move out of turn, the dicks'll pull you in."

"No, they won't. They've had a go at me already. But I foxed them."

Louie was in the act of taking his cigar-case from his pocket. He froze. "Had a go at you already, have they?" His voice was low and he spoke as though he were thinking of something else.

Tooley nodded. "This morning; wanted to know where I was last night. I told them and then they let me go."

"Just like that, was it? You told where you had been and they let you go. You foxed them?"

"They didn't get anything out of me."

"Who was it?"

"Harley; and Leith was there, too."

Louie took a bottle and a glass from a cupboard and poured out three fingers of whiskey. He gave the glass to Tooley, who took a gulp and then reached out and put the glass on the desk. He wiped his mouth with the back of his right hand. The panic light had gone from his eyes.

Louie said: "Now tell me what was said; every word."

When he had finished Louie sat down and lit a cigar. "Maybe it's all right. But don't go thinking that you're out of it yet. Remember what you told them; they'll pick you up again and put you through it just the same way. Stick to your story and you'll be O.K."

Tooley put out a hand for the glass. He drank more slowly this time; his hand was almost steady.

His brain seemed half frozen, with thoughts revolving incoherently like points of pain. He made an effort to concentrate, and found himself thinking of the Rigger. His eyes narrowed and his nails dug into the palms of his hands. "I never meant to do him in; I never meant to. . . . If he hadn't come at me like that I'd never have touched him."

Louie gently broke the ash of his cigar into the saucer on his desk. "Now don't get worked up all over again. You've got nothing to worry about. Everything'll be all right."

"Yes, all right for you; you've never killed a man; you don't know what it's like. Sometimes I think I've forgotten, but I haven't; it always comes back. I've been through that moment a hundred times since last night. And one day they'll get me; I know it and you know it, but what will you care? You'll just go on sitting there, fixing jobs for other poor boobs to pull, and all the time you'll tell them that there's nothing for them to worry about; you'll land them in it up to their necks and—" Tooley suddenly stopped talking.

Louie got up and took the glass from Tooley's hand. He refilled it and gave it him back. He said: "Go on, let's have the rest of it." Tooley took a long drink, and relaxed in his chair, slowly shaking his head. That line was no good. He mustn't quarrel with the boss now—Louie had the headpiece to think of a way out for them both. He, Tooley, was utterly dependent upon him; more so now than ever.

He glanced half sheepishly at Louie sitting in his chair. He had nerve.

The silence lengthened over Tooley's outburst.

He was feeling better. His eyes wandered to the calendar on the wall; to the picture of the curly-haired boy and the mastiff. His mind was groping for something else he wanted to say. After a minute or two he remembered. "What about my cut?"

"You'll get it all right." Louie felt in the pocket of his waistcoat and brought out a folded sheet of paper. "When the job's finished." Tooley gaped at him. "What do you mean, finished? I got everything you told me to, didn't I?"

"Yes, yes, you did fine. It was Zimmermann made the bog, not you. When he gave me the list he left out the piece he wanted most. At least—we got one, but it should have been a pair."

Tooley felt empty—flattened out.

"I'll bet it was a potato-ring," he muttered weakly.

"No—it's a glass. The mate of one you pinched. He says it's the only pair in existence. I said we'd get it for him, tonight."

"If you mean me—you're wrong. Dead wrong! I wouldn't go near that house again for all the money in the world. I'm through I tell you!"

Louie was watching him quietly. "Then there's nothing to cut," he pointed out. "No money. No—anything."

"I don't care—and you can't make me do it. I didn't want to do it last night. You don't know what it's like. I—I—no, I don't want any more of your damned whiskey. I can't do the job when I'm doped, and I won't do it when I'm sober. I'm through—do you hear?"

"Other door," said Louie softly.

He sat quite still when Tooley had flung away and left him.

Then he picked up the receiver of a telephone which connected with the club.

"I want Anna," he snapped.

*   *   *

Tooley was standing outside the inner bar of Guido's Club when Anna came in, at about eight o'clock. She was wearing a white fox fur round her shoulders and somehow it made her look slimmer, more dainty, more provoking, infinitely more desirable than ever he had seen her before.

As his hand brushed against her bare arm and he sensed the faint scent which she always used he had the feeling of complete and utter happiness; the happiness of selfless adoration.

She smiled and pulled the fur more tightly round her neck. "Isn't it lovely?"

"Yes, fine." His fingers sank into the soft downy fur. "Where did you get it?"

"From Mr. Kimber. Birthday present."

The tight smile on Tooley's face faded and his voice was hard when he said: "You shouldn't take presents from him."

"Why not? No one else gives me presents." She smiled very sweetly. "And I like him very much. I like men who take me out to dinner and give me champagne and buy me white fox furs. That's the sort of man I'd like to marry."

"He's not your sort. He's right out of your class. And besides, he'd never marry you. He'll run you around and take what he wants and then leave you flat. You're just a painted doll to him."

"Well, that's something." Anna fingered the fur. "I could hock this for a tenner."

"Come out with me tonight."

"Sorry—can't be done."

"You've got to."

There was a sudden insistence in his voice which frightened her. She sensed in him a pent-up emotion which at any minute would burst out.

"Why?" She sparred for time.

"I can't tell you, but you must. I've got to talk to you." The muscles of his face worked.

"Something's happened. What is it?"

"It's nothing. I want you, that's all."

"Come in here." She opened the door which led to Louie's shielded table, in a corner of the restaurant.

He kicked the door shut behind him and suddenly took her in his arms, pressing her savagely to him. Their lips met. She gave herself to him.

Minutes passed before she pushed him from her. She sank back on a chair. He stood staring down at her. "That's how I want you." She did not speak. "I'm not like Kimber, I'd marry you. I'd take you away from all this. . . ."

"You would? Oh, my dear, I didn't know you felt like that. I don't think I even knew that I loved you . . . I've been a fool." She stood up and put her hands on his shoulders. "Wouldn't it be wonderful to get away from all this? Just you and I. Quit of it all, of Guido, and Louie and this place—and—oh, wouldn't it be marvellous?"

Tooley's eyes were ablaze as he took her in his arms again. He was too much delighted to realize that her enthusiasm was a little forced, and her surrender surprisingly sudden.

"By God, Anna, we'll do it!"

"And you've got the money," she went on guilelessly. "Your cut from last night."

His eyes clouded and his arms dropped to his sides.

"What's wrong?" she asked. "Oh, don't say something's wrong! We can't do a thing if we haven't got the cash."

Tooley stared at her dumbly.

"You'd come away with me if I had the cash? You swear it?"

"Of course I would. Haven't I just been saying how wonderful it would be? But why? Do you mean you haven't got it? I'll swear to you that I'm not going to run away with any penniless—"

"Be quiet. I'll get it—tonight. I told Louie I wouldn't do it—but I will. I'll go and tell him now."

*   *   *

Down in the chapel Benny Watt was brewing cocoa on a gas-ring. Louie had told him he would be wanted tonight, and when there was a job on he could never sleep.

The car was ready, the key of the gate was in his pocket; all the locks had been oiled.

He got up off the box he had been sitting on, shuffled over to the baling bin, and pulled the chain which worked the ram. It ran easily in its pulley. A dozen sacks of loose paper were stacked close by, all ready to tip in.

In the office, Louie had finished his work on the plan. He threw away a dead cigar, and as he lit another he looked at the tin clock on the top of the desk. After Tooley's capitulation, so speedily effected by Anna, he had sent him away for an hour, while he completed his plans. But now he should be back. He got up and began to pace up and down the room, his head thrust forward and his hands pushed deep in his trouser pockets. If Tooley let him down!

He stopped and looked down at the plan; it ought to work, but there was no room for a false move. As long as Tooley kept his nerve. If only he had been able to have Sharkey Finn!—but Sharkey was dead.

Footsteps sounded in the passage and there was a light double tap on the panel of the door which led to Mrs. Hoskins' shop. It was Tooley.

He slid into the room, a cigarette hanging from the corner of his mouth; he leant against the wall and said: "What if they've changed the locks?"

"They haven't changed them. Where have you been?"

"Taking a walk."

Louie handed the plan to Tooley. "Just see that you've got it all straight. Tonight's job'll mean a clean-up. It'll be easier than the last time; you know your way around and there's only the one thing to take. But don't make any mistake this time."

Tooley let the plan fall on the desk. "I got it all here." He tapped. his forehead with his finger. He moved towards the door which led to the club. "All right for me to wait in there?"

"Yes, but don't booze up. We don't start till midnight."

"O.K." Tooley released the catch of the door.

"And don't get funny with Anna. She's holding Kimber till you're through."

"You don't need to worry about that side of it," Tooley slid through the door and was gone. He walked along the carpeted passage to the long lounge, and through the door by the cloakroom to Louie's table. He sat there for a long time just looking at Anna. He had spoken the truth when he had told Louie not to worry about 'that side of it'; for he felt sure of Anna now. As soon as he cleaned up this job she would come away with him; she was his. Only the faintest twinges of jealousy ran through him as he watched her dance with Kimber.

Tomorrow. He promised himself a lot of things tomorrow. He put the ivory pig on the table and smiled at it; she had given it to him and it was going to bring him luck, lots of luck.

Tomorrow he was going to live and get back some of the things he had missed during these three long years.

He was just beginning to forget, and he was going to get something that would wipe out all these memories.

Tomorrow. The throbbing music soaked into his brain, filling him with an utter content, sponging out the creases of his restlessness.

"Hullo!"

He looked up with a start to find Anna beside his chair, Anna with a puzzled, searching look in her eyes.

"What's up?"

"Nothing's up. I'm dreaming dreams. Where's Kimber?"

"Met a friend. They're in the bar. He didn't want me—" She flushed and sat down at Tooley's table. Kimber had been ashamed to introduce her to his man friend. She had seen it in his eyes. She had been left out of the conversation, as cold as the Elgin marbles they were discussing, and of which she had never heard.

And here was Tooley—alone and dreaming dreams. Her eyes fell on the little ivory pig. He cupped it in his hand, laughing.

"He's bringing me luck tonight. I need it, after last time—"

"Last night? Did anything go wrong last night?" she whispered.

"Yes. That's why I've got to get away—"

"What happened? Please tell me."

He shook his head, and she thought that he shuddered all over involuntarily.

"I must know if—if we're going away together."

He moistened his lips and spoke in a mutter, disrupted and barely audible.

"A man was killed. I didn't do it. I swear that, but it looked that way."

"Who knows?"

"Louie and Benny Watt and Tony. They were all there."

"Who killed him?"

"I don't know. There was a fight and it was all mixed up. Louie said it was me, but he lied."

"He won't help you."

"I know that." Tooley spoke bitterly. "But he was there and he won't dare say too much." He was feeling better now that he had told Anna. He sat down and spread out his legs. "I didn't want to go into that job, but Louie made me. All the same, I'm glad he's dead."

"Who?"

"The Rigger. He shopped me."

"And you're glad he's dead?" Anna spoke slowly as she asked the question.

"Don't look like that, damn you. I tell you I didn't do it. I've I never raised my hand to a man before . . ."

"So you did hit him? You fool! You damned fool! And now you want me to marry you; to go away, and run with the coppers on our heels. How long do you think that would last? They'll get you. They'll get you."

Her voice broke in a sob. She realized that she, too, had been looking forward to tomorrow and all that it had promised, before she knew that it was shadowed by—murder.

Tooley put his big hand over hers.

"Don't you believe it, kid," he said gently. "I didn't do it on purpose, so I'm O.K. Besides I've got the pig—and I've got you. Tonight I'm going to have a last clean-up. It'll mean a century at least. And tomorrow, we'll be off."

Anna smiled at him weakly. "I know. Sorry." She pulled out her compact to repair the ravages of that one genuine, inexplicable tear. She had for a moment forgotten Louie's orders about tonight, forgotten Kimber, and her job. She pulled herself together.

"You'll be all right—of course you will. I'll be ready, tomorrow." She snapped the lid of her compact shut. "I must get back to Kimber. That's all I can do to help you. Good luck!"

She smiled, and left Tooley's dreams unimpaired.

CHAPTER XI

LOUIE PATRA was uneasy. It was not the killing of the rigger that worried him; that had been squared off, and even if the police became suspicious there was no reason why they should bother him. Tooley would be the man to take the can back.

Reason bade him go ahead with the new job Zimmermann had put up. There would be no risk if it were worked properly. He had it all worked out. His only worry was the state of Tooley's nerves.

That is what Louie told himself, as he stood staring with unfocused eyes at the calendar hanging crookedly on the wall. But something was wrong. He had had that uneasy feeling once before, when he was planning a big smash, and things had come unstuck. A car had broken down and he had been lucky to get away clear, but without the swag.

Perhaps Benny might know something. Louie switched out the light before he unlocked the door which opened on to the outside stairs, and stood for a minute in the darkness, listening. There was a glint of light in one of the windows of the chapel. He went down the wooden stairs, his weight poised on the balls of his feet, silently, smoothly, for somewhere ahead of him in the darkness there was a man.

The scuffle of a foot against a scrap of paper, the creak of leather or the sharp sound of a steel-shod boot on stone; what it was that had betrayed the trespassing man to Louie's ears only Louie himself knew. He possessed the senses of a wild cat allied to a brain which interpreted every sound, without pause for puzzled thought.

He reached the lowest tread of the ladder, saw a moving shadow on the other side of the roadway and followed it, keeping a parallel line close to the wall.

His eyes were becoming accustomed to the darkness now and he could see the shape of the man as he stepped from the shadows and walked across the open space in front of the chapel. He saw him approach the window through which light showed and remain quite still.

Cold hatred, tantamount to the lust of killing, was in Louie's heart as he crept forward, his hands half clenched and fingers moving in anticipation of the grip which had already destroyed one life, and sought yet another.

In his very eagerness to conceal his approach Louie betrayed his presence, for, as he slid into a shadow, his foot struck a spanner lying unseen on the cobbles.

The man at the window turned a frightened face and Louie saw that it was Spider. Louie's suspicions were confirmed. Spider was a squealer—and a spy. It was incredible that he should come back for more after the lesson Louie had given him that very afternoon. But it just showed how dangerous the little rat was. A beating was not enough. . . . One split second later there was no Spider at the window. Running footsteps up the narrow alley leading to the back door of the café were the only confirmation of his presence in Starling Court.

"Got you this time," Louie muttered to himself, and a smile which was not a smile came and went. He picked up the spanner and ran to the mouth of the alley; there was no other escape save the door to the café, and that was always kept locked and bolted. Five yards short of the door was a water-butt which constricted the width of the passage so that only one man could pass that way.

A rat in a trap, it appeared to Louie, had more hope of life and freedom.

Spider! The double-crossing little rat! So he thought he could put a fast one across, did he? Louie reached the water-butt and braced himself to meet Spider if he tried to break through.

"Come on out of it. You'll never live to make another squeak."

But that was where Louie Patra made one of the few mistakes in his life, for there was no one at the end of the alley. The door to the café was open.

Puzzled at the silence which followed his order, Louie took two paces forward, saw the open door and swore savagely. There was no light in the passage as he passed through and kicked open the door which led to the shop. There was no one there. He called out: "Mrs. Hoskins! Where the hell have you got to?"

There were sounds of movement in the back room and the door was opened by a blear-eyed Mrs. Hoskins. She stared at him for a moment and then smiled stupidly, placatingly, as she sought to button up her blouse.

"Why was that door left open?" Louie shot out the question savagely.

"The door? Open?" mumbled Mrs. Hoskins stupidly. "I don't really know. It oughtn't to have bin, and it wasn't like that five minutes ago when I went in to have a wash."

There was no visible evidence that Mrs. Hoskins had washed for some days.

Louie walked to the shop door and shot its bolt. Then he turned back to Mrs. Hoskins. "You know Spider, don't you?"

Mrs. Hoskins nodded dumbly. Tears were just round the corner.

"When was he last in here?"

"Dinner-time. That's when it was. Yes, that's right, he came in and had his dinner. He sat right at that table where you're standing now." Speech gave relief to her feelings, an outlet for her fear.

"What was he saying?"

Mrs. Hoskins stopped fiddling with the buttons of her blouse to put a hand under her chin. "Well, now, that's a thing I didn't take no notice of, not to remember, that is, if you get my meaning."

"Did he ask you any questions?"

"I don't think so, Mr. Patra. You see, there was a lot in just then and I was busy dishing up all the time."

"How long did he stay?"

"All the afternoon." Mrs. Hoskins shut her mouth as though she regretted she had spoken.

Louie nodded slowly two or three times, and his voice had lost its harshness when he said: "Oh. So your friend Spider was here all the afternoon, was he? That's very interesting. And did he sit in here all the time?"

"No, Mr. Patra. Seeing as he was tired and didn't have no place to go to, I said he could have a lay down in the back room. You see, I had to go out to my sister's, her that's expecting, and I never thought I there'd be anything wrong in what I done."

"And where do you keep the key of the passage door?"

"Here in the pocket of my skirt. I made it special so as I wouldn't lose it." As she groped in the pocket a frown came over her face. "That's funny, now. I could ha' swore I'd put it there after I took Benny his tea through this morning."

"But you didn't," Louie prompted.

"I couldn't ha' done," Mrs. Hoskins agreed. The fingers of her right hand played round her lips as she sought a solution to the problem.

"You must have left it lying about." Louie stared at her for a moment. He unlocked the shop door and went out into the street.

He went first to Silvretti's shop. The Italian, who was spelling through a paragraph in an evening paper, looked up and at once smiled and said "Good evening" twice in his soft sing-song voice.

"Have you seen Spider?" Louie asked.

"No, saire. Spider he hardly ever come here now. One time, yes. But for one week I do not see him." Silvretti brushed the ends of his drooping moustaches with nervous fingers.

"When did you last see him?"

"The last time? The last time?" Silvretti drawled out the words. "Why, it was the day, no, the night, of your last big business. If you remember I was keeping the lookout at the corner of John Street, and while I was standing there he came past me."

"What place does he use when he's round these parts?"

Silvretti thought for a moment before he replied: "You know the Stella Theatre?"

"Yes."

"Well, on the Piccadilly side of it there is a small public house called the 'Flag and Lamb'. Sometimes you will find Spider there." Louie scribbled a couple of lines on the back of an envelope, and handed it to the Italian with the curt instructions: "Give this to Benny, and tell him he's got to give it to Tooley, as soon as he comes in. It's urgent."

Then he walked out into the street.

*　　*　　*

Leith was standing in a waiting-room at the Yard when a call came through. He was standing with his feet on the edge of the fender and his shoulders against the mantelpiece, trying to make up his mind to go home.

When the 'phone bell rang he picked up the receiver and with his eyes on the floor said: "Yes. Yes, Leith speaking."

From the other end of the wire came the thin voice of Spider. He spoke quickly, urgently: "I want to see you, Mr. Leith. And I want to see you bad."

"What about?" Leith inquired, with no show of interest.

Again came the urgent quacking over the wire.

Leith became thoughtful. "All right. I'll come along, but if it's dud I'll throttle you with my two bare hands."

A man sprawling across the table reading an evening paper looked up and said: "A squeak?"

"Maybe." Leith yawned. "It's Spider, and he's all worked up."

Spider came out of the 'phone box in the saloon bar of the 'Flag and Lamb' and ordered a dog's nose. His fingers beat a nervous tattoo as he watched the barmaid pour a measure of gin into a pint pot of hitter beer. It was his third that night, and the coppers he spilled on the counter were his last. He grinned at the barmaid. "Ain't even got the price of a fourpenny doss now."

She said: "Reely, now. Fancy that. And it's raining, too."

Spider became confidential. He laid a smutty forefinger against the side of his nose. "But I know how I'm going to make more: a whole lot more. There's a gentleman coming in here to see me and I'm going to tell him something he doesn't know; something that nobody knows, except me."

The barmaid leaned against the edge of a shelf and manicured her finger-nails. Like all barmaids she had the power of listening without hearing. Sometimes she said, "Reely now," and sometimes she said: "You are a one." That was her contribution to the conversation.

She did not notice when Spider stopped abruptly. She did not see the look of stark fear which came over Spider's face.

His jaw sagged and his hands sought and gripped the edge of the bar.

*   *   *

Twenty minutes later Leith arrived at the 'Flag and Lamb', but having waited in vain for Spider to put in an appearance, whilst he consumed two pints of best, he gave it up as a bad job.

He went down the Haymarket and across Trafalgar Square, intending to go on to Charing Cross Underground to get a. train home; but conscience turned his steps right-handed into White-hall, towards Scotland Yard.

The policeman at the door looked at the board and said in reply to Leith's question: "Yes. Harley's still here." He yawned and added: "Which is more than I'd be if I was him."

Leith found Chief Inspector Harley drinking a cup of coffee. He was wearing his hat, and his coat was lying across the back of a chair. He looked up and said: "I'm just going home. Have you got anything?"

"No, I didn't see Spider. He wanted to talk, but apparently changed his mind."

"What did he say on the 'phone?"

"Not much. Only that he had been working with the Rigger and that the Rigger had disappeared. He wanted me to go along to the 'Flag and Lamb'. He said he'd got a story, but I never got it."

"I wonder why?"

Leith shook his head slowly. "Lord knows. The Rigger and Spider were good pals, and I'm pretty sure Spider wasn't lying when he told me that the Rigger had disappeared."

Leith took a cigarette from a packet and lit it.

"It looks as though the Rigger was the man we found on the burning dump." Harley drew a folder from a drawer. "Here are the measurements of the body found on the dump, and the de-scription of the Rigger. They're almost identical. It might easily be the Rigger." Harley skimmed through the remainder of the papers and then got up. "You've got to find Spider and bring him here. Do you know where he lives?"

"He usually dosses in a house in Chester Street. Can I take a car?"

"Yes, and you'd better take two or three men with you. I've got a hunch this may take us somewhere."

As he went down the steps into the courtyard Leith muttered to himself: "My trouble is I can't keep my flaming mouth shut." He was thinking of his bed.

*   *   *

Spider stayed in the bar of the 'Flag and Lamb' for only a few minutes after Tony had come in. At all costs Tony must not see him with Leith. He had a firm conviction—and, as it happened, a true one—that Patra knew of the rendezvous. The danger of his position did not fully penetrate into his brain, drugged as it was with gin and beer. But he did know that Louie suspected him of putting up a squeak. And he had to go out into the streets, alone.

Spider's knees sagged beneath him as he got up slowly and walked unsteadily to the door. Like a rabbit in sight of a stoat, he could not have run a yard.

There were few people in sight; a beggar picking through the contents of a garbage can; a girl with slim silk-clad ankles picking her stilted way along the opposite pavement; a policeman coming out of the darkened doorway of a shop closed for the night.

Spider began to feel a little better and he quickened his pace in the direction of the lights and humming traffic of Shaftesbury Avenue, fifty yards away. He would be all right there, with people round him.

He looked back and saw a man walking quickly towards him. and for a moment panic seized him. Then he looked again; the man was passing under a street lamp. It wasn't Louie. He wasn't big enough and he was wearing a cloth cap. Louie always wore a black felt.

"It's all right. All right. Nothing to get windy about," he muttered to himself, as he wiped the sweat off the palms of his hands. Not far to go now. And there was another policeman standing at the corner. His breath came more easily and he slowed to a gentle stroll. He groped in his pocket for the half-crown Leith had given him, and drew comfort from the feel of the milled edge of the coin. He could have another drink; a couple, if he felt like it, and leave enough for a doss and a cup of tea in the morning.

When he turned into Shaftesbury Avenue he did not look round again and therefore did not see the man in the cloth cap raise his handkerchief three times to his face. Nor did he see a car which drew away from the kerb after he had passed.

The kidnapping of Spider was one of the smoothest jobs ever pulled. There was no gunplay, no threats. Just an invitation to step in and go for a ride.

Spider's brain became numb. He stumbled on the running-board and fell sprawling on to the floor of the car. The man in the cloth cap pulled him up and back on to the seat with a jerk that sent pain shooting from elbow to shoulder.

"If you sit quiet you'll have an easy ride." Louie's voice was husky and held no emotion, no threat.

Sweat gathered on Spider's forehead and he began to feel sick. His mouth was dry; "I haven't done you no harm, Mr. Patra. Honest I haven't."

"What were you quacking to Leith about?"

"He was just asking a few questions, that was all. He wanted to know what I was doing these days, and I told him that I was only fiddling a bob here and there. He wouldn't say what the trouble was." The ash from Louie's cigar broke and spilled over his coat. He brushed it off and then leaned back and was silent for several minutes. At last he spoke. "And what were you looking for in Starling Court?"

"I just went in casual like to see Benny Watt. He's an old raggy of mine. Him and me was in the same hall once on the Moor."

"Didn't he ever tell you I don't like strangers on the place?"

"Yes, but I wanted to speak to him very particular so I chanced it."

"And what did you want to talk to Benny about?"

Spider tried to make his brain work sufficiently to produce a plausible answer. He failed, and mumbled something about a job that he was looking over and wanted Benny's advice.

Louie laughed, deep down in his stomach; laughed until he choked and coughed. When he had recovered he put a hand on Spider's knee and levered himself forward in his seat. He tapped on the glass partition and signed to the driver to slow down.

"You get out, Charlie," he said to the man with the cloth cap. "I'll finish this job myself." He put a hand on Spider's shoulder. "You and me are going for a nice long drive right out into the country. Maybe it'll do you good." Then after a short pause he added, "And maybe it won't," and laughed.

Spider's world was the streets and shops of Soho, Charing Cross Road, St. Martin's Lane and Long Acre. He would have died of boredom in the country. Lights, noise and movement were as necessary to his continued existence as beer and an occasional meal. And yet, as he sat in that car with Louie Patra, driving through streets he knew as well as the back of his hand, he experienced a curious detached, disembodied feeling, as though he had never seen these streets before.

He didn't care. He was like a man sinking in a snowdrift, who, though knowing that to save his life he must exert himself, yet was incapable of making the slightest effort to throw off a not unpleasant, enveloping inertia.

It was like that time a year or two back when he had gone to bed drunk and a draught from the open door had blown out the gas. He had lain on his bed and smelt the escaping gas; had heard the door slam; had realized that, if he did nothing, he would probably be asphyxiated, and yet he had not moved a limb to save his life. Later, a man passing on the stairs had smelt gas and had come in and shut off the gas and opened the window.

He had the same feeling now. He knew that his life was in danger because he knew Louie Patra. Six feet away—ten feet— there were men walking along the pavements. They were as far away as though they had been on Mars, as unreal as the characters in a child's fairy-tale; as a character in a Disney cartoon.

The air in the car was heavy with cigar smoke, and the gentle sway of the springs brought an easy, pleasant drowsiness to Spider. The bogy of fear retreated before approaching sleep, but he became wide awake when the car pulled up for the lights at the Bank. He turned half on his side and groped in a pocket for cigarettes, and found a squashed packet.

"Can you give us a match?"

Louie produced a book of matches. He looked curiously at Spider as the match flared up. 'Stupid little rat,' he thought. He had no more feelings towards him than to a wasp imprisoned in a pot of jam. The wasp was within his power. At any moment he could squeeze out his life.

Louie thought of Tony behind the wheel. How far could he trust him? If he were starved of the black cigars, or the harsh red wine he loved, would he not talk? And the yellow liqueur! If the police discovered his weakness for it and they tempted him with it, how long would Tony remain silent?

No. If the job had to be done he must do it himself.

Louie leaned forward and said to Tony: "Turn left into the first quiet street, and stop where there's no one about."

When the car drew up between two lamps Louie gripped Spider's arm. "I'm going to drive and you're going to sit beside me." He turned to Tony. "I'll pick you up here in two hours' time."

When Spider was in his seat Louie leaned across him and locked the nearside door. Then he slipped the car into gear and drove back to Aldgate, along the Commercial Road, until the houses began to thin out. A cold white mist, hanging low over the ground, concealed the open, marshy country.

Ahead was the gaunt chimney of a ruined factory. Louie muttered to himself, "That's the turning place," and slowed down to turn right on to a cinder-rutted track, along which the car lurched and swayed its way. On either side there were wide dykes, and beyond, the marshes. Spider saw the grey shapes of sheep feeding and thought of Charing Cross Road, the lights and the smells. The country at night, out of reach of a pub, was his particular idea of hell.

Up to that moment he had been completely and curiously apathetic to his position, but now realization came to him; though whether it was the sight of the wretched rain-sodden sheep, the white mist, or merely the negation of all the light, sound and warmth of the city life which roused him at that moment, it would be impossible to say.

Panic seized him and he gripped the handle of the door and fought to open it. There was cold sweat on his forehead and he trembled all over.

Louie took his left hand from the wheel and struck him savagely a backhanded blow across the face. Spider fell back in his seat with a hand to his mouth. For a minute, or it may have been two, he lay back quite still.

There was an added grimness to the set of Louie's jaw, and he jabbed his right foot down on the accelerator. As the car heeled over in a deep rut, he pulled at the wheel with all his strength. Three feet away were the icy waters of the dyke.

The car righted itself and Louie released his grip on the wheel and felt in his pocket for a box of matches. His cigar had gone out and he liked to have smoke in his lungs.

The road, straight and black, ran across the marshes between the two dykes, and over it like a pall hung the layer of white mist. The black mud track, which was the road, was wet, and the car slithered bodily sideways when it was not held by ruts.

Louie swore aloud. "I shouldn't have brought this damn' hearse. I'll get bogged if I don't look out."

He had forgotten Spider, because after the blow Spider had made no sound nor had he moved. He sat still for several minutes, his breath coming short and sharp. And then he dug his elbows into the back cushion and thrust himself forward, hesitated for a second and then sprang.

Before Louie could make a single movement to defend himself Spider had him by the throat and, with the strength of a man frenzied with the fear of death, was choking out the life of Louie Patra.

Louie's hands clawed upwards, sought for Spider's wrists and tried to tear them free, but failed, though he put all his strength into the effort. It was Louie's turn to experience the fear of death. Spider's fingers, like iron pincers, gripped tighter, tighter, pressing in on each side of his windpipe until Louie had to fight for breath. There was a roaring in his ears and could see nothing.

The car, held by deep ruts, went on straight for twenty yards, before Louie instinctively braked. Then it struck a smooth greasy patch, skidded and slid slowly sideways to the left, down the steep bank of the dyke.

Spider saw the danger first. He released his grip on Louie's throat and tried to clamber over him to the offside door. Louie drew back his right fist and with a short-arm jab to Spider's jaw sent the little man tumbling backwards, to fall in a heap on the floor.

Louie gripped the handle, opened the door by his side, climbed out and slammed it shut. The car was sinking slowly and heeling over on to its side as the bank subsided beneath its weight. Louie stood on the running-board, holding on to a lamp bracket, and looked for movement inside the car. There was none. The car began to turn over more quickly, and Louie, with one last glance towards the window, jumped for the bank and fell sprawling on soft black mud.

There was a sudden swirl and splash of water, and he looked round to see the four wheels of the car disappear beneath the surface. He climbed up the bank slowly, digging his toes into the mud and withdrawing them with difficulty, and when he reached the roadway he stood staring down at the waters of the dyke, breathing hard. "Deeper than I thought it was," he muttered to himself. And when minutes had passed: "Plenty of time to drown that rat."

His hat was gone; and the front of his coat, his sleeves up to his elbows, his hands and his trousers were coated with black mud, wet mud, cold mud. On foot the track back to the main road seemed miles long. He couldn't even see the factory chimney, and the white mist was pressing down, swirling in wraiths across the coarse tussocky grass. Very far away the whistle of a steamer on the river boomed hollowly.

Suddenly he began to run from the spot, slipping, slithering and stumbling until he could run no further and had to halt, and stand there half bent with his hands on his knees, breathing hard. He had a sharp pain in his right side.

For the first time in his life Louie Patra had run away from something he could not see.

CHAPTER XII

BENNY WATT was sitting on a bale of paper, smoking his short clay pipe, when Tooley opened the door of the chapel.

"Where's Louie?" Tooley asked.

Benny took his pipe out of his mouth and after a fit of coughing replied: "Don't know. He went off in the car about half past nine."

"Surely he must be back. But he's not in the office."

"Maybe Guido'll know."

"No. I've just left him. He hasn't seen Louie."

"It's funny he's not back."

Tooley began to walk up and down with quick nervous steps and drew at his cigarette till the point glowed suddenly red. He was like an actor keyed up to play a part for the first time. "He told me to be here at twelve. He said he'd have the car ready. Where's Tony?"

"He went with Louie."

Tooley walked to the door and looked into the yard and then up at the window of the office. There was no light there and the gate into Lucas Street was still shut. "It's damned odd him letting me down like this." His left hand felt in his waistcoat pocket for the little ivory pig, but even the feel of it failed to quiet his nerves.

"Come in and have a cup of tea." Benny struck a match, lit a gas-ring, and put a kettle on it.

"Have you got the last lot away yet?" Tooley asked.

"No. It'll go tomorrow, with tonight's little lot."

"Where's the ship?"

"She's due in tonight. The guv'nor got word at dinner-time."

Tooley sat down on a bale and lit another cigarette. "I wonder what the hell's happened," he muttered to himself, and tapped nervously with a toe on the boards.

Benny Watt glanced towards him and then got up, opened a cupboard and took out a bottle and a glass. "Maybe a taste of this'll set you up. It's better than brandy; it acts quicker."

Tooley took the glass and sipped the yellow liquor. He'd forgotten how good it tasted, and as the fumes filled his nostrils his fears became less, his hand steadier and his breathing easier.

As he sat there he thought of what he had to do. It would be easy; just the same as the first time. He had the keys of the front door and the grille. He knew his way to the long gallery and the description of the glass. It would be easy. Nothing to it.

Maybe it would be better without Louie hanging round.

He had smoked two cigarettes and emptied his glass by the time Benny Watt lifted the boiling kettle off the ring and filled the teapot.

"Four spoons I put in. I know you likes it strong." Benny wrapped the pot with a piece of cloth. "Allus makes a good cup of tea I does. Made proper it's all right. If it ain't I wouldn't wash dishes with it."

"They must have broken down," Tooley said. He thought of going to look at the office window, but changed his mind. 'If he wants me he can find me here,' he thought, and forgot about Durham Square.

The picture in his mind at that moment was Anna, and she seemed infinitely desirable. Once Louie paid up he would marry her and take her away: down to the country somewhere, where they could be alone; where life would be easy with nothing to worry about.

"What are you going to do when you retire, Benny?"

"Retire? What's that?" Benny Watt held his cup in mid-air.

"You know. When you chuck the job. I suppose you'll go to the country."

Benny drank noisily because the tea was very hot. "Country! Not for me. I went for a trip once to a place they call Amber Castle. Me and Spider together. There wasn't nothing there but trees and grass. We sat for a bit and then we had a walk, but it was terrible lonely. Then Spider says, 'What chance for a pub?' and we asked a fellow and he told us where to go and we stayed till they chucked us out, and then it was time to start off home. There was a barrel of beer on the chara and we had a high old time, I can tell you, on the way back. The rozzers stopped us twice but we didn't care."

"Spider? I've heard of him."

"Ah! He used to be a great lad at the dip. He was in with the Notting Hill Whizz mob for years till he got too old for the game; then he went as winger to the Rigger down Balham way."

"Where's he now?"

"Somewheres about. I see him this arternoon, up at Mrs. Hoskins'. We've fixed up to have a jag next pay day."

"Got any more in the bottle?"

"Yes, but not a lot."

"Just a drain. That's all I want; just to get the top spin on."

"The guv'nor don't fancy drinking before a job."

Tooley smiled. "Well, he's not here, so what the hell."

Benny Watt peered at the cheap alarm clock ticking furiously on a shelf. "It's nearly one o'clock. What time did he fix?"

"Midnight, he told me. If he's not here in five minutes I'm going to pull it on my own."

"You'd best wait. You know what the guv'nor's like if you don't work his way."

"I'll work his way all right."

Ten minutes later Tooley stood up. "I'm off."

"What is it you're after?"

"A glass. A drinking-glass. And my share's a monkey. Can you beat it?"

"I never heard tell of glass being as valuable as that," Benny replied. "Now if it'd bin red stuff, or even that Sheffield Plate, it'd be different. Though why anybody wants to pay good money for a plated dish fair whacks creation. But glass!" Benny put down his cup and followed Tooley to the door. "You'd better take a bit of paper to wrap it in." He bent down and picked up a sheet of newspaper. "Here, this'll do."

Tooley folded the paper and stuffed it in his pocket. "Come along and lock the gate after I'm through."

Benny waited till Tooley was out of sight round the corner of the street before he left the gate and walked back towards the chapel. He was uneasy in his mind at the absence of Louie

Patra. Tooley was all right, he assured himself. But he'd never worked on his own before, and he'd had a drink. He wished now he hadn't offered it to him.

Suddenly a bell rang, and he stopped dead. His heart was thumping. "Getting old, that's what it is," he muttered to himself, and looked up to the window of the office. "Telephone. I'll have to get the key." He hobbled along over the rough-laid paving stones to the chapel, went in and took a key from a hook inside the door.

The bell was still ringing insistently as he clambered up the wooden stairway. "All right, all right. I'm coming." As he fumbled with the key he thought: 'It must be the guv'nor. He must ha' broken down or something.'

He opened the door, groped his way to the desk and lifted the receiver. "Hullo. Hullo. Who's that?" He spoke loudly and held the receiver an inch from his ear. He wasn't used to answering the telephone. "Yes. It's me, Benny. . . . Yes. I can hear you, guv'nor. Can hear you plain as anything. . . . No, Tooley isn't here. He's gone out on the job. He said he couldn't wait any longer. . . . Tony hasn't been in, but I'll tell him as soon as he does. Where's he to fetch you from? . . ."

Benny locked the office and went back to the chapel to wait. That was about all he did these days—wait; but he didn't mind. Now and again he'd have a night out with Spider, and that made up for a lot. Spider and he had always been pals. He sat quite still for a long time and then he got up and messed about in a corner of the chapel where there was a pile of boxes. A glass. A drinking-glass. That's what he'd have to pack, and that would mean a good strong box. Six inches long. And then there'd be the packing. He'd have to allow for that.

Not finding just what he wanted, he gave it up, and sat down to wait some more. Might as well see the glass before he got started. And anyhow, the boss wasn't back. . . .

*   *   *

Tooley walked northwards the length of Lucas Street and then turned left down a narrow alley. He felt better now that he was moving. He'd show Louie that he could pull a job on his own.

He had the little pig in his pocket, so nothing could go wrong. He started as something moved in the shadows. He stood still as a figure advanced towards him.

It was Anna herself, pale and shadowy. She came up to him quickly.

"Tooley? Oh, I'm so glad I caught you! I've been worrying."

He put his arms round her, exulting that she had been waiting for him, worrying about him. They kissed and clung together, until a policeman came down the alleyway, rattling the padlocks on shop doors.

"You—you haven't done it yet?" Anna whispered as they moved on.

"Not yet. We're running a bit late tonight. You're just in time to wish me luck."

"I don't want you to go."

"But you said—"

"I know. That's what I wanted to explain. I only said all that tonight because Louie told me to. He thought you were going to go back on the job and he wanted me to bring you up to the scratch. But after you told me about what went wrong that night I got frightened. I don't want you to do it, whatever Louie says."

Tooley swore softly into the darkness, and spun round on the girl, holding her fiercely by the shoulders.

"Does that mean you lied to me tonight? You only said all that to please Louie?"

"Yes. Tooley—you're hurting me!"

"I could kill you—and him. So you don't love me, you little—"

"Yes I do. Can't you see? That's why I've come to stop you, and to explain. It's because I can't bear you to take the risk . . ."

Again his arms closed round her greedily and he laughed a low, triumphant laugh.

"You're a dam' good sort, kid—and I love you."

"I love you, too—but please, please don't go tonight."

"Why not? I need the money more than ever now."

"It's dangerous, Tooley. And it's all wrong. I hate it."

"I've been in this game all my life," he murmured. "I've got to go on. . . ."

"But you said you wanted to quit. You must quit, after last night."

"After tonight I will."

"You promise?"

"Yes, I promise. If I've got the chink—and *you*, I won't want anything else."

She sighed. Tears were round the corner and her hands were holding his tightly.

"I wish you wouldn't do it," she whispered.

"How like a woman! I've got to. That's the way it is." He kissed her again, wrenched his hands free, and was gone.

* * *

Durham Square was deserted except for two cats, one squawling in the gardens in the centre. From the corner by the pillar-box Tooley surveyed the approach by Stephens Place. There was no one in sight there either.

"Right. Let's give it a go," he muttered to himself, and walked quickly along the wide pavement and up the steps of Number forty-six. He had the key of the grille in his right hand, that of the front door in his left.

Louie was right—the locks had not been changed. Fifteen seconds later he was in the hall, listening. One light still burned on the first landing, casting a reflected glow which silhouetted the stair-rails and threw vague shadows of them on the opposite wall. His hand felt in his pocket for the reassuring touch of the ivory pig. He brought it out, clasped in his hand.

He was like an actor on the stage, playing a part he knew well. Every move ahead was clear in his mind.

He walked on the balls of his feet down the tiled passage to the door which led to the basement, opened it and listened for half a minute. Satisfied that there was no one there, he went on down the passage and opened the door of the picture gallery.

The case which held the glass was in front of a window which faced the garden. It had a glazed top secured with a flimsy lock which gave with a splintering of wood as he levered it up with a chisel. Then he switched on his torch and shone the light on the rows of glass goblets and rummers.

There must be no mistake this time. "Air-twist stem on a tear ball and folded foot," he murmured to himself. There were two glasses with air-twist stems. He lifted the first one up and saw engraved on the side of the glass the letters 'T.R.' The other had no marks on it. The first was the glass he was after.

He put the goblet on the top of an adjoining case, took the sheet of newspaper from his pocket and wrapped it up. There was more paper than was necessary, so he tore off a piece.

As cautiously as he had entered the house, so did he leave it, to find the Square still deserted, except for the cat which still made horrible noises in the garden.

He found himself hurrying and forced his pace down to a stroll. To be in a hurry in the early hours of the morning is in the eyes of the police a suspicious circumstance; to be caught carrying a parcel or a suitcase is very nearly a crime. Tooley had the glass in his overcoat pocket.

Louie had given him instructions as to how he should approach Durham Square, but the getaway was to have been carried out by the car driven by Tony.

Every job which Tooley had done had been planned for him, and it was not until this moment when he had to choose his own route back to Starling Court that he appreciated fully the value of the immoral support of Louie Patra.

On the face of it a simple problem, easy of solution. Easy to an innocent man, but when you are carrying stolen property to the value of five hundred pounds the solution is apt to become more difficult to find.

A night taxi overtook him, and as it passed the driver raised a questioning arm. Tooley ignored it. Taxis were dangerous, if you didn't know the driver. It was safer on a bus, and Regent Street wasn't far away.

He headed northward and struck Brewer Street, turned left past Liberty's, and then right to Oxford Circus. There was a knot of people waiting for a bus; he joined them and felt safer.

It was easy now; nothing to worry about.

He went straight to Lucas Street and found Benny Watt waiting to open the yard gate.

"The guv'nor rang up soon after you'd gone."

"What did he say?"

"Breakdown or something. I got the Moke to take a car and pick him up down Barking way."

"I'll wait till he comes." Tooley walked down the yard and into the chapel. Benny followed him.

"How'd it go?"

"O.K." Tooley took the parcel from his pocket and tore off the paper wrapping. "The boss'll want this packed. Have you got a box for it?"

"Not yet. The boss'll want to see it first. Sawdust; that's what it wants for packing. Better wait for him to see it, though." Benny took the glass and held it up to the light of his oil-lamp. "The guv'nor's a wizard, ain't he? Fancy getting cash for a thing like that!"

"I'll have another shot of that booze."

Benny uncorked the bottle and poured out a tot.

"Did the boss say what time he'd get back?"

"No." Benny rubbed the white stubble on his chin. "But Barking ain't far; specially when there's not much on the roads."

Tooley sat down on a bale to wait. He was tired, and when Louie returned half an hour later he started up suddenly from a doze.

"I got it all right," he said, and pointed to the glass standing on the shelf.

"You went?" Louie's temper, like his legs, was exhausted. "Didn't you get my note telling you to wait for me?"

"Note? No."

"I gave it to Silvretti to give Benny to catch you when you came in."

"I didn't get it." Tooley glanced at Benny, but the old man was looking the other way. He knew that his memory was not his best point.

Louie swore. "I hope to God you didn't make a mess of it."

Benny provided a diversion, with suspicious alacrity. "He got it, anyway." And he, too, pointed to the glass.

Louie picked up the goblet and examined it closely. "Good lad." His tone softened. "Were there any others like it?"

"No. I'm certain it's the right one."

"Did you have any trouble?"

"No."

"Did you see any dicks?"

"No."

Louie took out his wallet and counted out twenty-five one-pound notes. "I'll give you the rest when I collect," he said. "I'm a bit short."

Tooley said, "O.K." and went to Silvretti's and bed.

Louie waited until he had left, and then went round the corner of the yard where Tony was talking to the Moke. He told the Moke to take his car out of it, and signed to Tony to come into the chapel.

"Get the lorry ready right away. We've got to get the stuff out of here before it's light." He turned to Benny Watt. "Get started on packing up that glass. We'll have to leave that bale till next time, but I want to get the rest out of here quick."

As the first grey light fought with London's glare the lorry driven by Tony rattled down St. Martin's Lane and turned into the Strand.

CHAPTER XIII

KIMBER WOKE to see the glacial face of his butler and to hear that once again burglars had paid the house a visit.

"There's a case smashed, sir, but I don't know what's gone. I came straight up to tell you and I didn't touch anything."

"Quite right, Brooks. Finger-prints. Most important." Kimber poured out a cup of tea. "You know, Brooks, I'd like to meet the man who's taken a fancy to the collection. It leaves me colder than a frozen cod."

"Shall I—er—inform the police, sir?"

"Yes, by all means. Tell them everything. Keep nothing back."

*   *   *

Leith was at the Yard when the call came through. He had had two hours in bed after a search for Spider which had led him into every foul-smelling doss he knew within a half-mile radius of Cambridge Circus. He felt and looked as though he hadn't had a proper shave or breakfast.

"Another bust in Durham Square. This will tickle up Harley." Leith almost smiled.

'Tickle up' was an inadequate phrase to describe the effect on the news on the Chief Inspector.

Harley came in ten minutes later, smoothly efficient as usual. "Well, I suppose you got Spider all right?" he asked as he picked up a letter from his desk.

"No, sir. Couldn't find him anywhere."

"We've got to get him. Tell Simmons to lend you some men. Get on to him right away."

"Yes, sir." Leith moved towards the door. "There's a report just come through; a break at forty-six Durham Square."

"Durham Square? Forty-six?" Harley stared at Leith. "You mean the same house?"

"Yes, sir."

"What did they take?"

"A wineglass."

"And last time?"

"A quantity of china and glass."

"It stinks of an insurance fraud. I'll go myself. Tell Sampson and Foley to be ready to leave in five minutes' time."

When Harley arrived at the house in Durham Square, Kimber opened the front door himself. "Good morning, Inspector. I thought you'd be along."

"Why?"

"Well, it's a curious case, isn't it? The theft of one wineglass."

"Yes, very curious. What was it worth?"

"Difficult to say exactly. According to the records my father paid three hundred and fifty pounds for it; but that was some years ago. I believe it's worth a lot more now."

"How did the man get in?"

"I expect the same way as last time, through this door."

"I told you to change the locks."

"I know. I was going to get them done on Monday."

"Why Monday?" Harley was grim, potently suspicious.

"Because it was the first possible opportunity," Kimber replied. "Have you never discovered that it is impossible to get the British workman to do a job on a Saturday afternoon?"

Harley grunted irritably. Then he walked down the hall to the picture gallery. The door was open. "Do you lock this at night?" he asked Kimber.

"No. Never." Kimber was smiling. "It looks like the perfect crime, doesn't it, Inspector?"

"Perfect be damned. Lucky. Damn' lucky. Did you have any guests last night?"

"No. I was out."

"At Guido's Club, I suppose?" Harley's eyes closed to slits.

"A very good guess, Inspector."

"What was taken?"

Kimber pointed to the case which had been broken open. "That's the one. There's a space and that label describes the glass which is missing."

"Has anyone touched this case?"

"Oh dear me, no! We were very careful about that."

'I bet you were,' Harley thought. He stooped and picked up a piece of newspaper from the floor. It was stained with violet ink. "Do you know how this got here?"

"No. I've never seen it before. Have you, Brooks?"

The butler shook his head. "No, sir. I didn't notice it, I'm afraid. You see, it was under the case."

Harley put the paper on the top of a case. Then he examined the fastenings of the window, opened it and looked out. There was a sooty patch of soil underneath which showed no trace of footmarks. The wall of the house was not scratched.

Foley set up his camera, but Harley waved him away. "We don't need that. See if you can get any prints." Foley took a bellows from his case and blew grey powder over the surface of the case.

"You didn't have any luck with that last time," Kimber commented. He leaned against the door lintel and lit a cigarette.

"No," Harley agreed. "But you never know when a man won't get careless."

"True—true." Kimber pointed to the piece of newsprint. "Is that a clue?"

Harley countered with another question. "Do you mind if we have a look round?"

"Not at all. Go where you like. I'm going to have a bath."

When he had gone Harley said to Sampson: "Search the house for any more paper stained like this."

He signed to the butler to follow him and went to the study. "Now Brooks, what do you know about this?"

The butler looked like a sick archbishop who had lost his mitre. "Nothing, sir. Nothing at all," he intoned. "And if I may say so, sir, it is all most unsettling. Most unsettling." The butler sighed and looked sorrowfully at the toes of his well-polished shoes.

He was a windy man, as hollow as a drum, and though he talked a great deal Harley obtained no help from him.

Harley returned to the Yard with the conviction firm in his mind that any further investigation of the circumstances of the burglary in Durham Square would be a waste of time. The case was a simple insurance fraud. The insurance company had a staff to deal with such matters.

Later in the day Leith returned. "That man Spider's passed right out." He scratched his head. "I don't know what to make of it, unless he was mixed up with the Durham Square job."

Harley put down his pen and blotted the words he'd written. "Kimber's the man we've got to watch."

"Kimber!" Leith looked surprised and his lower jaw fell. "You mean he's been behind these art thefts?"

Harley nodded.

Leith thought for a minute and then said: "A sort of Raffles? I see what you mean, but—"

He had been too long in the Force to express his firm disbelief of such a theory. There were no such persons as fancy criminals; the true thief was born and bred to the trade.

He was thinking of the body on the burning dump, of the disappearance of the Rigger and what Spider had said to him.

Harley picked up a typewritten sheet and skimmed through it before he added his signature. When he looked up Leith was still looking doubtful.

"You can carry on for forty-eight hours on this job. If nothing turns up in that time I'll let the insurance company have a free hand." He added irritably, maliciously: "They've got some damn' good men on their staff."

Leith ignored the insult, buttoned up his coat and picked his hat up off the table. "Sampson said you'd picked up a bit of paper." Harley opened a drawer and took out the scrap of stained newsprint. "This is it. Take it if you think it'll help you."

*   *   *

Leith had seen paper stained just that violet hue before. Maybe his idea wouldn't lead anywhere, but it was worth trying. So on Monday morning he turned eastward along the Embankment and took a penny tram to the streets of the newspapers, where, from doors in back alleys, the unappreciated products of the Press of yesterday are borne off to the pulp mills, stacked high on lorries.

The front of the *Globe* building is magnificent in gleaming concrete, metal and glass, where stately commissionaires guard doors which revolve at the lightest touch.

It is the shop window where the populace and advertisers are bludgeoned by its sheer magnificence into the belief that the *Globe* is a mighty power, a dictator of the policy of the country; where space is sold at figures which appear fantastic.

The front of the building is no more than concrete skin deep, and a very thin skin at that. It is the sign of a flashy success. It is different at the back of the building. Lenter Lane, into which the staff exit debouches, is a haunt of bookmakers' runners and touts, where hawkers rest, waiting for the peak period of the sales day.

Leith found a fat man in a shiny serge suit sitting on a high stool in a sooty little office. He had a bowler tilted back on his head and was ticking off entries in a ledger with a stump of a pencil.

The sight of Leith's warrant card caused the fat man to sweat a bit and he mopped his forehead with a large red handkerchief; he had an 'arrangement' with a bookmaker and his wallet was full of betting-slips awaiting collection.

His relief when Leith put his first question made him genial and most obliging. Yes, he would give Leith all the information he could; always liked to help the police. He slipped in the hint of a question as to the purpose of the inquiry, which Leith ignored.

"Most of our stuff goes to Stockens," he explained, and pointed to a trade card pinned on the wall. "That's their address."

Leith produced the scrap of newspaper. "Can you tell me the date this was printed?"

The fat man read the end of a paragraph describing a street accident in Finchley. "No, I'm afraid that's got me beat, but I'll tell you what you can do. Go up to the file room. They'll maybe help you."

A boy took Leith to the file room, where he filled up an inquiry form, waited twenty minutes, was interviewed by two clerks, waited half an hour, and at last received the information he wanted.

Then he went back to the fat man's office. "Now can you tell me where the papers of the second of November went to?"

"Second of November," the fat man repeated, and took down a ledger. When he found the right page he said: "There wasn't much went out that day. A matter of a hundred bales, that's all, and it went to Patra. It's a small firm, and we don't do a lot of business with them."

"Patra! What address?"

"Address? Address? Somewhere up West, I think." A dirty thumb travelled down the page. "Yes, that's right. Lucas Street. A turning off Shaftesbury Avenue. North side."

Leith looked at the entry. Patra! Louie Patra! He said, half aloud, "Well, I'm damned!", saw the startled look on the fat man's face and walked out into the lane. "Louie Patra! Now I'll show Harley where he gets off."

*   *   *

Benny Watt was sitting on a box at the door of the chapel smoking his pipe when Leith came into Starling Court.

It was eleven o'clock, the sun was warm, and Benny was achieving a delightful state of semi-coma. It took him, therefore, a minute or two to wake to the realization that an enemy was in the camp.

"Do you work for Mr. Patra?"

Benny nodded and got up slowly from his seat on the box. He was trying hard to think whether he had left anything lying about; the glass was packed in a bale of paper all ready to go and the bale looked no different from any of the others.

His fingers tightened round the bowl of his pipe. It was a long time since he had come into contact with the police; he was getting old, and his nerves weren't so good.

Apparently Leith noticed nothing wrong. "I'm making inquiries about a consignment of paper which was delivered here on the second of November," he said.

Benny said "Yes," but did not move.

"Where's it gone to?"

"It's still in there. Just the same as it came." Leith walked to the door of the chapel, pushed it wide open and stood for a minute or two looking at the pile of bales, at the desk in the corner, the packing bin and then at the floor, ankle deep in places with paper.

"Where do you keep your records?"

Benny put on his questing sea-lion expression and said: "What's that?"

"Don't you keep any books?"

"Books? No. You'll have to see the boss about that. All I do is to look after the place."

Leith had no desire to interview the boss and put him on his guard too soon. He pulled aside the sacking screen round Benny's bed and saw the stove. The ash-door was open and before it lay a heap of paper-ash.

Leith suspected stoves. They were his enemies, for they had a habit of consuming evidence. He lifted the top plate and flashed a pocket torch inside the stove. He saw some charred kindling sticks and more burnt paper. . . .

"What have you been burning in here?"

Benny shuffled forward. "Just made a fire same as I always do to boil a kettle." There was a faint note of defiance in his tone.

"It would have been a lot quicker if you'd used that." Leith pointed to a gas-ring. He turned the tap and there was a hiss of escaping gas.

"Sometimes it's cold of a night time and a bit of a fire's company."

Leith picked up a bit of stick and raked the ashes out on to the floor. They broke into a thousand pieces, wafer-thin, and the heap flattened.

'He couldn't have boiled a kettle on this lot of paper,' he thought, and, kneeling on the floor, pulled out the paper-ash with his hands. He broke it up to a fine dust. Then he told Benny to fetch a broom, and, when he was out of sight, picked up two scraps of cloth. One was no more than an inch in length, the other was longer and on one end there were torn threads and the letters 'by' sewn on it with yellow thread.

Benny went to the door into the court, his trembling fingers felt for a bell-push and pressed it three times.

Louie was asleep when the buzzer rang, but he woke in an instant. He pulled his trousers on over his pyjamas, put on his coat and went to the door leading to the office.

He unlocked the door and opened it slowly. There was no one there. He stared at the saucer, full of ash and stub ends of cigars, as though he had never seen it before. The swivel chair was as he had left it. He was relieved to see the calendar, the picture of the child and St. Bernard dog.

For an instant his brain became a blank so that he stood inactive and wondering what he was doing. He traced back his movements to the moment when the buzzer sounded.

He rubbed his heavy cheeks and muttered, "Must have slept heavy." Then he remembered the shot he had taken and became frightened.

It was very still in the room and the air was heavy. "I mustn't take the stuff again." He held out his right hand with fingers rigid and widespread. There was no more than a faint tremor.

"Not so bad." Then he again remembered the warning call of the buzzer, and again was frightened because he had forgotten it.

He crouched behind the desk and looked round it, through the window, down into the yard. The door of the chapel was wide open but there was no one in sight.

"Maybe it was nothing; a mistake." But still he waited and watched.

In the chapel Leith was wandering round the paper-littered floor. In his mind was a clear picture of the place, the position of the door, the window, the desk and the stove. He put his fingers into his waistcoat pocket and felt the piece of cloth he had found among the ashes, and something like a smile touched his mouth. He was thinking of Harley. Harley, the scientific office-made detective.

'I'd like to clean the whole show up and give it him on a plate,' Leith thought. "And then see what he has to say about it."

He stuffed tobacco in his pipe, lit a match and, as he sucked in the smoke, strolled over to the packing bin.

Benny Watt stood with his back to the window. His right hand still gripped his cold pipe. There was nothing to be found. Nothing. He was sure of that. Except the bale. And a split would never think of looking in that. Grand idea, that was. It took a man like the guv'nor to think of it.

Leith leaned on the side of the bin; looked up and saw the weight and pulleys. There were a few scraps of paper inside and little heaps of dust in each corner.

He called out to Benny: "What sort of paper do you pack in this thing?"

"Most every kind. We're not particular."

"Newspapers?"

"No. That's already baled. We passes that straight on."

"Where?"

"To whoever wants it and who'll pay a fair price."

"I see." Leith straightened himself and walked to the door. "Have you got any other stores?"

"Just where we garages the lorry."

"Show me the way."

Louie Patra drew in his breath sharply when he saw Leith come out of the chapel door into the sunlight. When he saw Benny close behind him he muttered: "That's not so bad. He's alone."

From his experience of the police Louie knew this visit of Leith's was one of purely an exploratory nature; a preliminary skirmish. He smiled and felt in his pocket for his cigar-case. As he lit a cigar he did not take his eyes off the lounging figure of Leith.

He saw Benny unlock the garage door and the two of them disappear inside. Then he stood up and went to the window. Leith knew him; there was nothing to be gained by keeping out of sight.

In the garage Leith said to Benny: "Who drives this?"

"Tony. He's a wop."

"Where is he now?"

"I don't know. Hanging round Silvretti's, I wouldn't wonder."

Leith made a mental note to pick up Tony. Then he walked round the lorry. He pointed to mud caked on the walls of the tyres. "Been out into the country, hasn't it?"

Benny looked blank and said he didn't know where the lorry had been. "You'd better ask the guv'nor about that. He knows his own business better than what I does."

Leith glanced around, noticing that there was room in the garage for another car.

"What else do you keep in here besides the lorry?"

"Nothing."

Leith noticed a dark patch of oil on the floor where evidently another car had stood, and not so very long ago.

"What about the car?" he asked.

"Oh, that's been gone a long time," Benny replied. "I don't know what the guv'nor's done with that."

Louie waited until Leith reappeared in the yard. Then he unlocked the office door and walked down the wooden staircase.

He had recovered his assurance. The smoke of his cigar tasted very good. He would sell his soul for a good cigar; nothing else mattered. And the sun was warm. There was nothing for the police to find. The bale which contained the glass? Louie chuckled fatly. They would never tumble to that; never in a hundred years. The rest of the haul was safely stored in the shed on the marshes.

The marshes! He fought back the memory of that last night on the marshes; the look in Spider's eyes when he fell back on the cushions; the blank white of his face; the car sinking under the waters of the dyke!

It had been different with the Rigger. He'd asked for it and he'd got it. That didn't worry him. But Spider was different; like kicking a dog or a cat or anything that couldn't hit back.

Leith spoke first. He said, "'Morning, Mr. Patra." He noticed that Louie was not wearing a collar and tie. It was a shock—almost like meeting a stranger, for Patra was usually well dressed.

Louie looked first startled, and then he smiled quickly as he took his cigar from his mouth and blew out smoke.

"What can I do for you, Mr. Leith?"

"I don't think anything. I'm making inquiries about a consignment of paper from the *Globe* that's gone astray. My inquiry here was just a matter of form to check up the dates. There's been a lot of trouble in the *Globe* office. Someone's been messing about with the books."

Louis said, "I haven't dealt with them for quite a while."

"That's their stuff in your shed, isn't it?"

Louie nodded. "A hundred bales."

"That tallies with what they told me." Leith tamped the tobacco down in his pipe with the edge of a matchbox. "Are you busy these days?"

"Fair."

Leith looked as though he were going to speak, but didn't. He puffed at his pipe for a minute or two, then he said: "Well, I'll be getting along. I've got a few more calls to make. Good morning, Mr. Patra."

Louie Patra watched Leith disappear through the gate in the archway, stood in silence, thinking for a time, and then returned to Benny Watt. "What was he after?" There was a harsh edge to Louie's voice.

"I dunno, guv'nor," Benny replied quickly. "He just had a look round like and then you come, and that's all there was to it."

"What sort of questions did he ask?"

"Just about a lot of paper we took in on the second of November. I showed him which it was but he didn't seem terrible interested."

"After that what did he do?"

"Looked around, that's all." Benny thought hard for a moment and then added: "He did ask what I'd bin a-burning of in the stove, and I said it was only some paper and kindling to boil the kettle on."

"Yes? Go on."

"He said, 'Why didn't you use the gas ring?', and I said I'd made a kind of a fire 'cause it was cold some nights."

"Did he—did he look into the stove?" Louis asked.

"Yes. He poked about with a bit of a stick, but he didn't find nothing, whatever it was he was looking for."

"Whatever it was he was looking for." Louie repeated the words slowly to himself. Was Leith looking for anything? There was a vague uneasiness at the back of Louie's mind. For years he had never had cause for fear. He had been too careful.

Quickly in his mind he ran over the events of the night of the first burglary in Durham Square. He had left no loose ends there, he was certain.

And then he wondered if Tooley had slipped up last night. And had he been frightened to say anything about it? That was possible. His hand massaged his fleshy chin. He'd have to see Tooley and make sure. It would be best to get him out of town.

He looked up and saw Benny still standing like a wax figure. "What did Leith want in the garage?"

"He looked at the truck and asked how it got the mud on its tyres. I said I didn't know. Then he asked where the car was, and I said it had been gone some time, and he didn't bother about it no more."

Louie said nothing for a minute. Then he turned to Benny. "Get that bale out of here. Take it into the café and tell Mrs. Hoskins she's got to keep it in her back room till tonight."

"You mean the one with the glass in it?"

"Yes, of course. What the hell do you think I mean?" Louie snapped, and walked off up the yard.

It wasn't often he was like that, Benny decided. Not once in a month of Sundays did he lose his temper. "He's getting windy," Benny muttered, for he, too, was uneasy.

*   *   *

Silvretti was shaving a customer when the door-bell rang. He put down his razor and pushed through the bead curtain, which closed behind him with a faint tinkling sound and then was silent.

The smile which came without effort creased his swarthy skin and his teeth showed white beneath his blue-black moustache.

He bowed, clasped his hands together, and said: "And what can I do for you, saire?"

"Do you know a wop called Tony? He works for Mr. Patra up the street."

"Tony? Yes, yes, I know him a little bit, that is all. Sometimes he come here, but not often."

"Where does he hang out?"

Silvretti unclasped his hands and spread them out palms upwards. "That I do not know so I cannot tell you. It is seven, eight days or longer since I see him."

"Like hell it is. He was in here yesterday."

"No, no. You make the mistake. Tony not come here for a very long time."

"You know Mr. Patra, don't you?"

Silvretti became wary. He rolled his head from side to side and said in his sing-song voice: "Everybody know Mr. Patra. Why not?"

As soon as Leith had left the shop, Tony got up from the barber's chair. He wiped soap from his face with a towel and came through the rustling, clicking bead curtain. He was scared.

"Do you know who that was?"

"Yes, I know him. Come. I will finish your shave."

But Tony stood quite still. He looked as though he were going to cry. Then he saw himself in the glass and was reminded of the glory of the new silk shirt and the tie with polka dots. "Two collars I get with this shirt. You like it?"

"Very pretty. Yes," Silvretti answered indifferently. He picked up the receiver of the telephone which stood on a ledge behind the counter and called a number.

When the connection had been made he said: "Someone has been here asking for Tony. Tony is here."

At the other end of the wire Louie replied: "Don't let him go out. I'll be along in a minute."

* * *

When he left Silvretti's shop Leith walked to the end of Lucas Street. There was a man standing outside a glassware shop.

"Keep around. If Silvretti goes out, trail him. I'm looking for a wop called Tony."

The other man nodded, almost smiled, and said something about a needle in a haystack.

Leith walked on to Shaftesbury Avenue and turned right, towards Piccadilly. Spider was the man he wanted; the man who could explain that name-tab he had found in the ashes of the stove. He'd got to find Spider.

Leith returned to Scotland Yard. He went to a room, signed for a box labelled 'Articles taken from body. Claxton Ash Dump.'

He laid out the coat on a table, found the place where the tab had been cut out. The scrap of cloth he had found in the ashes of the stove fitted one end of the ragged rectangular hole.

The binding thread was of the same colour, a light brown, and appeared to be of the same make.

"I must have a test made," Leith muttered to himself. He sat on the edge of the table feeling the tab between his fingers. "I wonder if you'll hang anyone," he remarked, and his thoughts went to the night of the burglary. The Rigger was interested, or that's what it looked like.

'It was probably his body found on the dump. Probably. That is the devil of it. Spider could have given us a lead, might have identified the clothes. And now he's gone.'

There was the mud on the wheels of the lorry. The absence of the car which used the same garage.

He packed the clothes back into the box and returned it to its rack. Then he picked up a telephone and spoke to the operator at the exchange. "I want a tap put on the line to Louie Patra. P-a-t-r-a." He spelt the name and gave the address. "Let me have any information as soon as you get it."

If Louie Patra was his man, he'd get him. It might take time, but Leith had lots of that and lots of patience.

*　　*　　*

Almost immediately after Leith's departure, Louie received the call from Silvretti. He began to sweat. Tony was the weak link. He was vain, he was conceited, and he was a coward. Louie's expression hardened. Tony had got to be kept quiet and out of the way of the police.

He went to the door of the chapel and called out to Benny. When he came blinking in the sunlight, Louie sent him to Silvretti's with orders that Tony was to lie up until it was dark and then go to the café in Canton Street.

Five minutes later Benny returned. He said that he had given the message.

"All right, you stop here. I'm going out for an hour or two. Keep the gate locked."

He went up to his office through the door which led to Mrs. Hoskin's café, and down the stairs to Canton Street. He left the office by the route which Zimmermann had used; down the stairs and through the door which bore the notice: 'Ladies' Tailor'.

He walked for half a mile before he was satisfied that he was not being followed. Then he took a bus to the Caledonian Road and made his way to a builder's yard. There he spoke with a man who agreed, for the sum of three pounds ten, to have a lorry outside Mrs. Hoskins' café in Canton Street at eleven o'clock that night.

Louie had forgotten all about Mr. Zimmermann and his promise to communicate with that gentleman.

Mr. Zimmermann waited uncomfortably and conspicuously for that call in the lounge of his hotel in Aldgate.

He read English papers with difficulty and little comprehension. He smoked a chain of thin cheroots. Sometimes he got up off his plush settee and walked out into the hall and asked the porter if there had been any message for him.

The answer was always the same. There had been no letter nor 'phone calls.

At four o'clock, at which time Louie Patra was approaching the Caledonian Road, Zimmermann decided to ring up Louie. The porter, who had nothing to do and who scented a tip, helped him to find the number in the telephone book.

"Leave it to me, sir. I'll get through for you," the porter said, and called the number.

He sat for a couple of minutes on his stool with the receiver to his ear. Then he said: "There doesn't seem to be any reply. I'll get on to the exchange and get them to change the line."

He jerked the hook up and down and asked for the supervisor. "I've called a number and can't get any reply. Will you please ring them again?"

"He said he would be at home," Zimmermann muttered. "It is very curious that there is no reply."

The porter put down the receiver. "They want to know who's calling."

"What is that? What do you say?"

"They want to know your name."

"It does not matter. Tell them, please. It does not matter. Give no name."

The porter said, "O.K.," and put down the receiver.

"And now please bring my bags. I must leave at once."

And that was the last the hotel saw of Mr. Zimmermann. He gave the porter a ten-shilling note as he climbed into a taxi and told the driver to take him to Fenchurch Street Station.

Leith was told of this 'phone call half an hour after it had been made and went straight to the Aldgate Hotel.

The ten-shilling note and the obvious agitation of Mr. Zimmermann had underlined in the porter's brain every detail of the incident, and he was able to give Leith a very vivid picture of Mr. Zimmermann. He produced the hotel register and pointed to Mr. Zimmermann's entry. Leith made a copy of the words.

The case was beginning to open up. But it was a question of first find your Mr. Zimmermann.

The porter had heard him order the taxi-driver to drive to Fenchurch Street, so Leith went there and found that there was no boat train before midnight. Nor was Mr. Zimmermann's luggage in the cloakroom. The porter from the hotel, who accompanied Leith, was quite sure of that after he had spent a sweating half-hour inspecting mountains of trunks and cases.

Leith sent out a call for the driver of the taxi; he told off two men to attend the departure of the boat train; he got in touch with the shipping company, the Customs and the immigration officials. Then he went into a tea-shop and had a pot of very strong tea and a bun. There was no public house open at the time.

*   *   *

Louie Patra returned from his trip to the Caledonian Road and after a careful survey of Canton Street he entered Mrs. Hoskins' café. Mrs. Hoskins had slipped into something loose and was sitting on a chair peeling potatoes. On a dirty sheet of paper were the flaccid forms of sausages looking amazingly unappetizing.

She caught her breath and nearly cut her thumb when she looked up and saw Louie Patra.

"Got the stuff all right?"

She nodded dumbly, and jerked her head in the direction of the backroom. "It's in there. Benny said you'd told him to put it there."

Louie kicked open the door and saw the bale of paper standing on the floor at the end of the bed.

When he had shut the door Mrs. Hoskins said: "Have you seen anything of Spider?"

"No." He snapped the word out and then asked, "Why?", so fiercely that Mrs. Hoskins looked frightened and mumbled. There was no shape to her words.

"Has anyone been round asking for him?"

"No. I was just wondering. Benny was asking, too."

Louie opened the back-room door, and looked at the bale again. Then he shut the door, locked it and put the key in his pocket. He said: "I'll pick it up later on." He went through the door which led to the yard and into the chapel.

Benny was there, a pair of steel spectacles on his nose. He was reading an evening paper.

"Anyone been round?" He had to repeat the question before Benny heard.

"No. It's been all quiet." He thought for a minute, scratched the grey stubble on his chin and added: "'Cept for that blame telephone. It kept a-ringing on and on. I thought it'd never stop."

Then Louie remembered Zimmermann and his promise to ring him up. He hurried down the yard, and up the wooden steps to his office.

He sat down and picked up the receiver and called up the Aldgate Hotel.

The porter answered him and said that Mr. Zimmermann had gone. "Taken all his luggage, too. No, he didn't leave a message."

Louie put down the receiver slowly and sat for a long time, thinking. 'Funny him clearing out like that and not leaving word where he's gone.'

Louie got up, walked to the window and looked down into the yard. The gate was shut and locked. He had got his bolt-holes. There was nothing to worry about. And yet uneasy fears came pushing round the corners of his mind. He couldn't forget Leith. What the hell had he been after, nosing around? And he'd been to Silvretti's too. He didn't like that. Anyway, Silvretti would keep a hold on Tony. He could trust Silvretti even though he was a wop.

And they'd never pin the Rigger's killing on him. Never. If things got hot he'd shunt 'em on to Tooley. He wouldn't hold out long, once the police got him in the chair.

Louie gave a grunt of a laugh. And what was so damn' funny was that Tooley believed that he, Tooley, had killed the Rigger. His nerves were all to pieces. Once the rozzers got him they'd screw a confession out of the poor fool.

*   *   *

Kit Kimber was bored. He was tired of the police and of the man from the insurance company; especially was he tired of this man who had insulted him continuously for half an hour.

That he, Kit Kimber, was suspected of attempting to defraud the company of the sum of several hundred pounds was made as clear as spring water.

He thought of Tooley, and muttered, "I suppose he did it," and smiled. Kimber was no fool. He had guessed after the first robbery that Tooley must be the culprit. But he was not going to admit his suspicions to the police. He was interested in Tooley—more interested in the man than in his father's antiquities, and he felt it a challenge to try and help him, rather than to commit him again to the prison life which had so nearly destroyed him. The cheek of the man amused him. A funny chap, Tooley. Hard as agate but nervous as a cat. Sentimental, in a queer way, and in love with a burglar's daughter. "I'd like the chap if he'd let me," Kit mused.

And Anna! She was an attractive kid, with that solemn expression of hers and her honey-coloured hair. She dressed well too, and didn't speak badly.

He went to a wall safe in the corner of the room, opened it and took out a thick wad of one-pound notes. Then he rang for Brooks. When the butler came he said: "I'm dining out tonight.

You needn't wait up. Leave out the whiskey and soda and some chicken sandwiches; enough for two. No, three."

When the butler had gone he took out a half sheet of note-paper from his pocket. There were four lines of straggling writing.

I should be so pleased if you would come to our going-away party at Guido's tonight. Eight sharp. Anna.

Poor kid. It looked as if she was going to get tied up to Tooley. Kimber frowned. He couldn't make up his mind about the man. Sometimes he was sane enough, good company, a likable chap, but at others he was touchy and behaved like a nervous child.

Then he remembered the remark of the man in the bar at Guido's. "Jug plays hell with your nerve."

"Anna's going to have a damn' rough row to hoe. Well, maybe the money'll help."

He let himself out of the front door and walked through the echoing silence of Durham Square to Lucas Street.

The public restaurant held only a sprinkling of diners when Kimber walked through it and mounted the stairs to Guido's Club. Only Guido himself was in the lounge. He was standing utterly immobile. Seconds passed from the time when he saw Kimber until he broke his pose and slid silently forward as on rubber wheels towards his guest.

A fat hand was outstretched to take Kimber's hat. "Miss Anna is in there, waiting," he said, with a jerk of the head towards the lounge.

Anna was sitting back in a deep chair in an alcove of the lounge. She smiled when Kimber came to her, but the smile faded quickly and she looked tired as she leaned back.

Kimber asked: "Where's Tooley? I thought he'd be here."

"Late. He had some business to attend to."

"And you're going away with him tonight?"

Anna nodded slowly twice.

"Why?"

"There can be only one reason." She blew out a thin stream of grey smoke. "The police."

"What do they know?"

Anna turned her right hand palm upwards and let it fall on the arm of the chair.

Her eyes met his evenly, and there was a deep appeal in them. "What do you know, Mr. Kimber?" she murmured.

"Just as much as is good for me," he replied reassuringly. "And no more than is good for you. And I was very flattered that you asked me here tonight."

"I wanted to talk to you before we went. You've been so awfully good to us that I couldn't go off without . . . without . . ." She paused, and darted a glance about the lounge. "I suppose Tooley wouldn't like me telling you. He's got so that he can't trust anyone. That's partly why I'm taking him away. You know he could be decent if . . ."

"I'm sure he could. I'm glad you're going to give him the chance —right away in the country."

She shook her head. Her hands were trembling as she took another cigarette from his case.

"That's not far enough for the police. They'll trail him, anywhere. I'm so frightened . . ."

"You needn't be frightened," he told her gently. "I won't push the charge."

Her eyes flicked up to his.

"So you know? That's what I've been trying to tell you."

"Yes, I know, but I'm glad you wanted to tell me. I guessed it was he who burgled my house. But, like you, I believe there's good in Tooley, and I'm sure you're the right person to bring it out. But I don't want you to feel you must go away with him because of that. He'll be quite safe here, as far as I am concerned, I promise you. It seems to have been so well planned that I don't think the police will get him, if I continue to swear he was here both nights—as I will. And I've made no claim against the insurance company. I wouldn't like to think you'd thrown yourself away on him, if that's your only reason."

Anna sat forward in her chair. "It's wonderful of you to say that, Mr. Kimber. But I feel I must stand by him now, when he's in trouble. He loves me, and I might be able to help him."

"Yes. But do you love him?"

She paused. "I don't know. Yesterday I thought I did. But now—I know he's no good really. It's only I'm sorry for him."

"Then for heaven's sake don't run away with him, just to try and save him from a charge of burglary, which will probably never be made."

"But that's not all. There's worse troubles than that. Worse than the burglary at your house. That was nothing."

Kit smiled at her naivety and suppressed it quickly.

"Do you mind telling me what this other trouble is?" he asked gravely.

"No. I can't tell you that. Not even you."

"But is it enough to justify your sacrificing yourself for him?"

"Yes, I think it is," she replied softly.

"Very well." Kit leaned forward to beckon to a waiter, and saw Tooley enter the room. He looked pale, and was smoothing his hair. Kimber called out to him.

Tooley came over to the corner, took Anna's hand in his and pressed it. "Hullo, kid. How she go?"

Anna smiled up at him. "Fine. Are you all fixed?"

He pressed his thin lips together and a frown crossed his face. "I don't know." He had been drinking, and his hand was shaking as he lifted the glass the waiter set before him. He was badly rattled. He had failed to collect his cut, as Louie told him Zimmermann was missing. And—almost worse—he had lost his lucky pig . . .

Anna, watching him, frowned. "What's wrong?"

"Nothing." He lied unconvincingly, and smiled apologetically at Kimber. "I wasn't expecting you tonight."

"Anna asked me to come—to give you a send-off. I gather you're getting out of Town for a bit."

"I don't know."

"Tooley . . . ?" But he wouldn't meet her eyes, and kept glancing nervously towards the door.

"Well, I think it's a grand idea to quit," said Kit. "Anna's right. Get right out of it for a bit. And here's my contribution." He took the wad of notes from his pocket and put them on the table.

Tooley picked them up as though he had never seen money before. He let them ripple through his fingers.

"A pony?" he muttered, and Kimber nodded. Tooley smiled thinly. "What's the idea?"

"I'd like you to have a chance."

Tooley swore under his breath, and then, "I don't want it," he rasped ungraciously. "I can manage."

"You can manage a damn' sight better with a little more cash," Kit smiled. "Besides, it isn't done to refuse a wedding present, is it, Anna?"

There were tears in Anna's eyes, and Tooley swore again as he pocketed the notes.

"Good," said Kit cheerfully. "You'll go?"

"I'll go all right," Tooley replied. "But I'm going alone. Sorry, kid. I'll come back for you later. We can't start together."

"Why?" she breathed. "Why not now?"

"Because I'm leaving by the roof, the way I came; and that's no way for you. The place is being watched. Stiff with dicks."

"You shouldn't have come!"

He shrugged his shoulders and picked up his glass with an assumed air of indifference. "They're not looking for me, as far as I know, but I'm not taking any chances."

"You'd better go," said Kit.

Tooley looked at him curiously. "Has Anna been telling you anything?"

"Only that you are in danger."

"Do you know why?"

Kit smiled. "I have my own idea about the burglary in my house."

Tooley glared at him, and his upper lip snarled as he asked: "And you've told the police? You've been playing with me—you and your damned friendliness. You—"

"No. I've told the police you were here at the time of the robbery."

Tooley's eyes dropped. "Sorry," he mumbled and laughed, ashamed of his savage outburst.

"And now you compound a felony by helping the thief to escape. They can give you a stretch for that."

Kimber laughed. He said: "I rely on you not to give me away. And now, hadn't you better go?"

"No. I want my eats. There's Guido, and dinner's ready. Come in."

The three went into the dining-room.

CHAPTER XIV

"WHY THE HELL didn't you tell me this before?"

Harley and Leith had been in conference that afternoon in Harley's room.

"I'd hoped to get something a bit more definite," Leith mumbled. "That's definite enough for me," snapped Harley, "though it may not hang anyone." He picked up again the Rigger's coat and the torn charred scrap of cloth which had borne the maker's name. "Go on, go on. What took you to this place in Starling Court?"

"The bit of newspaper picked up in Kimber's house." Leith recited the whole story.

"Patra," said Harley. "Patra? Louie Patra."

"There isn't a lot to go on," remarked Leith diffidently.

"We'll get plenty."

He was staring at a large-scale map of Soho when there was a knock at the door, and a policeman came in with a small pasteboard box in his large hand.

"This has just been sent round by the man on duty at forty-six Durham Square, sir. He said a maid found it in the hall, just inside the front door, wedged between a coconut mat and the wall."

Harley took the box and, removing the lid gingerly between finger and thumb, he lifted out a small ivory pig.

"Why the hell can't they clean the hall in the morning?" he muttered. "All right. All right. D'you know anything about this, Leith?" he demanded, as the messenger retired.

Leith took the pig in his hand. His eyes were shining.

"Yes," he said. "Tooley wears one like this, on his watch-chain. It's a lucky charm."

"Tooley. Yes, Tooley."

Leith pointed the pig at the map. "Tooley's been dossing at Silvretti's. There. All in a bunch with Starling Court, and that club, Guido's. Tooley's probably one of Patra's boys."

Harley was rumbling like a sleek cat.

"It's up to you to collect Tooley, at once."

"He's not likely to be at Silvretti's now. He's got a girl who works at Guido's. I'll try there, tonight."

"A girl's always a good bet," Harley agreed.

"There's a hole in Lucas Street. I'll want help."

"Take whom you like. I'll wait here till you report."

*   *   *

Kimber took the wine list from the waiter. "I think fizz to-night, don't you?" He looked up. Tooley had gone!

Anna was sitting forward in her chair. There was fear in her eyes and her fingers were scrabbling on the cloth.

Kimber looked round and saw Guido disappearing through the arch into the lounge.

The band was still playing. A couple at a table near by were talking as though nothing had happened. The wine waiter still stood impassive by his elbow, patiently solicitous of an expensive order.

"What's the matter?"

Anna did not move. She did not appear to have heard the question. Kimber laid a hand on her nervously working fingers. Slowly the tenseness faded from her eyes; she looked at him blankly as though awakening from sleep.

"What's wrong?"

"The police. They're here again." The words barely escaped from her lips, so low was her tone.

Kimber turned to the waiter. "A bottle of one nought six." Then he said to Anna: "How did he know?"

"Guido gave him the office."

"Don't worry. They're probably only having a general roundup."

"I wouldn't worry about the burglaries. It's not that," Anna whispered. Her eyes were dry, but she looked as though she were about to cry. "It's worse. Ever so much worse."

*   *   *

At the first sound of the buzzer, Guido, who had been standing by the service door, slipped through the crowded lounge to the bar. He signed to the barman, who pulled down a switch. Then he said to the men drinking: "Get going. On to the roof."

Outside in the entrance hall a steel shutter slid silently in its grooves across the passage which led to Louie Patra's room overlooking Starling Court. Tooley had already gone that way.

He was in the room now, a cigarette drooping from his lips, his light-blue eyes expressionless as a doll's. "What's the next move?" Louie leaned back in his chair and took his cigar from his thick lips. "It's all fixed, son. Don't you worry."

"All fixed? Did you know this was going to happen?"

"No. But I'm always prepared. That's my motto. Same as the Boy Scouts." Louie's mouth smiled.

"Who are they after?"

"Maybe me." The smile increased.

"What's the getaway?" Tooley's fingers sought in his pocket in vain for the lucky pig.

"Through the shop. There'll be a van outside at eleven o'clock."

Tooley opened the door into the passage and listened. His fingers, baulked of the pig, jingled loose coins in his pocket. He shut the door and faced Louie.

"Who started 'em off?"

"God knows."

"There must have been a squeak."

Louie shook his head slowly from side to side. "I don't think so. It's Leith working one of his hunches, but you needn't worry as long as you keep your trap shut. He's got nothing on you."

Louie spoke convincingly. He reassured Tooley, but not himself. His mind went back to the visit which Leith had made to Starling Court, his examination of the chapel and the garage. Something more than a hunch had prompted that visit. He was sure of that.

And there was the inquiry for Tony at Silvretti's shop. A squeak? It wasn't likely, unless Spider had talked before he put him away. "But maybe he did," Louie muttered to himself.

A bell rang and Louie lifted the receiver of the desk 'phone. He listened for a minute or two and then said: "O.K. Let me know when they're clear." As he replaced the receiver he said to Tooley: "It's Leith. He's asking for you. He's got a stopper on the Canton Street door."

"I was going to hide up. I was going with Anna."

"I know. I'll tell her. You'll be coming with me."

"I haven't had any dinner yet."

"You'll have to wait." Louie levered himself out of his chair. He walked to the window, and, looking out, saw the glimmer of a light showing through a window of the chapel. Benny was awake and on the job. He had seen to the barring of the yard gate himself.

In the club Leith had visited all the public rooms; he had been into the kitchens, the pantries and the deserted bar. He had seen Anna sitting at a table with Kimber, and the sight gave him no pleasure because he noticed that the table was laid for three.

'Am I too soon or too late?' he asked himself as he went back to the entrance hall.

Guido stopped talking to Louie Patra, put down the telephone and followed him. "Tooley, he not often come here, you understand, but if I see him I tell him you want to talk to him."

Leith would have laughed if he hadn't been so angry. "A hell of a lot of good that would do," he replied. In the hall he pointed to the panel which shut off the passage to Louie Patra's room. "When was that built up?"

"Built up? I do not understand." Guido was puzzled.

"Yes. The last time I was here there was a passage."

"Oh no, sir! No, you are mistaken, my dear sir. There has always been a wall there. Yes, always."

Leith tapped the shutter with his knuckles. It didn't sound hollow, which was not surprising, because it was four inches thick. He pressed against it with all his weight, but there was no sign of it yielding. "I suppose I must have been dreaming," he muttered to himself. He signed to a man standing at the top of the stairs leading down to the restaurant. "You can pack up. Go to Silvretti's and anywhere else he's likely to be. Leave a man in Crompton Street."

Leith threw his hat on to a settee. "And now for a spot of chow."

Guido fussed in front of him as he made his way down the passage to the lounge and the supper room. "There is a table in the corner. Just here."

Leith ignored the suggestion and made straight for the table where Anna and Kimber were sitting. The third place had been removed; also the chair.

"So he's not coming after all?" He looked first at Kimber, and then said to Anna: "Or was he called away in a hurry?"

Kimber said: "I don't know what you're talking about." He gave Leith no welcome, but the policeman was persistent. He turned and pulled up a chair from another table and sat down. "Would you mind very much if I joined you?" He looked at Anna when he spoke.

Anna finished the wine in her glass. As she put it down she asked: "What do you want?"

"Tooley."

"Oh yes. Yes, I see." Anna spoke like a child repeating a lesson. The shock of Tooley's narrow escape was still with her. "We don't know where he is. We can't help you."

A waiter came and put cutlery and glasses before Leith. When he had gone Leith said: "This is serious. It's not merely a question of burglary." He hesitated.

"Well, come on, let's have it." Kimber's tone was harsh.

Anna put a hand to her mouth.

"You'll know soon enough, and so will he. But I warn you if you assist him to escape it will lay you open to a very serious charge."

Leith said nothing for the next few minutes. "If I were you, Anna, I'd get out of here and stay out. Understand?"

She looked up and nodded.

Leith gulped some food in a constrained silence, and was gone.

Anna said to Kimber: "I'm going to take his advice."

"You're going with Tooley?"

"No. I've finished with Tooley. I—I can't go on with it."

"Why, Anna?" His voice was very gentle.

"There is nothing more I can do for him. Nothing. One day—it may be tonight or it may be tomorrow, or next week—they will arrest him. That will be the end. I can't help him now. No one can. He's finished."

"What? Another prison stretch?"

"No. It will be the end. You see he—he killed a man."

Kimber put down the glass he had raised to his lips. "Killed a man? When?"

"On the night of the first burglary at your house. Someone—never mind who it was—tried to stop Tooley. Tooley hit him. He didn't mean to kill the man—but he died."

"And what did he do with the body?"

"I don't know. He wouldn't tell me."

"And is that what the police want him for now?"

"Of course."

"How long have you known about this?"

"Not long. But I knew something had gone wrong that very night. It was an awful night. You remember he brought you here and we sat at this table and danced together."

"Yes, and he sat there"—Kimber pointed to another ta-ble—"with a blonde." He looked puzzled. "But I still don't see how Tooley could have done that burglary. Wasn't he here all the time?"

"No. He wasn't. He went out for a short time. Some day I'll tell you how it was worked." Anna held out a hand to Kimber. "Give me a cigarette, please. And then I must go."

"Let me take you to an hotel."

She smiled as she blew out smoke from the cigarette. "Thank you. It's good to have a friend. Life is going to be rather difficult for a time."

*   *   *

When Leith had gone Guido opened the panel in the passage to Louie Patra's room and himself carried a meal there.

As he put the tray down on the desk Louie said to Tooley: "You'd better make the most of that. God knows when you'll get your next proper meal." He told Guido to grill a rump steak. "And bring plenty of beer."

It was half past ten before Tooley was satisfied. He leaned back in his chair and lit a cigarette. "Where's the hide-out?"

"Down on the marshes. There's a ship there." Louie took a folded sheet of paper from his wallet. "Give that to the skipper, and when he's read it, burn it. You'll lie up on board till you hear from me."

"O.K." Tooley slipped the paper into his breast pocket. Half a minute later he said: "Where's Anna?"

"In the club."

"I'd like to see her before I go."

Louie took the cigar from his mouth, thought for half a minute, looked at his watch, and then said: "You can have ten minutes. That van's not to be kept waiting one minute. There are too many damn' busies about."

Tooley stood up. "I get you." He opened the door into the passage and went along to the hall. He saw Guido talking to a guest and waited impatiently until he was free.

Guido saw him with the tail of his eye, excused himself and glided over to where Tooley was standing. "Well—what is it you want?" His tone was an urgent whisper.

"Tell Anna I'm here. Quick."

"Anna? She's gone."

"Hell! Where?"

"She went with Kimber twenty minutes ago. She took a bag."

Tooley's fingers bit into the soft flesh of Guido's arm. "Tell me, you fat slug. Where did she go?"

"To an hotel. Wait, I have the name. I wrote it down so I would not forget. Yes, so that I would not forget." Guido fumbled in a pocket, produced a small black note-book, thumbed the pages and then held it up for Tooley to read what was written.

Tooley repeated the name over to himself. Then he looked at his watch, thought for a moment and said: "I'm going out. Tell Louie I'll be back in half an hour."

The colour of Louie's face deepened to a rich crimson when Guido gave him the message, and he freely cursed women. "Has he gone?" he barked at Guido.

"Yes."

"All right. When he comes back you can tell him from me to go to hell!" Louie signed to Guido to go, and locked the door behind him. Then after a quick glance round the room he opened the door which was masked by the shelves and went out and down the stairs to Mrs. Hoskins' café.

There was no light in the shop except the small blue flame of a gas-jet turned low. He moved silently across the floor and turned the handle of the door of the back room.

Mrs. Hoskins was sitting in a broken-down basket chair darning a black stocking. Benny Watt was perched on the edge of a kitchen chair staring at the floor, a cold clay pipe in his mouth.

They both looked up as though worked by one string when the door opened. Benny mumbled a greeting and pointed to the bale of paper. "It's all ready, guv'nor. And I've never taken my eyes off it since it was packed."

"O.K." Louie walked to the window and looked out. In the shadow of a doorway on the opposite side of the street he could see a dim figure. He looked at his watch. "Five minutes to go," he muttered. He left the window and touched Benny on the shoulder. "Come on, let's get it out into the shop." He bent down and put his fingers under one end of the bale. Benny lifted the other.

They carried the bale into the shop and put it down on the counter. Louie opened the door a couple of inches and waited, listening, with his fingers on the handle.

Two minutes later a motor horn sounded three times. A match flared up in the doorway opposite. Swiftly Louie Patra and Benny carried the bale to the van which slowed down as it approached the café.

The man from the doorway opposite ran across the street and vaulted over the tailboard. It was Tony. "Wait there till I come," Louie ordered. "And send back the van."

Louie waited until the van had made the turn into Crompton Street and then went back into the shop and locked and bolted the door. "That's the finish for tonight," he said to Benny Watt and to Mrs. Hoskins. He went through the door behind the counter and up the steep flight of stairs to his room.

He picked up a receiver and rang through to the restaurant. "Send Tooley through as soon as he gets back."

As he lit a cigar he thought: 'If Tooley's picked up, there's going to be trouble. I ought to have given him a longer stand-off and let him get his nerve back. And the Rigger turning up that night . . . Well, that was just a bit of bad luck. Just a bit of bad luck.'

Louie got up and began, to walk up and down the room. Sometimes he stopped to look down into the yard. He heard Benny shut the chapel door and he saw his light go out.

Tooley was a good scout. He wouldn't let him down. He could trust Tooley.

It was the first time he had had to trust a man as far as he had to now. On every other job he had kept so far in the background that no one could rope him in. But this time he had realized that Tooley might want stiffening.

Stiffening! It hadn't looked that way when he'd clocked the Rigger. He cursed Tooley, and forgot to curse himself for putting up the lying story that the Rigger had shopped Tooley. And he'd thought he'd been clever in doing just that.

Well, it wasn't his fault that gag had slipped. It wasn't anybody's fault.

Even if Tooley squawked there was nothing to connect him, Louie, with the Rigger's death. He'd just sit tight and keep his trap shut. Just keep his trap shut; that's all he had to do.

But all the same he'd feel a lot better if Tooley were out of the way. A sea trip would settle his nerve.

*   *   *

Tooley climbed the stairs from the club until he reached an attic room. He knew his way about, for without striking a match he felt his way to a cupboard, opened the door, took out a short ladder and hooked it on to two eyebolts under a skylight.

A minute later he was on the roof. He crouched down so that he was protected by a ridge of slates and took three steps in the direction of Silvretti's. There he stopped. The police would probably be keeping watch at that end. It would be better to take a chance through a house at the north end of Lucas Street.

Why he was making this journey he did not stop to ask himself. He had seen Anna an hour ago. He had explained to her. There was no reason why he should see her again. No reason but a jealous impulse. She had gone with Kimber. And he had lost his ivory pig. He had searched all his pockets frantically, but in vain. It had gone. And Tooley had a foolish fear that he had lost Anna too. He must make certain.

The houses in Lucas Street were old; they had been built before Shaftesbury Avenue had been driven through Soho. The ridges ran all ways; there was no system, no design. Chimney stacks appeared as solitary islands to be circumnavigated; at times as walls of brick to be surmounted.

It was no use coming down too near to Guido's. By the time he had traversed the roofs of a dozen houses Tooley felt as though he'd run a mile across country. He stood on the base of a stack and, looking north, saw as a dark indeterminate mass the trees in the Square at the top of Lucas Street.

"Five more and I'll give it a go."

A quarter of an hour later he began to look for a sky-light. One to a bathroom would be the most suitable, and easily identified by its frosted glass. But bathrooms were scarce in that part of Lucas Street. There were trap hatches firmly fastened, and sky-lights of clear glass. Through one a light showed. Tooley looked down and saw a woman cooking something in a frying-pan over a gas-ring. In one corner of the room was a bed. That was no good.

He climbed another ridge and slid down into the far valley. Here was a wooden trap, firmly fastened. The wood was old and warped so that there was a crack nearly a quarter of an inch wide. He put his ear to the crack and listened for minutes, then he looked through it, but could see nothing.

"Might as well try it," he muttered to himself, and took a flat leather case from his breast pocket. He selected a hacksaw blade from the line of tools and fitted it to a handle.

It was an easy job, but it took time to cut away part of the hatch and to prise up the staple to which the hasp of the trap fitted.

After a great deal of hard work Tooley dropped lightly on to the top floor of fifty-six Lucas Street, and proceeded quietly downstairs.

The way to the street was clear, the front door half open, and Tooley, with only a brief glance up and down the street, walked away with long, swift strides.

He reached Oxford Street east of the Palladium and took a taxi to the hotel in Bloomsbury where Anna had gone. He stopped the taxi short of the hotel and stepped into an alleyway, where he brushed the dirt off his clothes and adjusted his tie.

It hadn't been so difficult, after all, cheating the rozzers. When he'd seen Anna he'd ring Louie and fix somewhere to meet. It wouldn't do to try and go back to Lucas Street. Louie could send a car.

He walked into the hotel and asked for Miss Finn. The clerk said, "Yes, sir," and put through a call to Anna's room "What name shall I say, sir?"

Tooley hesitated. "Her cousin, Mr. Michael Finn. Ask her to come down; it's most important."

When Anna came out of the lift and saw Tooley she said: "You fool, why have you come here?" She was badly frightened.

"I had to come. Where's Kimber?"

"He went home hours ago."

"Why did he bring you here?"

"I asked him to. I can't stay in Lucas Street any more."

"Why not?"

"Because I'm not a criminal. The place is rotten."

"And I'm rotten too, I suppose?"

"I—I didn't say that." She was near tears, but suddenly he pulled her into his arms.

"Kiss me. Kiss me good-bye."

For some reason all her doubts and fears vanished as she clung to him.

Presently he pushed her gently away.

"That's all I want to know." He took her hand in his, pressed it and turned away. "So long, kid."

It was raining, and as he stepped out on to the pavement Tooley pulled his hat down over his eyes and turned up the collar of his coat. He walked southwards till he came to a tube station, where he entered a 'phone box and called Louie Patra in Starling Court.

When he recognized Louie's voice he said: "I'm ready to go. Can you fix a bus?"

There was a pause of seconds and then Louie asked: "Where are you?"

"Russell Square tube."

"Go to the Moke's. I'll tell him to take care of you."

"Where does he hang out?"

"In the mews at the back of Thetford Street. He'll be looking out for you."

*　　*　　*

Tooley knew of the Moke by repute as the best straight-up driver in Town. A straight-up driver being a taxi-owner who was willing, if not eager, to carry criminals when engaged on their business. Payment was made on results. The Moke was satisfied with five per cent and got plenty of work.

Tooley took a tube to Leicester Square and five minutes' walk from there brought him to the mews. The entrance was through an archway. The nearest street lamp was twenty yards away.

Tooley did not therefore see the two men waiting in the shadows and had no warning of their approach as they closed in on him. Before he could struggle they had him pinned against the wall and handcuffs on his wrist.

"Better come quiet," one of the policemen said.

Tooley relaxed. "O.K. It's a cop."

They walked back to the street. A car was waiting, and when they appeared the driver trod on the starter. He took them to Chandos Street police-station.

* * *

Leith was standing outside the Empire in Leicester Square wondering where to look next for the elusive Tooley, when a plain-clothes man brought a message that he was to ring up Harley.

He did so and was told that Tooley had been arrested and was then at Chandos Street police-station.

"How was he picked up?" he asked Harley.

"From the tap we had on Patra's 'phone. He's been charged with being concerned with the second burglary at Durham Square."

"Nothing about the murder?"

"No. Go along and see what you can get out of him. Take him easy."

"Take him easy," Leith repeated half aloud as he came out of the 'phone box into the rain. "I know what I'd like to serve up to Mr. Blooming Tooley. Half an hour alone and I'd have him giving me his life story with footnotes and an index."

It was in this mood of tired exasperation at the rules of the game that he walked up three steps under a blue light and entered the charge-room of Chandos Street police-station.

The sergeant on duty stopped reading the sports edition of an evening paper and said: "I've been waiting up for you." He drank noisily from a cup of very hot tea. As he put down the cup he said: "Do you want some of this?"

"Yes, that's one thing I can do with." Leith stripped off his dripping macintosh and hung it on a peg. He wiped his face dry with a handkerchief and then advanced to the fire. "You've got a snug job all right." He pulled up a chair and sat down.

The sergeant went to a cupboard, produced a cup and filled it from a teapot stewing on the hob. As he put in the milk he said: "That boy's all on edge. I wouldn't be surprised if he talked."

"What did he say to the charge?"

"Nothing. I got the idea he was surprised, but I may be wrong. I told him you were coming along. He didn't say anything to that either."

Leith stared at the hot coals as he sipped his tea. Steam rose from his trouser-legs. "You know, Sergeant, I'm sorry for that bloke, in a way."

"Tooley?"

"Yes. He hadn't been out of jug two or three days before some push got their hands on him and shoved him on a job." Leith glanced up at the clock. "I suppose I'd better have him in."

The sergeant shouted out a name and a minute or two later there were heavy footsteps and the jailer appeared. "Bring Tooley in."

The sergeant slipped off his stool and locked the door which opened on to the passage leading to the street.

When Tooley came into the room Leith made room in front of the fire. He pointed to a chair. "Sit down there."

Tooley yawned as he sat down. "This is a damn' fine time for a tea-party."

Leith sipped his tea. "If you can help us to find the stuff it'd be a help."

"Nothing doing. I'm not putting up a squeak. I can take what's coming to me."

Leith rubbed his chin. "I wonder if you can."

There was a tightening of the muscles round Tooley's mouth.

Leith didn't look up, and after a pause continued: "There was a fence who used to hang out down Balham way. The boys used to call him the Rigger. Did you ever know him?"

"I've heard of him. That's all."

"Sure about that? That you've never seen him?"

Tooley shook his head.

"How long have you been working for Louie Patra?"

Tooley opened his mouth to speak and then shut it again. For a split second he had been off his guard. It was an old trick to put in an unexpected question which bore no relation to the trend of the inquiry.

Seconds passed and then Leith prompted: "Well, what's the answer?"

"I don't know the man."

Leith showed surprise. "You mean to tell me you don't know one of the biggest fences in town?"

"Fence? Patra's not a fence."

"Oh, then you do know him?"

"I've heard of him."

"And what have you heard?"

"Just—just that he's got a business in Lucas Street."

"Did you ever hear that he had an old lag working for him?"

"I don't know anything about him."

"Yes, I suppose Benny Watt was a bit before your time." Leith held out a packet of cigarettes.

As Tooley took one, and flipped out the light of his match, he said: "Your wasting your time."

"Maybe," Leith replied. "Tooley, has it ever occurred to you that it would be a damn' good idea to go straight?"

"Going all sentimental?" Tooley sneered.

"No. It's too late now, I know. But didn't you think of it before you got caught up with this Patra crowd?"

"You've still got this Patra bug on your brain?"

"Yes, and it's come to stay. You see, I know something about him that'll put him behind bars."

"Have you pulled him in?"

"No. I'm waiting till I find out who killed the Rigger."

Tooley's fingers tightened on a fold of his coat. He stared straight ahead of him into the fire. Mechanically he read a word stamped on a fire brick. Messon. Messon. Messon.

Like a hen hypnotized by a chalk line, his brain ceased to work. Then he became slowly conscious of Leith talking: ". . . if we could get the man who did the killing . . . if you knew anything . . . might help . . . charges dropped".

He felt a hand on his shoulder. "Here! Wake up and listen to what's being said to you." The sergeant picked up the teapot and filled a cup. "Here, drink this." He poured in milk.

"You can't get away with murder," Leith said. "We'll get the man in the end, but if you like to talk and save us time, of course we'd do what we could to help you."

Tooley drank his tea. It tasted good to him. Leith gave him another cigarette.

"By the way, where were you on Saturday night?"

"At the club. Guido's."

"I see. Same story as the first night."

"That's right."

"Well, I can bust the second one right now." Leith took the ivory pig from its box. "That's yours, isn't it?"

"No."

Leith half turned in his chair. "Sergeant, did you take a watch-chain off the prisoner?"

"Yes." The sergeant unlocked a drawer, took out a silver chain and gave it to Leith.

In the centre of the chain there was a larger link than the others; from it hung a tiny screw. Leith fitted it into a hole in the back of the ivory pig and held it up for Tooley to see. "It is your pig, isn't it?"

Tooley said: "Yes. Can I have it?"

"No. I'm afraid not. It's going to be Exhibit A." He nodded to the sergeant. "I'll hold on to the chain." Then he turned to Tooley. "That pig was found in Kimber's house in Durham Square."

"Someone must have planted it."

"You'll have to think of something better than that. That's an old gag that stopped working when Charley Peace was a kid." Leith touched Tooley on the arm. "Now listen here a minute. If you did the second job you must have done the first as well. You had keys to the door and to the grille. You knew your way about."

"You've got my alibi on the first job. I was at Guido's. Kimber saw me there and spoke for me."

"Yes, I know. It foxed me at the time, I admit."

"What d'you mean?" Tooley snapped out the words.

"You weren't at Guido's at the time of the first burglary. Kimber thought you were; he was quite honest about it. I didn't spot it at the time, but he mentioned a funny thing. He said he never saw your face. You had your back to him all the time. You never danced and you never left the table, as far as he saw."

"If I never left the table how could I have pulled the job?"

"Because you were never at that table. Someone with a head of hair like yours was the man Kimber saw."

"That's not true."

"Mabel says it is. I had a talk with her too, and she tried to back you, but when she heard that there was murder in the air she opened right up and confessed it was a plant. She told me how you got the keys."

"In fact, she sang like a blooming canary."

"She did. The only thing she didn't tell me was who killed the Rigger."

"Oh, for God's sake leave that man out of it! I'm sick of his name. I don't know how he was killed nor who did it. It's true I was in the Durham Square jobs, both of 'em. Now let me get to sleep."

"There's no hurry. Now that we've got so far there's a few holes here and there I'd like to button up. Now if you could put us on to the stuff, that would do you a bit of good."

"I don't know where it is—honest I don't, Mr. Leith."

"I'll take your word for that, but you could give me a pointer, couldn't you? Just something to work on."

"I've only been out a week. I haven't had much of a chance to get around; and besides, as soon as I'd done my end of the job that was the finish."

"What did Patra pay you?"

"A tenner for the first—" Tooley got up and kicked his chair back. "Blast you, and your talk and your cigarettes and your tea!" He glared at the sergeant, who continued to lean on his desk quite unmoved.

"Sit down. You're disturbing our other guests," Leith said.

"I'm going to turn in."

"You're going to sit right down on that chair and not act like a kid." Leith did not raise his voice; he made no movement, but Tooley sat down.

"You shouldn't go at me like this. I want to sleep."

"So do I, but I'm going to have your story first." Leith gave Tooley another cigarette. "Just tell me what happened that first night." He signed to the sergeant, who picked up a pencil and opened a note-book.

"You've got most of it. I did the job for Louie Patra. He put me on to it."

"When?"

"The day I came out of jug. He met me with a car and drove me up to Town. I didn't want to do it. I wanted to lie up for a bit, but he talked and I said I'd do it. I met Kimber and told him the tale and got him along to Guido's. Slipper whizzed his keys when Kimber was dancing with Anna, but she didn't know a thing about it. I swear that's the truth. She didn't know what was happening."

"All right. What happened after that?"

"We had copies of the keys made and I used them to get into the house. Kimber was at Guido's with Anna. I swiped the stuff and that's all there is to it."

"Who got you away? You didn't walk through the streets with the swag?"

"No, that's right. Louie sent a car."

"Who drove it?"

"Tony."

"Where did you go?"

"To Starling Court. I left them there and went to the club. Kimber was still there."

"How did the Rigger come into it?"

Tooley half rose from his chair. His face was set hard, his hands pressed down on the sides of his chair. "The Rigger wasn't there. I don't know anything about him."

"He was killed that night. His body was found on a burning dump. His hands were burnt so that we couldn't get a dab from them. His face was burnt and every name-tab and laundry mark had been cut out of his clothing."

"Then how'd you know it was him? It might be anyone."

"Yes, that's the way it looked till I found one of the tabs. It had the maker's name on it."

"You found it? Where?"

"In that chapel place in Starling Court."

"How did you know to go there?"

Leith ignored the question. He said: "The Rigger was killed the same night as you did the first job at Durham Square. Who killed him?"

"I dunno."

"You know all right. Had the Rigger anything to do with the job?"

"No"

"What about Spider? Was he there?"

"No."

"He's cleared out. Do you know where he's gone?"

"No."

"Did Louie Patra kill the Rigger?"

"I tell you I don't know anything about the Rigger." Tooley spoke with savage intensity.

Leith waited a minute before he spoke again. "But surely you must know something. You must have heard something. You were working for Louie Patra. You lived with Silvretti, not a hundred yards away."

Leith paused and looked towards Tooley, who remained wooden-faced and silent.

"Two people might have killed the Rigger: Louie Patra or—yourself."

"I tell you I know nothing about it. I finished the job and went straight to Patra's place."

"You went to Starling Court in the car with Patra. You met the Rigger there. There was some talk, a quarrel. Someone hit the Rigger, knocked him out. He was dead when he was picked up, so you or possibly Patra got the idea of taking his body out to the burning dump." Leith threw the stub of his cigarette into the fire. "Anyway, that's how I figure it out. Am I right or am I wrong?"

"I don't know anything about the Rigger. I've told you that a dozen times."

"You killed the Rigger."

"I didn't." The words came as a tired sound from between Tooley's thin lips.

"Yes, you did." Leith's voice was even. The voice of a man stating a simple truth which could not be denied. "Four people know how the Rigger died. Tony, who drove the car; Benny Watt, who lives in the chapel and helped to dispose of the body; Louie Patra—and you. If it had been one of the first three you would have spoken to save your own hide." Leith paused and then said: "You killed the Rigger, didn't you?"

Slowly Tooley nodded his head. "Yes, I killed him, but I didn't mean to do it. It was an accident."

Leith interrupted: "That makes a difference, of course. It might help if you made a statement and got the whole business off your mind."

"All right." A feeling of relief had come over Tooley. He sat up in his chair and passed a hand across his eyes as though he were waking, up from a deep sleep. "I'll tell you everything. I want to, and then I can sleep. I haven't had a moment's peace since it happened."

Leith looked towards the sergeant. "Are you ready to take it down?"

"Yes." The sergeant gave Leith three sheets of paper. "These are notes I made. You can use them as a check as we go along."

It was half past one before the statement was complete, and when Tooley had been taken to his cell Leith picked up the sheets with a feeling of intense satisfaction. Every sheet had been signed. "He's going to have a job if he wants to wriggle out of this. I'm going to ring up Harley right away; he's sleeping at the Yard."

The sergeant picked up the receiver of his desk 'phone and called Whitehall 1212.

Three minutes later Leith was talking to Harley. "Tooley's confessed." He gave a brief resume of Tooley's statement.

When he had finished there was silence for a matter of seconds, and then came Harley's dry, incisive tones: "You've forgotten one thing, haven't you?"

"What's that?"

"The autopsy on the Rigger. He didn't die of that wound on his skull, but from carbon poisoning through having been placed face downwards on the dump. The man who murdered the Rigger was the man who put him on the dump."

"Tooley could have done that," Leith replied.

"I don't think so. We know he was back in the club at 11.30. He spoke to Kimber then. He must have gone straight back after the burglary, as he says. He wouldn't have had time for anything else."

Leith said: "I see. Shall I pull in Patra?"

"Did Tooley say anything about him?"

"Not as regards the murder."

"Then we'll wait till we get the others. Benny Watt. You can pick him up as soon as you like, and that Italian—Tony. We want him as well."

Leith acknowledged the order and put back the receiver. He looked towards the sergeant and then at the impassive face of the official clock on the distempered wall.

"Here's where I start a new day." He lit a cigarette and went over to the fireplace. He put his feet on the fender and leaned against the mantelpiece.

The sergeant said: "Why? Surely Tooley has tied it all up?" Leith explained, and added: "If I could only put my hands on Spider I believe I'd have the answer."

"Well, he ought to be easy enough to find. He never travels far these days."

"I had ten men on the job the other night and we couldn't find him."

"Have you tried that yard down Balham way where the Rigger used to hang out?"

"That's being watched now."

The sergeant ran through a list of Spider's haunts.

"I have Wilson going round them twice a day. He's cleared out."

Leith lit a cigarette. "Well, I suppose I'd better be moving." He went out into the street. The rain had stopped, the air was cool and fresh and it was pleasant walking. Light was creeping over the sky, and lorries piled high with vegetables, bound for Covent Garden, were signs that another working day had begun.

He first paid a visit to the room where a detective was keeping watch on Silvretti's shop and received a report that Tony had not been seen to leave.

"When Silvretti opens his shop, I want you to search the place. There's a room upstairs, and I wouldn't be surprised if Tony's lying up there. If he's there, arrest him. Don't make any charge; I'll attend to that. Now I'm going to have some breakfast."

*　　*　　*

Louie Patra had not slept well. Every half-hour or so he had woken up with the vague feeling that there was something wrong, that there was something he had to do. Then he would waken slowly to the memory of that night in Durham Square, of Leith's visit to Starling Court, of the raid on Guido's Club.

The drugging effect of the yellow liqueur was fading, leaving fears yet more clearly etched in his brain. He got up and had reached the office before he remembered that the bottle was empty. A sharp pain ran between his eyes.

He looked out and saw the dark barrier of the gate. If they came for him they would have a job to break that down, and he had other ways out.

Fear had never come to him before; fear to haunt and break his sleep, to colour every waking thought, to take the savour out of life like the intermittent aching of a tooth.

His peace of mind was as dead as the cigar ash in the saucer.

He fought against that realization with phrases which were losing their force by constant use. The police had no evidence against him. If they had they would have arrested him long ago. He'd got to be careful, that was all, and keep his trap shut, and not answer questions. That was how the dicks got most of their convictions, by jollying people along and getting them to talk. One word might give them a lead; one false step and they had you.

He went back to his room and, sitting on the bed, ran his hands through his hair. Tooley had got away with the Moke and Tony had gone with the van. Spider was dead. There was only Benny Watt left.

"I'll get him away first thing," he mumbled to himself, and rolled into bed, to lie awake until the shuffling footsteps of Mrs. Hoskins warned him it was time to be moving.

At seven o'clock Mrs. Hoskins brought him breakfast and he drank hot coffee greedily, for his throat and mouth were dry and the headache still lingered. When he had finished he told Mrs. Hoskins to tell Benny to come to the shop.

Benny, just roused from sleep, was uneasy. It was the first time the guv'nor had sent for him like this and he didn't like his look neither.

"I'm going to get you out of here for a spell," Louie said. "Down to the country. There's too many dicks hanging around."

"They'll get nothing out of me."

"I daresay, but I'm not taking any risks."

"I'd sooner stop here," Benny replied doggedly. "I like the place."

"Get your clobber together and be ready to move in an hour's time. Get me?"

For a moment it appeared that Benny was going to make a further protest, but after a pause he said, "O.K., guv'nor," and backed out through the door into the yard.

Louie stood looking after him; then he went out through the shop door into Canton Street. There were few people about: a road-cleaner with his barrow, women with shawls round their shoulders and shopping bags in their hands, a few children playing.

Louie's eyes made a quick survey. "Seems all clear," he said to himself, and turned northward.

Three times before he reached Oxford Street he doubled on his tracks, but saw no signs of a shadower. That way of escape was clear, and all that was necessary was to arrange to have a fast car handy.

The Moke was the man for that job.

Louie took a bus to Cambridge Circus and followed the route which Tooley had taken the night before. He felt better now that the arrangements for a quick getaway were taking shape, and when he walked through the archway into the mews he had for the moment quite forgotten the fears which had spoilt his night's rest.

He found the Moke with an old panama hat on the back of his head, sitting on the running-board of his taxi. He was wearing steel-rimmed spectacles and was reading a morning paper.

He looked up at the sound of Louie's footsteps on the cobbles, folded his paper and laid it by his side.

"Fine morning," he said, but didn't get up. He respected no one but himself.

"I want you on a job," Louie said. "Stand by in Canton Street. I'll fix a lay-by for you."

The Moke ran his fingers through his short, grizzled beard. "Going far?"

"Thirty or forty miles. Same place as last night, where you took Tooley."

"Tooley? I never took him no place."

"Why not?" Louie snapped.

"He didn't turn up, that's why. I waited an hour."

"Didn't turn up?" Louie muttered. Suddenly he felt cold and a little sick.

The Moke went on talking: "Made me miss another job, him not coming. It would have meant a tenner."

"Didn't he send a message or anything?" Louie asked.

"Never a sight nor a cheep out of him."

"Have the dicks been round?"

"No." The Moke picked up his paper again, as though disinterested, and lit a cigarette. "D'you think they've got on to Tooley?"

"I don't know." Louie spoke savagely. He was angry and he was frightened.

"He's on a ticket, isn't he?" the Moke asked, through a cloud of blue-grey smoke.

Louie nodded.

"You got to be extra-special careful when you're on a ticket. What's he been doing?"

Louie ignored the question and said: "Come round to Canton Street after dinner. Call in at Mrs. Hoskins' place, and she'll tell you where to put your bus."

"I'll be there."

Louie turned and went out through the archway of the mews, too busy with his thoughts to notice a man standing at the corner of the street reading a paper. Nor did he notice that he was followed back to Canton Street. His entry into Mrs. Hoskins' was noted by Detective-sergeant Simmons, who 'phoned the information to Scotland Yard.

*　　*　　*

When Harley received the news he took from the drawer of his desk a large-scale plan of Lucas and Canton Streets and the houses between. Then he picked up a pen and made a cross opposite Mrs. Hoskins' shop.

An hour later when Leith came in he was still examining the plan. He told Leith of Louie Patra's visit to the Moke's garage.

Leith said: "Yes, I heard from Simmons about that, but how the devil did he get out from Starling Court without being seen?"

Harley pointed to the cross he had made. "Through this shop, and there must be a way from it into the yard. There's no door shown here but one could easily have been made in this wall; it's only one brick thick."

"That's another hole we can stop."

"It would have been better if we'd found it before," commented Harley drily. "He's probably got the swag away by now."

"It's just about time we took Patra inside," Leith suggested. Harley shook his head. "We've got to find that Italian fellow first, and Zimmermann. We'll keep tabs on Patra; double bank the men you've got watching him."

"It's an amazing thing that we haven't got a lead on Zimmermann. He's a foreigner and he can't speak much English."

Harley arranged the papers on his desk in a neat pile. "Yes, it is curious how he's dropped out of sight. It may be that Patra has got a hide-away and that's where he's gone. It's not likely that he could find a place for himself."

"And apparently he's got the wop, Tony, away too. The next'll be Benny Watt. I was going to pull him in this afternoon."

Harley said: "Yes, you can go ahead with that, but get him out of the place before you take him. If Patra doesn't know where he's gone he'll start worrying, and a man who's worried usually does something damn' stupid that might give us a break."

"Do you think we ought to have another go at Tooley?" Leith asked.

"No. Leave him alone. Maybe he'll open up when he's been inside a week."

* * *

Zimmermann's knowledge of London was limited to what he could see from the window of his taxi. When he left the hotel with his bag he stopped the taxi after a few minutes' drive and set off on foot, heading east along the Commercial Road, homeless as a strayed dog. And when he saw the name Rosenheim he stopped and mopped his face with a dirty handkerchief. He stood looking into the shop window at five cuts of smoked salmon ranged on a slab. He was very fond of smoked salmon. He went in and sat on a high stool at a counter. Mr. Rosenheim himself served him, and Zimmermann explained as he ate that he was looking for lodgings.

Mr. Rosenheim was surprised, for Zimmermann was too well dressed to be a legitimate inhabitant of Whitechapel.

Mr. Zimmermann would have remained in the room over Rosenheim's shop for an indefinite period if he had had money to pay for his lodging. Germans are clannish but they are also fond of money.

Rosenheim's god, even above smoked salmon, was money.

Zimmermann was a fool. Therefore he became careless. Two days' stay in the room at Rosenheim's stilled his fears and raised his courage.

These English police. They were fools. He had just seen a policeman walking along with his thumbs in his belt. So he went out for a walk. He was nervous at first, but when he had reached the corner of the street without being arrested, he went farther, with assumed confidence, and even dared to enter the saloon bar of the 'Fox and Grapes' and order "One lager beer, if you please."

A public house is the Londoner's club. Some are as exclusive in fact if not in theory as the Athenaeum or the Senior.

The stranger is made to feel that he is a stranger. The barman is carefully polite.

Zimmermann drank his lager but did not sense the frozen hostility of the regulars. Therefore he stayed on for more lager and laborious conversation.

As Zimmermann's description was by now well known to every member of the Metropolitan Police Force, it was not the least odd that he was picked up within a few hours of his rash excursion into public.

But the police found him as obstinate as the walls of the cell in which he presently found himself. Not a brick was to be prised from it. Zimmermann protested that he was an honest trader doing a deal with Louie. "I knew him, yes. Sometimes we do business, but this time, no. He was too hard. His price was too high."

"What were you buying?" Leith asked.

"Waste paper. What else?"

"Antique glass?" Harley suggested.

For a second Zimmermann's face was blank, then it showed fear. Protestation followed in a spate of jumbled words. "Antique glass? I do not understand. What are you talking of? What do you mean?"

Harley pulled a folder towards him, opened it and read from a page of typescript: "You've never dealt with waste paper in your life, but you do know Schuster. Schuster is an art dealer in Ostend."

"Perhaps I have met him. I cannot remember."

"Why did you come to London?" Leith shot the question at him.

Zimmermann licked his dry lips.

"You came to see Louie Patra. He was supplying you with goods stolen from a house in Durham Square."

"I know nothing of that."

"You spoke to Patra on the telephone and he told you to clear out."

"That is not true."

"Then why did you leave your hotel and take the room in China Street?"

"It was—it was cheaper. I am not a rich man."

"But you are a liar."

Blood flooded Zimmermann's cheeks. "I am an honest businessman."

"There's no such thing," Harley muttered to himself. He turned to a small pile of papers which had been taken from Zimmermann. There was nothing in it to interest him. He spoke to Zimmermann. "Dealing in stolen goods'll net you two years at least."

"Two years?"

"Yes. Prison for two years. It'd improve your figure. Four inches off that would do you a world of good."

"Prison?"

"Yes. Have you ever tried it?"

Zimmermann summoned anger. "Prison. Of course not. I tell you I am an honest man."

"All the same, if you could tell us the truth it might help. We only want to know what's become of the swag."

"I know nothing."

"You're a damn' fool, and if you say you're an honest man again I'll clock you."

Zimmermann drew back in his chair. His understanding of the words was imperfect, but Harley's tone held a threat that a deaf man could take in.

"You got Patra to steal stuff for you. You were going to ship it in the *Van Wyk*. We know that. There's no good keeping anything back."

"I admit nothing."

"Oh, go to hell," Harley snapped. He said to Leith: "Lock him up before I hit him."

* * *

At two o'clock that afternoon the Moke drove his taxi out of the Chandos Mews. Behind him there followed what appeared to be a fruiterer's van driven by a police officer in plain clothes.

At Cambridge Circus a touring-car took the place of the van, and when the Moke turned into Canton Street, the touring-car, which carried three police officers in plain clothes, went straight on for twenty yards and then drew up at the kerb.

The driver kept his eye on the driving-mirror, in which he could see a man who was standing at the corner of Canton Street. After a short interval the man took out a box of matches and lit a cigarette.

The driver turned to the policeman beside him and said, "He's gone to ground," and drove on.

Leith, who was waiting in a teashop, received the report that the Moke had garaged his car in a lock-up fifty yards north of Mrs. Hoskins' shop. He gave orders to the man who brought the information that a police car was to wait at the north end of Canton Street. "Tell them to follow the taxi if it leaves the garage, but they mustn't overtake it. I want to find out where it goes."

From his bedroom window Louie saw the Moke arrive in Canton Street, and he smiled as he thought of the surprise the police would get if they tried to chase it. There weren't many taxis in London with a forty-horse-power engine under the bonnet, nor any with a man like the Moke to drive it.

He would like to go with Benny, but he had to find Zimmermann first and collect the money he had promised to pay.

A thousand pounds would last a month or two, by the end of which time it might be possible to return to Starling Court.

Optimism grew, fed by the thought of action. As soon as he had got hold of Zimmermann they would all sail in the *Van Wyk*. He knew the port of Esberg as a small, sleepy village. The *Van Wyk* was known and her arrival would not cause comment. He and Benny and Tony could live on board, or possibly land by night on a deserted part of the coast when Zimmermann had arranged a hiding-place.

He might go to Ostend! There would be crowds of trippers there and he could gamble in the casinos. It would be the first holiday he had had for ten years. The future looked good to Louie, and he took his wallet from his breast pocket and counted the notes it contained. Forty-seven pounds.

There was the Moke to be paid, stores and fuel for the *Van Wyk* to be bought. He scribbled figures on the back of an envelope. Even without Zimmermann's assistance he could get out of the country.

Louie massaged his heavy cheeks, doubts and fears returning. Perhaps it would be better to go now. The Moke was ready; he had only to say the word.

Then he looked out of the window to the yard. There was no sign of life. It seemed absurd to run away, and if he gave his mind to it he could make the business keep him.

He played with the idea for half an hour, examining it from every angle, improving it.

A month ago, a week ago, he would have assessed the value of the project in a fraction of the time, but now it was different.

The police, whom he had been accustomed to keep at sparring distance, had broken through his guard and placed blows which had left him shaken and unsure of himself.

He fought against accepting the fact that Tooley had been arrested. He refused to believe it, and yet he believed. If it were true that Tooley was in the hands of the police, what should he do? Stay or go?

Could he rely on Tooley not to talk, not to tell the whole story of what happened on that night? But even if he did it wouldn't mean the end; the evidence of an accomplice would be of little value. And the same was true of Tony and Benny Watt; they had all been in it with him. None was guiltless.

Tooley had struck the blow which had knocked the Rigger unconscious. Tooley believed that he had killed the man. Tony would tell the same story. He, Louie, had never laid a hand on the Rigger neither in the car nor at the chapel. Benny Watt had been there and his evidence would help.

No one outside his own gang had seen what had happened, so what had he to fear?

But he knew the police and knew of their dogged persistence in investigating a crime once their suspicions had been aroused.

Though he had been so far successful in outwitting his enemies he respected them.

He was startled by the sound of slow footsteps on the wooden staircase. His hand held a tremor as he raised his cigar to his lips.

Footsteps advancing, slowly, deliberately, inexorably as Fate! Real fear was in his heart, panic fear which deadened thought and killed reason.

He wanted to go to the window and look out, but could not.

Fingers fumbled with the latch, and Benny Watt came into the room. He shut the door behind him and then turned to face Louie. He stammered, "What's up, guv'nor?" and was afraid, for Louie's face was like that of a waxen model, with staring, unwinking eyes. Fear had wiped it clean of all emotion and expression.

Suddenly he came to life in a sudden burst of rage. "What do you want to come creeping up like that for? Haven't I told you a dozen times not to bother me here?"

Benny said nothing. He stood quite motionless. Seconds passed, and then Louie spoke again, quietly now. "Well, what is it?"

"It's the dicks. They're all round the place. They've got a car round the corner of the street."

"What sort of a car?"

"A big tourer."

Real danger restored Louie's power of reasoned thought.

He knocked ash from his cigar into the saucer on the desk. Then he went to the window and looked out over the roof tops with unfocused eyes. It had got as far as that, had it? They expected him to make a break.

He turned his eyes on Benny, who had not moved from his place by the door. "You'll go with the Moke, just the same. He can outpace 'em. When you get to the boat tell Tony I'll be along as soon as I've seen Zimmermann. They've got to have everything ready to sail, with the stuff on board, when I arrive."

Benny nodded his head. Then he said: "You shouldn't ought to stop here, guv'nor."

But Louie said, "Don't you worry about me. I'll fox 'em." He opened the door and Benny went out.

He watched Benny go into the chapel, then he muttered to himself: "I'll stay and see Zimmermann. I've got to get that cash." Greed had overcome fear.

*　　*　　*

Benny Watt walked out of Mrs. Hoskins' shop at a quarter past three. He knew that he was being watched, but that fact did not worry him, for he knew the Moke.

The Moke was waiting with the engine of his taxi warmed up and running.

As soon as Benny Watt had passed the entrance to the garage the Moke drove out and followed him. Benny opened the door of the taxi and jumped in.

The Moke spat out the fag end of a cigarette and slipped the gear-lever into third. A policeman, who saw the taxi flash past him, fumbled for his whistle, but before he could get his fingers on the chain the Moke had reached the end of the street.

The Moke saw the touring-car drawn up by the kerb at the entrance to the Square. "That's a rozzer all right," he muttered to himself, and swung the taxi round the left-hand corner.

He did not see a fruiterer's van on the other corner start up.

Oxford Street was jammed with traffic, and he swore as a light flicked green. A bus closed up behind him. He turned his head and said, "Are we clear?"

Benny looked through the rear window. "Can't see nothing."

"I'll take a run up north." The Moke turned to the left out of the traffic along West Kent Street. Twisting and turning, he came out in Tottenham Court Road, went north, then east again.

When he passed the Bank the fruiterer's van was twenty yards behind. The Moke saw it in the driving-mirror. "So that's their game, is it?" His grip on the wheel tightened.

"That van's on our tail," Benny said.

"I know. Don't you fret."

But Benny sat sweating on the back seat. He tried not to look out of the back window, but every now and then he twisted his body, and every time he did so he saw the fruiterer's van.

"Well, they haven't got anything on me. There's no evidence," he muttered, but his heart was cold within him. He was an old man. He liked his beer and his pipe and he knew all about life in prison—the cold sterility of steel bars and stone walls.

The Moke drove like a man without nerves. He made no mistakes and the most of every opportunity. In his mind was a map, clear as an etching, of the route he meant to follow.

He knew every bend, corner and traffic light. His hand on the gear-lever was never still for more than ten seconds at a time.

Houses thinned out as he drove northwards, until he reached melancholy marshland dotted with grimy factories, rubbish dumps, railway lines and a canal.

The van was fifty yards behind when he came to a fork in the road. "No damn' good trying it today," he muttered to himself, and took the left-hand road. "I'm going back," he said over his shoulder.

Benny leaned forward until he knelt on the floor. His hands gripped the back of the front seat. "We've got to get through."

"Like hell we can get through, I tell you. We're going back." The Moke, jamming the accelerator hard down on the floor boards, sent the car along a long straight stretch at seventy miles an hour. "We'll give 'em a run for it, anyway," he muttered savagely to himself.

But his luck was right out. Ahead was a line of cars and trucks held up by a traffic light; half the road was being repaired.

The Moke skidded to a stop inches behind the tailboard of a ten-ton trailer. Benny was jerked forward and hit his mouth on the back of the front seat.

Dazed and with a trickle of blood on his chin, he stumbled out of the taxi. A policeman came from the fruiterer's van and took him by the arm. "What do you think you're doing, you old wreck of the Hesperus?"

Benny stared at him and then began to cry. He was too old for the game. He'd lost his nerve. There had been a time when he could have given as good as he received, but that time was long past.

The Moke was dumb to the questions put to him by a sergeant in uniform. He and Benny were taken to the nearest police-station while a policeman drove the taxi to a police garage.

*   *   *

The trip should have taken the Moke two hours. Two and a half at most. Louis had it all worked out. He had ordered the Moke to return at once to Canton Street, and Mrs. Hoskins was keeping a lookout for him. She would tell Louie at once.

Nevertheless, when the two and a half hours had elapsed, he rang up Mrs. Hoskins on his private line, and her hoarse voice assured him there wasn't a sign of the van.

Louie swore as he hung up the receiver. He had spent the time waiting, in vain, for news of Zimmermann, and revolving contradictory plans in his mind. His nerves were beginning to show the wear and tear of warring hopes, doubts and fears. He had almost decided to run for it when the Moke returned—and now there was no Moke.

For another half-hour he tried to believe that a puncture was responsible for the delay, but at six o'clock he gave up all pretence. He must have the inevitable truth. They'd got the Moke. And, of course, Benny too. He should never have sent him. He was a fool to have risked it.

And now if Benny talked! For a minute his brain was numb, and when he could think again he had to struggle to collect his thoughts. It was this gradual disappearing of his men which was so ominous. He could only presume that they'd got Tooley and Benny. Tooley was all right, he wouldn't sing, not unless his nerve went, and even then it wasn't the end. Tooley had struck the blow. Tooley had believed that the Rigger had been dead when they had brought him to Starling Court.

And Benny knew nothing. He had seen the body, that was all.

Louie lit a cigar. Then he rang a bell, and when Guido came he told him to send in a bottle of whiskey.

When it came he dropped a powder into the drink and gulped it down.

As the drug took effect trouble slipped from his mind. What the hell had he got to worry about? They'd got nothing on him. There was not a single scrap of evidence in the place. The loot was all on board the *Van Wyk*, and they didn't know anything about her.

All he'd got to do was to find Zimmermann and take him to Holland in the ship, collect the dough, and then everything would be all sargany.

Zimmermann! Where the hell had he got to?

Louie leaned back in his chair and stretched out his legs. He was beginning to feel deliciously sleepy. Time enough in the morning to find Zimmermann. Time enough—

He shook himself out of his doze with a jerk and got up. He walked to the window and looked out into the blackness of the night. The roofs were clearly etched against the stars.

There was no light in the store below.

He walked to the door and unlocked it, and at that moment the 'phone bell rang. He picked up the receiver and said, "Yes?"

"Hullo, is that you, Mr. Patra?"

His fingers stiffened as he recognized Leith's voice. He said, "Yes, it's me."

"We've got a friend of yours here. He wants you to fix up a lawyer for him."

"That's all right. Tell Benny I'll look after him. He needn't worry."

"It isn't Benny I'm talking about. It's Zimmermann."

*   *   *

As he put down the receiver Leith turned to Harley. "He thinks we've got Benny Watt. Now who the blazes could have tipped him off to that?"

"What does it matter?" Harley finished a sentence he was writing and looked up. "What did he say about Zimmermann?"

"Nothing. Rang off before I'd finished."

Harley allowed himself a hint of a smile. "I fancy we've got Mr. Louie Patra rattled. It's just a question whether we shouldn't pull him in right away or let him chew it over for a time."

"He's had plenty of time." Leith tapped with a forefinger on a blotting-pad. "It's full of rat runs, that block in Lucas Street. It's a hell of a place to keep tabs on."

Harley looked at him and nodded. "Yes, I know that. Of course, if we could find out where the *Van Wyk* is we could wait on board her. That's where he'll make for."

Leith said: "I've been on to the Customs, and they can't help us. They cleared her when she came in but they don't know where she's gone now. Except that she hasn't passed Gravesend."

"Have you tried all the docks?"

"Yes, I checked up on all of them."

Then he saw an envelope on the desk and picked it up. "I'd forgotten about this. It's the sample of mud I took off the lorry wheels. I sent some of it to the lab for analysis."

"Have we got the report?"

"No, I don't think we have. I don't remember seeing it."

"Get on to them right away. We might get something out of it."

Ten minutes later a messenger appeared with the report.

Harley read: "The composition of the sample marked A is as follows: ninety per cent black silt, probably from a river bed. Four per cent coal cinders. Six per cent yellow clay. It is probable that the lorry from which this sample was taken had been driven over a marsh road. These roads are composed largely of silt dredged from rivers and drainage ditches, with a six-inch top dressing of cinders. Clay is seldom found on marshland. A geological survey map is attached to this report, and it will be seen that surface clay appears in three places in Essex and in numerous cases on the Kent side of the river."

"I think I know how we can get a line on this. I checked up on the running time of the lorry when she made a trip the night before I had a look at it, and it worked out at five hours and a quarter. Average speed not more than twenty. Give it an hour for unloading and we have a forty-mile radius."

Harley rummaged in a drawer and found a pair of compasses. He drew a circle. "Hmmm, that's interesting. That just takes in one of these clay patches, the only one on the Essex side. Now how are we going to check up on this?"

Leith leaned over the map and followed a track with his finger. "And do you see? It ends up in a creek."

Harley gave a grunt. "Too easy."

"But worth checking up on," Leith said, and picked up the telephone. "I'll try the river police."

While he was waiting for the call to come through Harley turned back to the map. "Looks like a house and a wharf."

Leith spoke into the telephone. When he had finished he said to Harley: "The *Van Wyk* is in that creek. She went in three days ago. They want to know if we need any help. I said I'd talk to you and ring them back."

"No use taking any chances. Tell 'em to have a boat waiting off there between ten and twelve tonight. That should cover it. We'll flash a light three times if we want them to lend a hand."

"What about Patra? Are we going to let him stay loose?"

"Yes. Take the guard off Lucas Street."

"Don't you think we'd better have a tail on him just in case?" Leith suggested.

"No. He won't play if he thinks there's a string on him. The stuff is in the ship, I'm sure of that, and it's a bait that can't fail."

"When do we start?"

"In time to get there about ten. The tide's out now. The ship won't float before eleven."

*   *   *

Louie put down the receiver. So they had got Zimmermann too. He stubbed out his cigar slowly, watching the leaf spread and split amid the white ash. Zimmermann. He never had trusted that man. He wasn't like Tooley or Benny.

It wouldn't be long before the police broke his nerve. He'd tell them about the *Van Wyk* and that would mean the end of everything. Everything.

He didn't fear the police, he never had. They couldn't pin anything on him. He'd been too clever for that. Tooley would swing for the death of the Rigger, and now that the stuff was out of Starling Court they couldn't get him for the robbery either.

Starling Court and the paper business was finished. He would have to build up another front, but that would take money. He would have to get out of Town and work from some other place where he wasn't known.

There wasn't a thief within fifty miles of Charing Cross who would bring stuff to him now.

He was known to the police.

He had held the joker for a long time, but now he had lost it. He would have to begin all over again. He would have to find someone to take Benny's place, someone to drive a car, and someone to do Tooley's job; he'd banked on Tooley. There weren't many like him, men who had nerve and who wouldn't sing the first time things went wrong.

He fought back the tiredness that was creeping over his brain. Start again? He wondered if he could. It would take time, and where could he go? Manchester? He knew a few of the boys up there, but he'd lost touch these last few years. Blind Larry with his gig-lamps. He could have worked with Larry, but Larry was dead. Consumption. And the Professor. They'd got him for a lifer. And Sam Pelly, he was inside, and the Clerk as well.

Suddenly he became aware of the nervous ticking of the clock on the mantelpiece. "You've got to go. You've got to go," it said to him.

He must move, and move fast. He must get the stuff out of the *Van Wyk* and hide it away till he could find a buyer.

He opened a drawer and raked through the papers with his fingers. There was nothing there that would help the police; they were just receipts and accounts connected with the business.

He picked up a box of cigars and carried it into his bedroom. He'd need to take clothes. There was a suit-case on the top of the ward-robe. He pulled it down, shook off the dust and put it on the bed. It was a long time ago since he'd used it; not since he used to do his own smashing and had had to travel around. Well, maybe he wasn't too old to start that game again, he told himself, and knew that it was a lie.

When the bag was packed he put on his raincoat and went up the stairs to the roof. It would be best to go through the wop's place. There was plenty of traffic in Lucas Street, and with a good lad at the wheel he'd have a chance of making it. If the dicks beat him to it—well, that would be that; he'd tell 'em he was going down to the country to visit a sick aunt.

Silvretti stopped stroking his moustache and dropped his hands on the counter when he heard Louie's step on the staircase. He knew who it was, and, as Louie pushed his way through the jingling bead curtain, he forced a smile. It made him look as though he were going to cry.

Louie dropped his bag near the street door and came over to the counter. "Well, what's the news?"

"There's a car just round the corner." Silvretti waved a hand vaguely in the direction of the window.

"What's it like?"

"A black saloon. It's been there since six."

Louie grunted a reply, picked up a box of cigars and smelt the contents. "Get me a bus. I got to get out of here quick."

Silvretti sidled round the counter and untied his apron. As he put on his hat he said: "I'll try the Greek."

"Yes, he'll do. And tell him to fill right up. He'll have a long trip."

Silvretti was glad to get out into the street. He feared Louie as he feared snakes and rats, and the fear was instinctive.

Half an hour had passed before Silvretti returned. He said: "He wants a tenner."

"That's O.K. Where is he?"

"Round the corner. And the police are still there."

"The Greek can drive?" There was a challenging expression in Louie's eyes. "Can't he?"

Silvretti stammered: "Yes, yes, he can drive all right. You will be all right."

"Sure I'll be all right, all right." He mimicked the Italian's tone. Then he walked out into the night, but before he stepped into the Greek's car he glanced at the saloon waiting on the corner. "You got to lose him," he spat at the driver. "And lose him quick."

At Tottenham Court Road he looked back. There was no sign of the police car. "That's funny, now." He had expected a chase, and was puzzled and uneasy, for it seemed too damn' simple.

The car moved fast through the thinning traffic. 'Maybe I'd better give it a miss tonight,' he thought, but said nothing to the driver.

Street lamps and shop lights were behind them now; on either side were the marshes. Here and there a single light showed from the window of an isolated cottage.

Far away he heard the faint sound of a steamship's whistle on the river.

He felt in his pocket and pulled out his cigar-case. His hand was steady as it held a lighted match. Now that he was out of London the strain had eased. Once again he was master of himself.

Tony would be there with the lorry. They'd load it up right away and take the stuff into the country. Somewhere in Essex. He'd find a place all right, and it would be time enough then to think about finding a buyer later. He had forty pounds in notes in his wallet; that would last a while.

He leaned forward and peered ahead. Then he touched the Greek on the shoulder. "It's not far now, Mick. Look out for a hoarding on the right. It's the second road after that."

The Greek nodded. "I've been there before. I went with Tony on his first trip."

"Yes, of course, I forgot." Louie sat back on the cushions and crossed his legs.

Ten minutes later the car slowed down, turned right and began to bump over the marshland track. There was no sign of a trailing car. Louie leaned forward again. "When you drop me beat it right back to the Smoke."

The Greek nodded, and as the car lurched and heaved over the bumps he said: "If I've got any springs left."

"It's all right if you take it slow," Louie grunted.

*   *   *

On board the *Van Wyk* Tony was standing in the lee of the deckhouse. He saw the lights coming down the road and called down the hatch.

The captain came clattering up the ladder. "A car, huh? Who's in it?"

Tony muttered: "How the hell should I know?" He was frightened and angry.

The captain went into the deck-house and brought out two short lengths of rope. There was a heavy knot in the end of each of them, and attached to the other end was a short lanyard. He gave one to Tony, and slipped the lanyard of the other on to his wrist.

Tony muttered, "I've never used one of these before. What about getting the crew up?"

"They're no damn' good." The captain pulled Tony by the sleeve of his coat. "Here, you stand by the ladder. They won't see you. And when I give the word let 'em have it."

The captain climbed up the ladder until his eyes were level with the top of the wharf. The car was a hundred yards away. He watched it stop and saw a man get out. Then the car turned and went away. He said to Tony: "It's all right, it looks like the guv'nor."

Then Louie called out: "Anyone down there?" His squat figure was silhouetted against the stars.

Tony dropped his piece of knotted rope. He was thankful to get rid of it. He was almost crying with relief. He clutched

Louie's arm and babbled, "I thought you'd never come. How are things going? When do we start?"

Louie put a hand on his shoulder. "You're O.K., Tony. You're all right, I tell you." He turned to the captain. "Had any trouble?"

"No, guv'nor. Everything's been quiet. There's none of us been further than the end of the wharf."

"That's good."

"I'll tell the chief to get ready. The tide'll be right about eleven."

"We're not sailing."

"Why not?"

"I'm going to take the stuff in the truck. Get the boys up and rig the derrick. Tony, get the truck started up."

"But we're all ready," the captain protested. "The hatches are on and—"

"Get the hatches off."

"O.K., guv'nor." The captain walked forward. Louie waited until he had reached the forecastle hatch and then he said to Tony: "Come in here a minute." He opened the door of the deck-house. When they were both inside he shut the door and lit the hanging lamp.

"The dicks have got Zimmermann. It's no good taking this stuff across now. We've got to hide up in the country for a spell."

"Where's Tooley?"

"I left him in the Smoke. We don't want him."

"And Benny?"

"He's all right."

"Benny knows the bales. I don't."

"We can work it out."

"He should have come. It's going to be hell in the dark finding them. I'll take the truck back and fetch him."

"You'll stop here and do what you're told." Louie's voice was like the growl of an angry bear. "If you want to know, Benny's inside, and Tooley as well. We've got to work, and work fast."

Tony put a shaking hand to the knot of his purple tie. "They've got all of 'em?"

"They haven't got me and they haven't got you. That's all that matters."

"I'm not going to stay here. I'm going." Tony's voice rose like that of a frightened child. "You can't keep me."

"You frightened little rat!" Louie shot out a hand and gripped a handful of Tony's mauve shirt. "You're going to step my way and all the way. You're not going to get a chance to sing."

Tony sagged. The last trace of rebellion seeped out of him. "All right, I'll go. Anywhere you like, but why take the truck? The stuff's all in the hold, and the skipper says we can get away by eleven."

"Now listen here. For the first time for three days there hasn't been a dick on my tracks. There was a car-load of them in Lucas Street when I left the place but they didn't follow me. They let me go; they let me come here."

"Maybe they didn't see you go," Tony suggested.

"They may be dumb, but not so dumb as all that. And they've got Zimmermann, and Zimmermann must have sung. That's how I figure it out."

"You're sure they've got him?" Tony whispered the question.

"Yes, and they think they've got me, but that's where they're ruddy well wrong. And that's why we're clearing out with the stuff. I'm still one jump ahead."

"But if we meet 'em on the road, what are we going to do?"

"You'll ride 'em off. There's a ditch on each side and plenty of water in them." Louie took a flat flask from his pocket and gave it to Tony. "Get some of that inside you."

Tony's hand was trembling as he held the tin cup and raised it to his mouth. Louie watched him drink. "Now come on and get that truck out. You can have another before we start." He kicked the door open and pushed Tony towards the ladder.

They climbed on to the wharf and went to a storehouse. Tony took a key from his pocket and unlocked a padlock.

By the time the engine had been started up and Tony had backed the lorry out, the crew of the *Van Wyk* was taking off the hatches. A man in a greasy overall was bending over the engine which drove the winch. Louie could see the light from his torch and hear the clink of metal on metal as he oiled the bearings. He looked at his watch. Seven hours to go before it would begin to get light; there was plenty of time, but he shouted down to the skipper: "You got to get a move on. I want to be away from here in an hour's time."

But a church clock far away across the marshes had struck ten before the last of the bales had been located and hoisted out on to the lorry.

"Send out another half-dozen; we've got to make it look like a proper load." His cigar tasted bitter and he threw it down into the inky water, which was rising slowly. He called out to know where the petrol was stored.

"There's three tins in the shed," the skipper replied. "Hard on your right as you go in."

Louie went to the store, found a tin and loosened the cap. Then he carried it to the lorry and clambered up into the driving-seat. He wasn't taking any chances.

He looked out along the marsh road; there was nothing to be seen. "Looks as though my luck's in this time," he muttered to himself, and was about to stow the tin of petrol under the seat when he stiffened and froze. He had heard the purr of a motor-car.

It was so faint at first that he thought he must have been mistaken, but a moment later he heard it clearly.

It was a car, slowly approaching, a car without lights. . . .

His fingers went to the tin and unscrewed the cap. Then he stood on the seat, stepped on to the top of the load and emptied the petrol on to the bales of wastepaper.

"What the hell are you up to?" The skipper's voice broke through the sound of the clanking winch.

"There's a bus on the road. Maybe it's the dicks."

The last of the petrol gurgled out of the tin and Louie threw it on to the wharf. "Tony! Where the hell's Tony?"

Tony came running from behind the tailboard. "What's up?"

"Start the engine! Quick! Get her back in the shed." Louie climbed down on the wharf. "Get a move on, for God's sake!"

Tony switched on the ignition and cranked the motor. Twice it coughed and died again. Then it started.

Louie looked in the direction of the approaching car.

"Maybe they won't hear it. They're half a mile away yet." He shouted to Tony: "Get on. Drive her right in."

When the lorry was back in the shed he said: "Go on board; take the dinghy and pull up-river out of the way. Come back in an hour's time."

Louie did not want to have Tony questioned by the police.

He ran to the edge of the wharf. "Get the hatches on and then take the crew below." He waited for a minute; the car was quite close now; he could see the black bulk of it.

He heard the dinghy bump alongside, saw Tony jump into her and pull away. Now they could search the ship all they liked; they would find nothing.

There was a bend in the track a hundred yards from the wharf, and as the car swung to the left Louie ran quickly to the shed.

* * *

Two police cars left Scotland Yard as Big Ben boomed eight times; they made good time through the comparatively quiet City streets and along the Commercial Road.

Harley checked his watch. "We're a bit early, but it won't matter."

He switched on a torch and gave it to Leith to hold while he unfolded a map. He pointed to a double dotted line running southwards across the marshes. "That's the road we've got to find. It's almost exactly two miles past a public house called the 'Bear', and there's some buildings just beyond it; they look like an old factory."

At last the headlights picked up the sign of the 'Bear', and as they passed it, Harley said to the driver: "Just two miles to go; check it on the clock."

A few minutes later the car slowed and Harley put his head out of the off-side window. Bulking black against the sky he saw buildings and a tall chimney. "We're almost there. Go dead slow and stand by to turn right." He directed his torch on to the side of the road. "That's it. Turn in."

The car swayed as it swung on to the soft mud of the track. "Can you manage without the lights?"

The driver replied, "I'll try, sir," and turned a switch on the dashboard. A minute or two later he added, "I'll be all right," and slipped into second gear.

Harley leaned back on the cushions and lit a cigarette. "It's been a long trail, but I think we've got 'em at last. There's no other way from the wharf except by boat, and we've got that hole stopped."

The car jolted on with whining gears.

Once she skidded and the rear wheels churned their way sideways towards the threatening black shadow which was the dyke bordering the track.

The driver righted her, and muttered: "The bank's fallen away there."

Harley's fat legs were cramped with tension, but he was looking ahead. There was a luminous gleam above the enveloping grey of the marsh.

"Here's the creek."

And, almost simultaneously, Leith said: "And there she is!"

The masts and spars of the ship were etched very faintly against the sky.

"All right, go ahead," grunted Harley, as the driver slowed. "They'll have heard us a mile off." And as they rounded the last bend and headed straight for the wharf, he ordered: "Light up."

The headlights of the car blazed out suddenly over a deserted scene. The ship lay, idle and apparently deserted, at her moorings, still listing slightly before the tide lifted her from the mud.

Harley climbed slowly out of the car, one hand in his pocket.

"We're too soon," breathed Leith at his elbow.

"I don't think so," Harley grunted, and he jerked his elbow at the muddy tracks of heavy tyres on the wooden slats of the wharf. A double line of them led to a wooden shed at the end of the jetty.

Harley glanced from the shed to the ship, and, walking to the stem, read the faint lettering: "VAN WYK".

He grunted, and then opened his mouth to a bellow.

"Oy! *Van Wyk* ahoy!"

Leith suppressed a smile at the unexpected nautical smack. But presently it was his turn to shout, and it was an eerie sound as the grey mist hanging over the marshland seemed to smother and blanket the echoes of his voice.

At last a door in the deck-house opened and the captain appeared, wearing shirt and trousers.

With a somewhat exaggerated display of having been disturbed from sleep, he rubbed his eyes, yawned and inquired what the hell was up.

"I'll have a look at your bill of lading," Harley told him shortly. "Bring your books out here."

The captain hesitated. "Who the hell are you?" he demanded.

"Scotland Yard."

"Come off it," added Leith wearily.

"Do you want to come on board?"

"No."

Muttering something about 'those damn' lights', the captain retired to his cabin.

Harley backed out of the glare towards the shadows.

He said: "Don't stand there like an Aunt Sally waiting for him to take a pot at you." -

"He's not that sort. That young wop, Tony, is more likely to try a spot of knifing," Leith remarked cheerfully.

"There's nothing in the ship," muttered Harley. "He invited us on board as though he wanted us to come."

"Maybe they're laying for us there."

Harley shook his head. "Let's try the shed while we wait."

They walked to the door of the shed and found it barred on the inside.

"Must be a door at the back."

There was, but it, too, was unyielding. Harley said: "Fetch the driver to bash it in."

Leith walked back to the car, but he had barely given the order to the policeman, who was still at the wheel, when a sound made him turn.

Harley was signalling to him, but it was the shed itself which drew his attention. A flicker of red light was visible under the double doors, and almost at once a crackling sound became audible.

"They've fired it!"

Leith and the driver ran.

Harley was cool. "You wait by the gangway to the ship," he ordered Leith. "One of the rats may run from there. We'll deal with this one."

A little reluctantly Leith retreated. He could see the startled face of the captain at the deck-house door, but otherwise the ship was quiet enough as she righted herself slowly to the incoming tide.

Leith watched. The glare of light inside the shed was increasing quickly and throwing a ruddy glow over the mist which swirled up from the marshes, and mingled with the smoke which was beginning to find its way from the shed. Leith could only just make out the two black figures, waiting outside the two doors like terriers at a rabbit warren.

"He'll have to bolt for it or be frittered," muttered Leith, and he felt for the gun in his pocket, just in case the rabbit should be too fast for the terriers.

But there was no bolt, no shooting. It was done as smoothly and quietly as the arrival of an expected guest in a drawing-room. Leith, half blinded by the swirling clouds of ruddy-tinted smoke, heard the sound of coughing, and footsteps ringing hollow on the wooden planking.

"Leith!" Harley's voice was almost drowned by a sudden roar and crackle as the roof of the shed caught fire: "Damn this smoke!"

Leith saw three figures advancing, and recognized the one in the centre.

"Patra!"

"Who did you expect? Livingstone? Come on." Apparently Harley was not satisfied with his capture.

Patra turned and looked at the blaze with an expression of quiet satisfaction before he followed Harley to the car. In a billow of smoke and a burst of flame was gone the only shred of evidence against him. He made no protest to his arrest. His business at the moment was to keep his trap shut. They'd got nothing on him. He climbed into the back of the car and sat beside Harley as though he owned the outfit.

"Go and get that swab of a captain," Harley ordered. "We'd better take him along. And his books. And then for heaven's sake let's get out of this damned awful hole."

In spite of the silent, almost smug presence of Patra beside him, Harley was not in a good temper.

*   *   *

The car jolted slowly along the track; the scene over the marshes was even less inviting than before, as the white mist fled in slow wreaths and eddies before the headlights, and rose up on either side, as the car passed, like malignant ghosts. Here and there the mist thinned, allowing glimpses of oily water in the dykes and occasionally a stunted willow.

The party in the car were silent, even the captain, who had started with a burst of voluble protestations which had been even less enlightening than Louie's masterly reserve.

Behind them the glare from the burning shed grew greater, as the walls and roof ignited, and the whole marsh seemed to glow around them like some would-be inferno.

It was thanks to the fire that Leith was able to see something protruding from the oily waters of the dyke. The driver was going more slowly than ever, for he was anxious to avoid the spot where he had skidded on the outward journey.

Just as he saw the black tracks made by his tyres in their sideways surge, Leith exclaimed:

"What's that?"

"Place we skidded, sir. Looks like the bank's had a bit of a slip."

"I should say it has. There's a car in the water there."

The driver halted cautiously, on the other side of the track. Leith got out. In the glare from the fire he had seen two wheels and a rear axle black against the oily water.

Harley did not move. He could not see Louie's face, but he was aware of a sudden rigidity in the man at his side, and presently he heard a faint wheezing breath as though the other had stopped breathing for a moment. He waited for Leith to investigate, every faculty on the alert.

"It's a car all right," Leith reported presently. "And it doesn't look to me as though it's been there very long. It was heading towards the river. You can see there clearly where it left the track."

"Can you see inside?"

"No. Not without diving." Leith shuddered.

"Number plate?"

"Yes. I've got the number."

"All right. Get in. Mark the spot, Knight. We'll send a breakdown gang along."

*   *   *

As Leith had feared, he was not quit of the marshes yet.

A message from the local policeman, at the nearest village of Hockling, awaited Harley on their return to Scotland Yard. It was dawn, and the party was extremely tired and cold.

"Cocoa," Harley ordered abstractedly as he glanced at the message pad on his desk. His hat was still tilted to the back of his head and his overcoat shrugged about his shoulders. "They can't dig that car out," he told Leith. "P.C. Brightman wants us to send a heavy breakdown lorry."

Leith grumbled. "Probably he's only got a one-horse-power lorry in that one-horse burgh. I'll order one in the morning."

"It is morning. And I think you'd better go too. Check up on the number of the car first."

Hot cocoa luckily had the effect of dousing the spark of rebellion in Leith. But the report from the Car Registration Department awoke a fresh enthusiasm.

The wrecked car was Patra's.

"And he left the number plate on the car for every passer-by to see," mused Harley, but he lumbered out of his overcoat as though he were feeling warmer.

"Looks like an accident."

"That's what he'll say. You'd better wait till we've had a talk with Mr. Blooming Patra. And I'll bet you he sings as loud as a mute canary."

Leith glanced eloquently at his watch.

"Yes, forty winks first. An hour or so of cold anticipation won't do Patra any harm."

* * *

Harley was right. Patra was still complacent, and looked distressingly well-fed and alert. He had been about his lawful business on the marshes, he stated, getting his paper bales on to the ship. The fire had been an accident.

"There must have been a petrol leak, and I dropped the stub of my cigar."

"And locked yourself in the garage while it ignited?"

"The door jammed. I was trying to put the fire out."

Harley and Leith looked at each other before Harley proceeded: "And what about the car in the dyke?"

"What about it?"

"It was yours."

Patra's simulation of surprise and indignation was well done. The car had been stolen, he explained, a few days before.

"And who stole it?"

"How should I know?"

"Why didn't you report it to the police?"

Patra smiled. "If you will forgive my saying so, Mr. Leith, I have never found the police much good."

"Take him away," growled Harley.

When he had gone, Leith remarked grimly: "That car was not stolen, I'll swear."

"Swearing never got a policeman any place." Harley lay back in his chair. "I know, I've tried it. Patra's got a hell of a lot of good stories to tell. Tooley killed the Rigger, and Benny Watt dumped him on the dump. His car was stolen and ditched. The garage caught fire by an act of God—or the devil. And we haven't a thread to hold him by—much less to hang him. The only evidence we have against Patra is Tooley's story of the burglary, and the only evidence of murder is those name-tabs from the Rigger's clothing in a stove on Patra's property. Damn' flimsy."

"And the newspaper in Kimber's house."

"Scraps of paper are no more use to a policeman than to a politician. We'll send out a call for the others this morning. Silvretti and Tony, and that other wop, Guido. I'm getting used to the sound of my own voice asking damn' silly questions. You'd better pop down to the marshes again and pull out that car."

"I think I'll take Benny Watt," Leith suggested. "He was in charge of the packing of those bales. He might help to identify them."

"He won't talk," grunted Harley. "Blooming pack of oysters."

"You never know. I'm certain the stuff was packed in those bales."

"Try anything once." With the sardonic look of a duck Harley bade the messenger: "Bring Watt."

Almost immediately after Leith had gone, the messenger reappeared in Harley's room.

"There's a Mr. Kimber to see you, sir. And a lady."

Harley hesitated. Kimber—and probably Anna, the girl from Guido's.

"All right. Show 'em in." Harley was right.

Kimber introduced the girl: "This is Miss Anna Finn, Inspector. She has something to say to you."

"Yes?"

Anna was slightly overpowered by the atmosphere of the Yard. She made a palpable effort to control herself as she addressed Harley.

"Please, what are you holding Tooley for?"

"I thought you'd come to tell me something, not to ask questions."

"I must know that first—please."

Harley was watching her closely. His lips tightened before he spoke: "Well, you're quite right. It's murder."

"Tooley didn't murder the Rigger!"

Harley's nerves were taut but his voice sounded casual.

"Who did?"

"I don't know."

"You're not going to be very much help to me, are you?"

"It's Tooley I want to help."

"So I gathered." Harley spoke drily, and glanced at Kimber. "Has she no evidence except a romantic devotion?"

"It's not that, exactly," Kimber began, but Anna was gaining confidence and interrupted:

"All right, I'll tell you. I know Tooley didn't kill the Rigger. I was there. It was Mr. Patra who hit him and—and put his body on the dump."

"You were there? Where?"

"In the car."

"And what were you doing there?"

"I'd just gone along to help. Mr. Patra asked me to go, so I went. I was in the car when the Rigger stopped it and I saw Patra hit him. I'll swear it."

Kimber was staring at the floor, but Harley thought that he looked shocked and surprised.

Harley asked him: "Did you know what Miss Finn was going to tell me when you brought her along?"

"No. Not exactly. She was worrying about Tooley, and said she was sure she could help him if she talked to you."

"Telling lies has never helped any suspect."

"It's not a lie, Mr. Harley. I tell you I know Tooley didn't do it. I was there."

"I was told you were at the club at the time. Dancing with Mr. Kimber, I believe. You told me that yourself, Kimber?"

Anna spoke quickly. "He was wrong. Not that night. *He* was lying then, just to help me out."

Kimber met her defiant gaze with a smile. She had given him proof positive of her position, of which he had not been quite sure up to now. She was ready to sacrifice anyone, even her benefactor, for Tooley's sake.

"What have you to say?" Harley asked him.

"I must have been mistaken," he replied. "Anna is quite right."

Anna's reaction to this admission was to burst into tears.

Harley sighed. He hated scenes. He hated feminine tears as much as a dentist's drill.

He spoke to Kimber. "Puts you in a tough spot. Accessory. False evidence."

Kimber shrugged his shoulders.

"All right. I'll want her statement in black and white presently." He rang the bell. "Come and take a statement," he told his clerk. "Paper and ink, and"—with a withering look at Anna—"and lots of blotting-paper."

*   *   *

Anna recovered her poise with the amazing speed of her kind. By the time her statement was made and signed and she and Kimber reached the street, she was radiant.

Kimber glanced at her with some amusement. He did not tell her that it was extremely improbable that her story would be believed, or that it was well-nigh impossible to bluff a policeman. He admired both her loyalty and her audacity.

She took his arm and squeezed it.

"I'm sorry, Mr. Kimber. Awfully sorry. But the police can't do much to you for having lied about dancing with me. And it may save Tooley from . . . from . . ." and she shuddered eloquently.

"That's all right."

"You see, even if Tooley did do it, he didn't mean to. And Patra deserves all he'll get. Tooley's only mistake was ever working for the boss."

"Yes. There's another reason for getting Tooley off, if we can."

"What's that?"

"You love him. Don't worry, Anna. He'll be free one day, and he'll have learnt his lesson this time. We'll find him a decent job."

"We . . . ?"

"Yes. If you'll allow me to help. I'm a member of the Prisoners' Aid Society, you know, and I think my position authorizes me to support not only ex-prisoners, but also ex-prisoners' future wives, while they wait. . . ."

To Kimber's dismay Anna again melted into tears. The fact that she could cry so blatantly in the middle of Whitehall proved to him once and for all, not only that she was in love with Tooley, but that he would never be capable of jealousy of the affections of one in such an utterly different strata of life.

*   *   *

Oddly enough. Benny Watt was not so dumb as Harley had prophesied. Surprised by his sudden liberation from the depressing atmosphere of Scotland Yard, he became positively conversational as he and Leith set off in a car, followed by a salvage lorry.

"Where are we going, Mr. Leith?"

"Pleasure cruise round the Essex waterways."

"Eh? Tell me one thing, Mr. Leith, have you took in Spider? Him and me was mates, and then a while back he disappeared like. Have you got him inside?"

Leith shook his head.

"Funny thing about Spider," the old man quavered on. "I wouldn't like to think nothing had happened to Spider. Him and me was mates."

"Was he in on this show?"

"What show, sir?"

"One of Patra's lot?"

But Benny had grown deaf again. They drove on in silence until they reached Hockling, where they picked up P.C. Brightman and the local butcher, who was also the chief of the fire brigade, and who had recently breakfasted on onions.

"We couldn't save that garage, sir. She was fair burnt to a cinder afore we got there. Must have been something 'ighly combustible."

Leith nodded. "Stolen goods usually are."

Although the mist still hung low over the marshes like dirty cotton-wool, the submerged car was easily located, and Leith got the salvage gang to work before driving on with Benny.

But there was little information to gain from the shell of the burnt-out garage, in which stood the twisted chassis of the lorry. Nor from the *Van Wyk*, over which a river policeman stood guard. Benny eyed it all in silence, his head wobbling slightly from side to side.

"Picked up a suspect in a dinghy on the river this morning, sir," the policeman said. "We've got him on board."

It was Tony, his eyes hunted, his lip quivering, and his mauve shirt soaked with the damp.

"Good, I want you," Leith greeted him. "Few questions to ask you."

"Where's—where's—?"

"Mr. Patra will be at the party. Don't worry."

So his journey was not entirely in vain, in spite of Benny's obstinate silence, and the warning glance he shot at Tony.

"I could do with a spot of that liquor," Tony whispered, as he and Benny climbed into the car.

"Don't you open your mouth, not even to drink," retorted Benny wheezily. "They've got the boss."

Leith had a sample bale of paper from the hold strapped on to the back of the car, and the party drove back to watch the operations in the dyke.

The men were working with a dogged slowness which irritated Leith. The penetrating cold and damp, the smell of mud and the difficulties of the undertaking were not his idea of free entertainment on a winter's morning.

He thought of Harley, seated comfortably in his office at the Yard. He thought of Patra, whose seat would not be so comfortable. He was going to be a tough nut to crack.

At last, to the sound of heavy breathing, squelching mud and creaking ropes, the car began to come up from its sticky grave. Leith bore a hand, glad of the exercise to put a stop to his shivering.

In the swirling mist the scene looked like a faked cinema production, unreal and rather grotesque. The straining figures of the men, the black bulk of their booty, now on its side like a dead hippopotamus.

"Hold her there," said Leith, and stepped gingerly down the muddy bank. He peered into the car, and after a moment drew back.

"There's a chap inside," he said. "We'll get him out first."

"He must be dead, sir."

"He's dead all right."

It was some time before the body could be extricated. The door on the near side was locked.

Leith grunted, as his eyes fell on the upturned white face.

"Spider! Poor devil. Poor little devil."

*   *   *

Something violently jolted him in the side. It was Benny Watt. He knelt down in the mud beside the body of Spider, and the tears were coursing down his furrowed cheeks.

"Spider—Spider—" He looked up blearily at the ring of faces.

"Him and me was mates. And the boss murdered him. Spider . . ."

Leith bent over him. "Patra?"

"Yes, of course it was Patra—the swine. He had it in for poor little Spider. Thought it was him told the Rigger and put him up to a double-cross. So he murdered him, same as he did the Rigger."

Leith bent lower. "How do you know it was Patra?" he asked clearly.

"Benny! Take a pull at yourself, man!" It was Tony, standing on the fringe of the crowd. Tony, who had realized that it was his turn to issue a warning. But Benny didn't hear. He was sobbing and babbling as he patted vainly at Spider's cold hand.

"Take him away," Leith ordered sharply, and again bent over Benny, listening to his rambling lament.

Presently he interrupted again. "How do you know?"

"Of course I know. I know the boss. I saw him with the Rigger. Tied him up like an old sack and took him to the dump. Wouldn't send for a doctor even though I told him the chap'd die, else. He hasn't no heart, the boss hasn't. Murder. And now he's murdered my mate, Spider. Went off Sunday night in the car."

'Sunday,' thought Leith. 'The day Spider tried to put up a squeak to me at the "Flag". Poor little devil.'

"See that bruise on his face?" Benny was going on. "That's the boss's mark, I'll swear. He beat him up once before as a warning, when he thought he'd squeaked. This time he killed him. Just to be sure."

But Leith was not interested in the suspected murder of Spider. He could see that there was no evidence. Louie would stand by his story that Spider had stolen the car and met with an accident. But Benny's talk about the murder of the Rigger was a different matter.

"Poor Spider," he said. "Tough luck."

"Call it luck? When the bloody swine murdered him?"

"Would you like to see him swing for it? It'd serve him right, wouldn't it?"

"Too good for him—swinging."

"You're through with him?"

"He murdered my mate."

Leith laid a hand on his shoulder. "Then come and sit in the car and tell me all about it. Maybe we'll get a cup of tea somewhere. Come on, Benny, you can't help him now. Only by answering my questions."

Hospitality was forthcoming in P.C. Brightman's front parlour, and the master of the house got busy with his official notebook, while Benny, still snivelling, noisily gulped his tea.

"Are you sure the Rigger wasn't dead when the car got back to Starling Court?"

"No. He was alive all right. So was Spider alive when that car was driven into the dyke. The—"

"Yes, maybe. And you said Patra tied up the Rigger? What with?"

"A cord I give him. Same stuff I do the bales with. But Spider wasn't tied. He must have tried to fight back . . ."

Leith nodded as he poured out another cupful. That cord should serve to hang Patra.

*   *   *

"How in hell did you make that old mule talk?" asked Harley, as he and Leith were comparing the statements of their two witnesses some time later. "I couldn't get a whisper out of him."

Leith, inwardly triumphant at the admission, replied: "Nor could I, until we found Spider. Then there was no stopping him. Him and Spider was old mates, you know. We all jumped to the conclusion that Patra had murdered Spider. Benny started to cry, and then I gave him a cup of tea and we were all girls together."

"We have no evidence that Patra murdered Spider. The doctor's report is that Spider died by drowning. The bruises might have been caused by anything. As usual, we've no evidence."

"Benny didn't know that. Anyhow, Patra will swing for the murder of the Rigger."

Harley muttered something about 'irregularity', but it was the only criticism he could find, and Leith's triumph was unimpaired. "How does the girl's story fit in with Benny's? He makes no mention of her in the car."

"Because she wasn't there. Did you believe her statement?"

"I believe nothing I'm told." Harley was guarded. "Especially by hysterical women."

"No. We have plenty of evidence besides Kimber's that she was at the club all the night of the first robbery. She just put up a tale with the vague hope of saving Tooley, and Kimber backed her up."

Harley snorted sceptically. "That's love."

"Well, she hit on the right man for the murderer."

"And I suppose you call that feminine intuition. Any damn' fool could have seen it a mile off, but when it occurs to a woman it's intuition."

Leith grinned and yawned. "The love of a maid for a man," he mused. "Funny thing. And what's even funnier is Benny Watt and Spider. David and Jonathan. . . . Well, what do you want me to do now?"

Harley grinned at Leith and tossed down the papers in his hand.

"You can clear out if you like," he said, and glanced at the clock. "They're open. And dammit, I think I'll come too. We deserve it."

THE END

Lightning Source UK Ltd.
Milton Keynes UK
UKOW06f0906061017

310497UK00017B/330/P